I0778407

TO THE END

To The End

MARKED SERIES: BOOK ONE

Nicole Green

Nicole Green

Dedication

This book is dedicated to all who love reading. My wish for you, my friend, is that you always have more stories than stars in the sky.

Contents

1

Chapter 1

"Please, I wanta play in it," I ask gazing longingly at the dirty pile of snow on the side of the road. I didn't want to walk into our rundown home just yet, but Heather, once again, tugs on my arm pulling me up the stairs into our house.

She shakes her head, "Later. I'll take you to the park later. Right now, I'm late for band practice and you need to go to sleep."

"But Heather, It's not even eleven yet!" I complain rubbing my eyes.

"TJ," my big sister smiles as she pushes me through the open door and into the small kitchen, "You are eight years old and shouldn't be up this late anyway. Now, go tell Papa you're home. Okay?"

She kisses me on the forehead, in the traditional gesture of kinship, and walks into her room to gather up her things as I scamper away to the back of our small home. Papa stands filling a backpack and rucksack with all of his belongings spread over the bed, "Papa?"

My father's delicately pointed ears twitch and he turns, "I didn't know you were going to be home tonight."

I smile at him, confused about why my elven father is packing, "Where ya going?"

He tousles my dark hair, so opposite from his own, as he leans down, but he can't meet my eyes - he never can - and looks over me. Papa places a ruff hand on my cheek and I flinch slightly before calming, since I know he hasn't been drinking, "Tammy, why do you have to be so curious?" He sighs as he straightens and turns back to his packing, "I have to go away for a while. I need to find us a new place to live."

"Why?" I ask, while my eyes fill with tears at the thought of my Papa leaving and, in a stricken voice, I quietly say, "You're leavin' me 'n Heather?"

He doesn't look at me, but his response sounds sincere, "No. I'm going to come back for you, once I find a place for us. I don't like watching Annah hurt you."

I choke back my tears in understanding. My father hates watching Mama hit me, but he loves her too much to make her stop, "Promise?" I ask, rubbing my eyes with the back of my small hand.

Papa hesitates slightly before putting a silken shirt I have never seen before into the rucksack, "Promise."

Suddenly, I am standing in the kitchen and my mother is in front of me screaming and I know my father has been gone for over a year. Her delicate features are contorted in anger as she screams at me for something I never meant to do.

"Mama! Please. Don't," I nearly cry as she throws a bowl at me. Luckily, I gained my father's elven reactions and dodge out of the way before it can make contact. I hear it clatter against the cupboard before standing up straight again.

She continues to glare at me, "You let him leave! It's all your fault. You STUPID MISTAKE!" She angrily sweeps her arm across the table knocking the clean dishes to the floor and the noise, finally, wakes the twins. "Go take care of your sisters. Make yourself useful for once."

I quickly scurry off, happy for a reason to leave and be with my baby sisters, but the image changes and I walk in to see Heather kissing their foreheads, they are two years old instead of one, Heather has a pack over her shoulder.

"You goin'?" I ask confused and fall into the port dialect she hates me talking in.

Heather turns and her golden eyes glint in the lamp light, turning her normally pale skin yellow, "To find Papa."

My heart begins to race and I feel panic rise in my chest, "You're leavin'?"

"Tammy, I promise you I will come back," she looks like she is telling the truth, but so did Papa.

I shake my head and take a step back, looking up into my older sisters' face, "That's what Papa said. He promised too and he never came back."

"I will. I swear to you."

"You're lying!" I scream as panic takes over and I turn to run out the door looking for solace in the quiet of the park by our home.

I make it to the road before my sensitive ears hear Heather catching up behind me, "TJ! Stop! Please!"

I stop in the middle of the cross road as the snow falls in fat flakes and my panic drowns out all the noise as I scream, "Leave me alone! I hate you!" A large tear slides down my smooth golden cheek, "I hate you!"

She continues running and shoves me onto the side of the road. I smack my head on something hard, I see her half smile and mouth something before getting trampled by a horse pulling a cart that seemed to come out of nowhere.

***

Deep blue eyes flickered open and he sat up breathing hard, grateful for whatever it was that woke him from the memory-dream which forced him to grow up so quickly. TJ looked around his darkened room before reaching over to light the lamp on his bedside table, wishing he could afford the electricity the nobles had.

Tap, tap, tap.

"Just open the door," a young voice murmured.

"You open it," a similar voice countered back.

"No. You," the other voice echoed sounding almost identical.

"I don't want to."

"Don't be such a baby, Kali."

TJ smiled and wiped his sweating forehead, trying to wipe away the memory-dream with it, "Come in you two." The twins immediately stopped talking and walked in, "What's up little ones?"

"We had a nightmare," the identical golden skinned twins replied simultaneously.

"Come sleep here then," he gasped suddenly as a fuzzy image of a red river passed across his vision and he sneezed. "Sorry." The twins climbed under the blanket on his floor by the small pile of clothes and lay their heads on his chest. "Sleep *aida's*. I'll watch over you. Nothing will harm you," he whispered. Using the elven term of love meant for kin.

They smiled up at him as he leaned back and hummed a lullaby while he thought about the last words he said to the only person who ever truly loved him in his home - the only person who would ever give up their life for him.

The next morning TJ walked to work with a slightly foggy mind. He didn't normally remember his dreams and this past one had seemed to haunt him. As he rounded the corner, a young man called from under a sign reading 'Make A Noise,' "TJ! TJ! Hurry up you have a customer!"

TJ sighed and, grabbing his pants to keep them from falling off his thin waist, sprinted the final block into the store as his best friend snickered at him and left for the back of the shop. The half-elf looked around for the customer and quickly spotted a group of four girls with perfectly done hair and make-up. Clearly from the Mercante District of the rich and almost noble, they were thin and held their heads high as if queens. The two taller girls dressed almost exactly alike, but the other two held distinct differences.

The first was elven and didn't need to draw attention to herself by adding make-up and her delicate frame was pretty enough without accenting it with expensive clothing. The second didn't seem to care about making herself presentable, since she seemed to be aware that her hair would never be tamed and her lips would always look rosy on her porcelain skin. They were the rulers of his high school. The two identical ones he couldn't stand, but he also wouldn't give up a sale for that reason.

He drew himself up and strode over, "I heard you all needed my help."

One of the four girls turned and made a face, "Why do *you* have to help us?"

"Because I know how much you all despise me," TJ shrugged as bluntly as possible. From experience, he knew, this was the only way to get them to stop pushing him. "What are you looking for?" The bell rang behind him announcing another customer. "Jake!" He called toward the back room.

His best friend ran out from behind and handed TJ a belt as he passed to tend to the new customer. The same girl answered TJ's question, "Piano music with three vocal parts."

"Well, you're not exactly in the right spot. It's over there," TJ pointed to his right. "Start looking and I will be back in a moment."

The girls began to walk over, and on the way – when the others weren't paying attention – the girl with rosy lips quickly took TJ's hand and gave it a squeeze as she looked into his blue green eyes. He smiled at her and gave her a little nudge over to her friends as he went behind the counter to put Jake's belt on and sign in to work.

The bell rang again and a girl with large hips and broad shoulders strode in, "Aly will you prop open the door? It's going to be a hot day."

The girl did as requested; then walked up to him and leaned against the counter, "Are you having fun yet? I saw you almost lose your pants while running in here." She laughed lightly.

TJ looked back at the group and locked eyes on the girl with rosy lips, "Sure."

She followed his gaze, "Ahhh. Hayle's here."

TJ gave her a little shove, "Be nice."

"She ignores the fact that you two have been dating for almost four months when with her friends. If she didn't make you happy, I would tear her hair out," the girl growled to give her words emphasis.

The half-elf turned to face his oldest friend, "Aly, breathe. You know very well why they can't know." TJ sighed and suddenly looked very tired.

Aly rolled her eyes, "Yeah, yeah. I know. She is from the Mercante District and almost a noble and you are from the Dead Lands – a slum boy. You would either be arrested or she would have to give up her title for you."

"Stupid law," TJ said bitterly. "Anyway, I should make sure they are actually picking out music all of them are capable of singing."

Aly nodded and walked over to the wood flute section, "Always a good idea."

"Picked anything out yet?" TJ questioned the four girls.

The elven girl and Hayle held up a few booklets of sheet music, "We were looking at some of these."

"But we want to know what they sound like. Can we use a piano?" Hayle asked shuffling the music.

TJ nodded and took them over to the piano and opened the lid covering the ivory keys, "Go ahead and try them out."

Hayle set the music down and sat on the bench he pulled out for her. Opening one, she put her fingers to the cool white and black keys, but it sounded disjointed as she attempted to sight read the music.

"Hayle, is it supposed to sound like that?" One of the other girls asked with a slight sneer to her lips. "Maybe we should try one of the other songs."

Hayle blushed and turned her hazel eyes on her in a death glare, "No, it isn't. I told you, I am not very good at sight reading piano."

"Here," TJ sat next to her and very gently brushed her side, "I can play. You four follow along."

One of the two replicas snickered, "I'm sure you are an..." her voice trailed off as TJ's fingers flew across the keys like he had practiced the song a thousand times.

He went through each song before the girls came to a decision on which one they wanted to purchase. TJ, finally, checked them out and Hayle casually left her bag while her elven friend rolled her eyes as they walked out and, five minutes later, Hayle and the elf came back in.

"You are such an idiot," she commented.

"Sabella, I didn't ask for your opinion," Hayle laughed and squeezed her shoulder affectionately.

"No, you didn't," Sabella smiled, tossing her hair back in a dark wave, "But as you're my best friend, I gave it anyway."

TJ raised a black eyebrow at the two from near the violin stands and casually took Hayle in his arms since no one else was in the store. She smiled at him and very carefully stood on her tip toes to kiss him on the cheek with one arm wrapped around his lower back.

"How are you doing?" She asked.

He smiled, "I'm fine."

She leaned back to look in his eyes that were an olive green, "You're lying."

Aly laughed and TJ glared at her, "Really I'm fine. Bruised, but I'm alright."

"Is it your ribs still?" Hayle asked worried and TJ nodded. "Are you sure it isn't broken? Why don't you come by tonight and have my dad take a look?"

"Hayle, I'm alright. I swear," TJ brushed a dark brown strand of hair away from her face.

Jake poked his head out from the back of the shop, "You always say that and you always are leaving something out."

"You all are so infuriating!" TJ exclaimed.

Hayle carefully set her palm on his cheek, "It's only because we care about you."

TJ rolled his eyes and released Hayle before turning back to the counter, uncomfortable with all eyes on him. He straightened the pamphlets explaining class times and different musical functions for the coming months.

"When do you guys get out of here?" Sabella asked as she checked herself, needlessly, in a hand mirror since her reddish brown hair and cinnamon colored eyes were still flawless.

"Never," the owner of Make A Noise said walking out from the employee's office, which was really more of a store room. "Stop distracting my workers."

"Sorry, Gary. We just can't help it," Aly laughed.

"You two can leave early today. How about by five pm if we aren't busy?"

The boys looked at each other wide eyed; they almost never were let out early, "Seriously? That's amazing!"

"Are you two sure you weren't separated at birth?" Aly asked and the boys smirked at each other.

"Yes, I am serious. A Festival is coming up this weekend. Fifteenth of Midmoon because of the solstice. Overtime for you two and especially you, TJ," Gary smiled. He always needed TJ's help, since he knew so much about all of the instruments and had been working at the store since he was twelve.

The boys immediately froze, eyes wide, and TJ shuddered. As much as he loved the Festival – where the shops were open for twenty-four hours and everything else was closed, bands played, and acts were done – was stressful. His band would be playing on the opening evening and he would need to take double shifts at Make A Noise and his job at The Bakery.

***

A week later, TJ ran through the streets with a smile plastered on his face. He just finished his last shift for the evening at The Bakery and was headed to pick up his sisters. Hayle was in front of him using her small size to squeeze through the crowd easily.

"Come on! You're so slow!" Hayle called over her shoulder.

"You aren't carrying a guitar and violin case!" TJ shouted back through the crowd of people flocking the streets of the Shop District in a mass of color and sound.

Hayle stopped and waited for him to catch up and took the violin case out of his hands, "You big baby. Now come on."

"I am not a big baby!" He said in mock offense.

Hayle laughed as she looked up at him, "Yes, you are."

TJ pushed open a gate with his hip and walked into the yard of the elven healer, Colette. Herbs and flowers filled every spare space around her yellow house and the scents perforated the air as they strode past the gardens and up the steps.

"Finally! I was wondering what had become of you!" The tall elven woman exclaimed leaning her long frame against the doorway as one of TJ's little sisters peaked out from behind her.

"Hayle!" She squeaked and threw her arms around the older girl's waist.

TJ smiled and walked in, "Guess I'm not wanted. Hayle, you can take them. They seem to like you better."

"Really?" She laughed and with the little girl standing on her feet walked awkwardly inside.

"Sure. They are little terrors though. I don't think you want them," TJ warned.

"Oh, they aren't so bad most of the time," Colette smiled kindly as the other twin came tearing around the corner straight at TJ.

"Hi, Erinn," he said catching the little girl in his arms and spinning her in a half circle. She giggled and gripped his neck.

"Are you two just stopping by? Or do you have something planned?" Colette questioned, leaning against a heavy wooden shelf containing a variety of jars filled with different tinctures and balms. TJ and Hayle set down the instruments and sighed in relief of losing their burdens.

TJ shrugged, "It's up to you. I can take the twins back or you could watch them still."

Colette laughed, "If I watch them, what are you going to do?"

"Probably meet up with the other Dead Landers. Go to the ports… avoid work till I have to go in tomorrow," he smiled at the woman who had helped him through the hardest years after Heather's death. One of the few people he could speak the Elven language of Layendrian to.

"Good thought. You work too much anyway," Hayle commented leaning against the door frame after picking Kali up and propping her on a hip.

"Go," Colette smiled, pealing Erinn off TJ. He looked up to meet her almost cat like eyes. She fought with the little blonde girl for a moment before TJ tapped the child on the nose and she quieted, "I'm serious TJ. Leave. Go have fun."

"Fun? What is that?" TJ sighed looking at the wooden floorboards.

Hayle set Kali down and although the little girl pouted, she didn't fight like Erinn, "Come along and I will show you."

Smiling widely, TJ thanked Colette and the two took off to the ports at high speed. Night began to creep into the sky and by the time they reached the ocean, the sun was a golden fingernail in the horizon and sinking fast.

"Hurry up! You're the last ones to get here!" Jake called as the wind pushed his blonde hair out of his face.

TJ rolled his eyes, "You didn't even know if we were coming!"

"We knew Colette would make you," Aly commented as the wind whipped her shirt while she played on the shoreline, leaving a trail of footprints in the shadowed sand. Hayle tied her hair back as she kicked her shoes off to join her and set TJ's violin carefully down. "So, are we swimming or not?"

"We're swimming," Hayle immediately exclaimed before adding, "Or at least I would like to."

Aly turned her large blue eyes on the smaller girl and, for a moment, Hayle thought Aly was finally going to tell her off. She knew Aly and the others only put up with her because of TJ, but, instead, Aly smiled, "Then let's go swimming."

The boys each stripped down to their boxers leaving their jeans and t-shirts in a pile on the sandy beach as three more Dead Landers joined them. One was a tall girl with an athletic build while the other two looked like night and day even though they were twins with identical personalities.

"Wait for us!" They called as the athletic girl slinked up to TJ as she pulled her shirt off to show a very revealing bathing suit.

"Hey Sami," TJ said in a voice constricting in his discomfort as he looked away and moved toward the water.

The twins snickered from behind as they stripped down and ran at TJ tackling him into the darkened salt water, forgetting about his bruised ribs. The others quickly followed as TJ came up spluttering, but he said nothing, knowing they hadn't meant to hurt him. For a time, they floated in the water letting the white waves crash over them in a cacophony of sound.

Soon though, the peace was broken as Jake, climbing up onto the pier, jumped into the depths below as the white water smashed into the wooden pillars. He pulled himself to the surface. TJ climbed up to the end of the pier and threw himself into the air flipping, then diving into the crashing wave. Instead of resurfacing, he grabbed Jake's feet and pulled him under which ended in a water wrestling match before the other two boys and the three girls got pulled in and began to play Trolling.

Hayle climbed up onto TJ's shoulders, Aly on Evan's, Sami on Jake's, and James refereed as Aly gripped Evan's curly brown hair in her long fingers and held tightly with her legs as Hayle attempted to dislodge her from Evan's shoulders. The two girls locked hands and kicked salt water into the others faces while the two boys attempted to dislodge the footing of their current enemy by jamming their shoulders into their sternums. The liquid flew up into their faces and stung their eyes, but they couldn't wipe it away until one of the girls fell. Not wanting to wait their turn Jake and Sami threw themselves into the mix and a battle royal ensued, until TJ and Hayle stood as victors. Exhausted, they fell into the turbulent waters and crawled onto the sandy shore as Aly set out a thick quilt for everyone to lay on and gaze up at the stars which blanketed the canopy above.

TJ sighed as he put one arm under the back of his head and entwined his fingers in Hayle's dainty hand. She turned and smiled at him, her hazel eyes dark and mysterious in the night. None of them knew how long they laid there in silence, because time didn't mean anything just then. When TJ suddenly inhaled quickly and began sneezing soon after, they all knew he had another one of his unintelligible visions, but they didn't question him about it. They didn't want to break that moment.

They just let the silence thicken until James spoke in his bass voice, "Aly, we should have a bonfire."

She looked up from Evans shoulder at the young man, "Sure. TJ do you want to bring your guitar?"

The half-elf sat up, "I can do that. If you want, I can pick up Aysté on the way over."

"Sure! We haven't seen her in a long time," Aly commented sadly, but excited at the prospect of getting to see their older and calmer friend.

"She's always so busy with work and studying," Sami added as they shook off the quilt and folded it.

TJ turned to Hayle as the others spoke about the motherly Aysté who fell into the place of his older sister when Heather passed away, "Do you want to get going?"

Hayle bit her lip in contemplation, "I probably should. My friends might begin to wonder where I am."

Her boyfriend nodded, trying not to look upset by her decision and Hayle frowned. *I wish we could just be together. It's just not fair. Stupid laws.* She wrapped her arms around him and buried her head against his chest as he hugged her back.

Finally, he leaned down and kissed her gently on the top of her head, "Come on. I'll take you back to the Shop District."

She nodded and said farewell to the Dead Landers and with TJ by her side, they left.

***

Aysté was thrilled when TJ brought the girls to her house for dinner the week before school began. He only brought them by a few times all summer and the last time she really spent time with him was at Aly's bonfire a few weeks previously. She normally spent the summers in the elven kingdom of Layendria. However, dinner was a tradition they started when he was twelve years old. She had worried about him ever since Heather passed away and his refuge became silence and drugs.

Tebuleten nights became the time when she could just sit and be with him and if he needed help with alchemy, she would help him and give advice if he asked for it. It also gave him someone to talk to in Layendrian. No one else in his home spoke the elven language and his sisters were just beginning to learn it with the help of Colette, the healer, and Grama, his next-door neighbor who aided in raising him. Both women helped him a lot and Aysté was very pleased and grateful for that, but she still wished he would let her help him more than just one night a week.

"Set your things down and breathe," Aysté commanded of the young man who had become her little brother over the years.

TJ smiled and obeyed, "You excited for school yet?"

Aysté raised an eyebrow, "I refuse to answer until you speak with proper grammar."

"*Are* you ready for school yet?" TJ gave her a brilliant smile.

She returned it with her own, "I need to start filling out applications."

He frowned as he absent-mindedly picked up Kali and propped her on his hip, "I'm just worried about classes."

Aysté rolled her eyes, "Tam, you have no reason to worry. You are incredibly smart." TJ sighed in frustration, "Don't you sigh at me. You are smart and naturally gifted at so many things."

"But I am going to be working two jobs and tutoring Hayle again," he complained.

"Oh, because it is so much effort to tutor Hayle?"

A rare smile lit up his eyes, "No. Not really. I just need to organize my time better than I did last year."

"Just let me help you. Please," she nearly begged as he nodded at Erinn that she could be free to romp around Aysté's large home for the Dead Lands.

Kali buried her head against his shoulder as he answered, "I'll try."

Soon Aysté's mother called them into the kitchen for dinner and as time tends to do, it raced forward. Classes began and TJ tried to keep up his promise to her by asking for help, but he was never good at asking or even admitting he needed it.

A very independent person by nature and nurture, TJ didn't understand when people offered to help; they truly meant it – most of the time. Gary, the owner of Make A Noise, never offered, he just gave it. He would let TJ work on homework or study when the shop was empty and this, above everything else, is what kept his school work afloat, especially because things at home only got worse as Fellmoon moved into Bloodmoon.

His stepfather, who appeared a few years after his own father's sudden departure, began to return home drunk every night and TJ was running out of places to go. He didn't want to continue staying at Jake's and felt guilty leaving the twins at his house alone, even though Roger never hit the girls. TJ, finally, decided to deal with the abuse and stay home with his little sisters. His friends didn't like his choice, but they knew better than to try and convince him otherwise. They absolutely hated seeing the whip marks on his back and small scratches on his neck from where his mother clawed him. However, TJ never complained and never said a word about it to anyone.

***

"Where's that club, TJ?" The Bakery's manager shrieked above the noise inside the overcrowded restaurant.

TJ stuck his head out from the backroom concealing his annoyance with the incompetent manager. "On the way. I had to make more slaw."

"Hurry up. Can't make them wait all day!" She continued screaming at him as she expertly stood around doing nothing.

The half-elf disappeared again and returned a few seconds later with food piled on a tray quickly dodging around the counter – the employee gate swinging closed behind him with a snap. Without much thought, he delivered the food and drinks to each customer, some thanking, a few ignoring, and a handful of girls batting their eyelashes – trying to gain more than a glance and polite smile.

TJ sighed and walked quickly back to the cash register as a boy from his year walked in. "How may I help you?" He asked of the young man.

The other boy sneered, "You *could* go kill yourself."

"I'm sorry, but we are all out of stock. Maybe you should take a closer look at the menu. If you need any help reading, feel free to ask," TJ rebutted with a perfectly emotionless face as his eyes glittered emerald.

The other man's large nose twitched in anger and annoyance, "Just give me the Turkey on wheat."

"Five coppers please," money exchanged hands. TJ quickly made up two sandwiches and placed one on a tray with a pickle slice.

Then walked back to where the boy sat down with the group of young men and women who had ignored him all day, "Here you go."

The boy reached up and purposefully knocked the tray out of TJ's hands, sending it flying to the ground. The group burst out laughing, "Damn, for a half-elf you aren't to graceful."

Jake appeared above TJ's shoulder with the extra sandwich, "And for being rich and proper you don't have much class." He gripped TJ by the shoulder and pushed him back toward the counter before leaning down to pick up the fallen debris.

"Protecting your lover as always Jake?" The young man asked in spite.

Jake turned his icy blue eyes on his once friend, "Not at all. Just helping a friend. Maybe you should try it sometime, you seem to be out of practice." He stood and left back to the counter, "Why do you always have to get involved with them?" Jake questioned and TJ handed a new tray of food to a different person so he could go and eat his own lunch.

The two boys walked outside and TJ set his tray down at the only open table on the veranda enclosed by a wrought iron gate, "Believe me, it's not intentional. You know that as well as I do. It's not like I try to be anywhere near him."

"I still can't believe he hasn't gotten over you showing him up in the guitar duel three years ago," Jake smirked.

TJ smiled back and Jake's smirk turned into a wide grin, "That was funny. If only he translated the lyrics correctly, maybe, he would have stood a better chance." TJ took a bite of the vegetable loaded sandwich.

"How are you keeping up in classes? You know mid-terms are next week, right?"

TJ nodded and swallowed, "Yeah, I know." He sipped his tea and changed the topic off himself, "What did the asshole say to you by the way?"

"The usual," Jake attempted to steal a bit of TJ's food and got kicked from under the table. "Said I should stop sticking up for my lover," he shrugged nonchalantly.

TJ rolled his eyes which turned emerald again, "I wish people wouldn't pick on you for being gay. I mean, what's the big deal?"

"I don't know and you should be more defensive of yourself, not me."

TJ laughed, "Probably, but I'm not. I just don't care enough. Plus, most people leave me alone now, just not Randy." He shoved the rest of his food into his mouth and stood, "Band practice tonight, right?"

"It's Sateriten, so yes. My place. You are staying the night, right?" Jake questioned.

TJ nodded, "The girls are staying at Grama's."

"Good, because it's going to be an incredibly long practice."

TJ picked up his tray and quizzically raised a dark eyebrow, "Why is that?"

"Just talked to Gary. Festival is next weekend. 30th of Bloodmoon," Jake bit his lip in an attempt to contain his excitement. "We are the second show case. Only one band is in front of us."

"Devil's Night. Damn. Let me guess, we are opening for Sound System?" TJ asked as he followed Jake back inside.

"Yep and the only reason they aren't opening for us is because they are older and have more money."

"I'm glad *you* are excited," TJ muttered to Jake as he walked behind the counter and Jake leaned his tall frame against it. "But me, not so much."

"It's not like anyone is going to know it's you singing. Calm down," Jake sighed and began to organize a way of getting TJ over his fear and decided he needed to talk to the band.

***

"So, we are all clear on the plan?" Jake questioned of the three other band members.

The drummer tilted his head to the side, "Alright, so when TJ realizes you aren't pretending to sing anymore and if he stops singing we continue to play?"

"Yes, but loop it so he can come back in," the bell rang downstairs and Jake's butler answered the door.

"Okay," everyone responded in understanding. As TJ entered, his band members inconspicuously tuned or practiced their instruments. He set his violin and his guitar case on Jake's bed and flipped open the latches on the guitar case and tuned as he looked around, "Everybody ready?"

"Whenever you are," they responded at different moments. TJ strummed a final chord and moved closer to the group.

"Let's get started then," he fingered the strings and thought. "We have about a half hour, maybe an hour, of time so we need to make sure we have at least fifteen songs ready."

Jake nodded, "We have songs prepared TJ. Don't worry."

"And we also have the basics everyone always requests," one of the other band members mentioned. "We will be fine."

"Well, how about we practice *Fire The Water*? That one could still use some work and *Sundown*," TJ suggested and the boys all nodded.

The half-elf drilled them like a general and kept them going until late in the night until they could almost play their songs in their sleep. All of them realized it would be one of their best concerts.

***

Aysté and Evan gripped TJ's hands pulling him up onto the cart headed off to EsCe. "Thought I wasn't going to make it again," TJ gasped as he lay sprawled across his two friends, attempting to catch his breath.

Aysté ran her fingers through his thick black hair pulling out straw, "What were you doing?"

TJ sat up and sighed, "Dealing with a small girl and a temper tantrum."

"Which one?" Sami asked looking over and crawling closer to TJ.

"Erinn," TJ took his back pack off and straightened his jeans. "She didn't want to wear a jacket over her dress."

"Why should she have to?" Sami asked repositioning her back pack.

TJ bit his lip in annoyance, but as he had learned to do because of his mother's abuse he molded his face into an expressionless void. "Because it's getting colder and I told her to wear it."

"You aren't her parent," Sami said defending the little girl. She wanted an argument and TJ knew it. He refused to answer.

Aysté eyed the younger woman in frustration, "He basically is their parent and you know that Sami. We all know he has raised them ever since Hea – stop being such a pest."

Sami's large protuberant eyes glared at Aysté since she knew the elegant elven teenager was right. Instead of trying to continue the argument she would inevitably lose, she attempted to gain the blonde twin's attention. It never worked, but she didn't notice or care.

Aly slowly touched TJ's shoulder and he twitched before turning to look at the girls freckled face, "Yes?"

"Sorry. I just wanted to see that handsome face of yours," she smiled at him. "It's the first time in a few weeks you have no bruises or cuts." TJ attempted to smile, but it failed and he gazed out at the city they were passing through. Buildings were stacked against each other and being erected out of the debris of the old buildings that had failed to be repaired. The stadium he would play at dominated the back of a row of the Shop Districts busiest stores and faced the elegant park with its large lake and rolling hills. He shivered slightly and took a large gulp of the cool salty air. "You're nervous aren't you?"

"Just a little," he admitted as Aysté wrapped her arms around him very carefully in a hug as the cart pulled off onto a nicer road toward the school at the edge of the Mercante District.

As the cart pulled in, TJ jumped down and held his hand out to each woman in turn, who gave him a smile and the trio strode into the prized school of the old capital, VeeCee.

They crossed paths of Hayle and two of her friends who possessed looks of disgust on their faces as they passed him and TJ tried not to look like it cut him, but it did. He leaned over his locker, twirled the combination, and opened it.

Jake picked up the books TJ dropped onto the ground before shoving his other books and bag in the locker and slammed it shut. "Come on. We're going to be late," Jake said handing the books back. TJ nodded and followed his best friend to their alchemy class.

TJ gave an exaggerated sigh, "I hate this class."

"And she hates us," Jake laughed.

"No, she hates how I'm late every Tebuleten and Throwten."

"You work. Not your fault," Jake added.

TJ shrugged, "Still. She doesn't like it."

"True," the other boy eyed the closed door. "Damn. You first."

"Oh thanks," TJ said as he opened the wooden door. "Just throw me to the dogs."

Jake quietly laughed, "No problem. Anytime."

The teacher glared at the boys scurrying in, "And what is your excuse this time boys?" The heavy-set woman questioned as she held a beaker aloft.

TJ shrugged as he took his seat on the opposite side of the room from Jake; they were separated in record time at the beginning of the year. Apparently, their reputations preceded them. Even still, the two fed the flames of the other class members. They were every teacher's nightmare, because they got good grades seemingly without thought, participated in class, helped other students, and yet were troublemakers, got students and teachers off track, played pranks, and caused general ruckus.

"Before I was so rudely interrupted," the teacher glared at TJ's uncaring golden face, "I was saying we are going to be working on our labs today with your assigned partner." A general sigh and groan from the class sounded around the room. "Come on! Let's get moving!" She clapped her hands and there was a chorus of scrapping chairs as around twenty students stood and began collecting the lab equipment.

TJ pulled the lab coat on over his loose red t-shirt and laid his notebook on the counter. He looked around and gathered the proper materials as his lab partner quickly scribbled something on the top of the worksheet and shoved it to him.

"Why were you so late? You said you didn't have work this morning."

TJ read the note and scribbled back his reply *"Ill tempered demon. Then I got distracted. Still need help this afternoon?"*

The delicate hand snatched back the paper and erased the writing to place her reply at the top again *"Yes please. Meet you outside the steps at thirty after?"*

TJ nodded his response as he set up the burners. Hayle began measuring out the chemicals and poured them into the beakers taking careful notes all the while. The two didn't talk even though fully aware of what the other did. She didn't mind that TJ wasn't the best at alchemy and, truth be told, he would have been failing if she didn't explain every step along the way. Every time the teacher came into hearing distance, she would stop muttering things under her breath to him and then begin again once the woman stepped away. It was hard, but they carefully carried on and successfully made the amethyst liquid boil at the perfect temperature and emit the noxious fumes the teacher was looking for.

Grudgingly, she came over and gazed at their set up, but she didn't even look at TJ as she said good job and let them clean up and leave the now overheating room. They quickly strode into the hallway and down toward the second years locker bank.

Hayle stopped in front of TJ's locker and leaned back against it, "Nervous?"

He tilted his head, "About what?"

"Tomorrow. You guys are performing, aren't you?" She questioned hoping the answer was yes.

TJ nodded and set his books on the floor and ran his hands through his hair as he gazed at the petite girl in front of him.

She smiled, "Your eyes just turned lilac. What are you thinking about?"

TJ looked around making sure they truly were alone and slipped his hand under her thick hair. A small smile twitched at the side of his mouth as he leaned down and kissed her cheek, "I'm just glad I get you alone for a few minutes. It never happens at school and I get sick of pretending I'm indifferent toward you."

Hayle bit her lip and standing on tip toe she wrapped her arms around his neck and whispered into his pointed ear, "I hate it too." Then kissed him back on his golden cheek.

She watched his ear twitch and his face fell as he changed his mind about what he was about to say, "Class is about to get out and I heard a door open. We should… well, you know."

"Yeah," she leaned back to see his face and attempted to look alright with it, but she knew she didn't. She gave him another peck on the cheek and let go, "See you later."

TJ watched her leave with her bag swinging at her side as the classroom doors opened and the students flooded out. He leaned down and spun his locker combination to switch books.

***

"Did you get a chance to talk to her?" Jake questioned as TJ stretched out his legs after sitting down next to him.

Out of habit, TJ tried to hide the brilliant smile which quickly spread across his face, "A little yes." He opened his notebook labeled Linguistics 4 and scanned through a paragraph. Jake leaned over as their teacher began to speak and stride up and down the aisles.

"Linguistics?" Jake questioned and TJ nodded as he began to quickly scribble out a paper in the elven language of Layendrian. "Wish my handwriting looked that nice."

TJ chuckled quietly to himself as the teacher neared their aisle talking about the geography of The Empire and how this was important to their education. *Maybe for humans it will be important, but not for elves of any kind.* TJ thought to himself remembering how, not too long ago, the Empire closed off its borders to elves. *I won't be going there anytime soon.* Jake tapped him on the shoulder as the teacher closed in on their desks. TJ slid the sheet with the paragraph under his folder, but didn't have time to hide the notebook.

She paused looking at his notes and TJ met her eyes innocently, "Doing other homework, are we?"

TJ shook his head, "No ma'am."

"I believe you are. This is Layendrian not Astèndrian," she snapped.

He sighed, "Layendrian is my first language. I take notes in it. Check any of my other notebooks," TJ pulled out his journal that wasn't labeled and handed it to her. She flipped through it and narrowed her eyes as she handed it back with the sinking feeling she was letting him get away with something.

She began her discussion again, more fervently, as TJ finished up his homework. The bell rang not long after and, as talk bubbled up, Jake muttered quietly to TJ, "You are so lucky."

"Not really," TJ smiled addictively and Jake couldn't help, but stare. "I really do take most of my notes in Layendrian. But, now I can do my homework in class every day and she will never know."

"You little-" Jake began, but was interrupted by Aly bounding up in a bustle of joy.

"Substitute in literature class!" She squeaked gleefully as the flood of adolescents pushed them to the wall.

The two boys exchanged maniacal glances, "This is going to be fun."

"Just don't get suspended or expelled, okay?" Aly laughed as they walked quickly to their seats at the back of the class.

A skinny woman with curling gray hair entered the room and turned her wrinkled sallow face upon the class, "Quiet down everyone." She scanned the room looking for empty seats and seeing none glanced at the letter the teacher had left her, "Okay, please pull out your homework and hand it up here and then we will begin to discuss *Sonoretta*."

The class broke into conversation as they dug in their bags or binders for their work and it took a good five minutes before the substitute could get them to quiet back down.

"It hasn't been too long since last I read this grand novel and I will try to answer any questions you may –" Jake and TJ simultaneously interrupted her, raising their hands and half the class groaned while the other half hid smiles. "Go ahead," the substitute said, though she didn't have any need to since they were already going at it.

"*Sonoretta* seems to be about a young woman trying to find her way in the world," Jake began before TJ stepped in.

"But she has no real reason to leave in the first place. Look at her family."

"What does family have to do with it? She's bored. She wants freedom."

TJ chuckled, "Freedom? Then why leave? She is now tied down to a job. She had more freedom at home."

"It's the principle of the thing," Jake stressed and watched TJ's eyes lighten to a lime green as he held back laughter in a face which appeared to be annoyed. The substitute tried to stop them, but TJ cut her off.

"Principal of the thing? She's stupid. Why would you leave a home that will give you everything? Her family loves her, her siblings help keep her entertained, her grandmother spoils her-"

"And she attends a good school. So what? It's the principal of freedom that she craves."

"There is no freedom though. She is searching for something that isn't there."

Jake smiled knowing TJ felt that way, even though he acted, "But how would she-"

"Get out of this class now and have this childish exchange in the hall if you can't keep your mouths shut. I will not have you disrupting this class anymore!" The substitute yelled.

"Sure teach. Catch you later!" TJ and Jake said simultaneously picking up their books.

As they reached the chalk board Jake asked, "To lunch?"

"To lunch," TJ answered and, as they made it to the door, they both turned and bowed. The class broke into scattered applause and the teacher immediately felt her stomach drop as she realized she had been played. The door snapped shut and the boys took off.

"Don't feel bad," Aly said, slightly condescending. "They are professionals and do it to the best teachers."

"That was well played good sir," TJ laughed as they put their books into their lockers and pulled out their sheet music and books for their last three classes.

Jake smiled broadly, "And you as well. Any homework?"

"Not yet. Probably in math, but I'm tutoring Hayle anyway so it's no big deal," he said as he shoved his thick math book inside his black bag with his two notebooks and sweatshirt.

"We still have a half hour," Jake commented.

"I'm going to see Ulrich. I need to practice the solo. Want to come? You can critique."

Jake slammed his locker shut and waved down the hallway for TJ to lead the way. TJ walked through the pristine hallways of their high school and down the stairs to the music department. The all girls' choir was practicing when TJ opened the door and stepped in. The half-elf waved as a few of the girls eyed TJ and many batted their eyelashes at Jake. Ulrich, the choir and band director, nodded at the two boys as he ended their piece.

"Perfect timing. What's going on you two? Causing more trouble?" Ulrich asked.

"Little bit," TJ admitted. "I was just hoping I could take one of the practice rooms. I wanted to warm up a bit before class."

Ulrich nodded and the boys disappeared to where the instruments were kept. TJ unlocked his violin case from the masses and stepped into the room with Jake close behind.

TJ set the music on the stand, tuned up, and soon mesmerized Jake as his eyes followed the notes with precision. Soon his eyes were closed and he felt the music, anticipating the next note easily. They both knew the piece's difficulty level, yet TJ's fingers flew over the strings with quick easy grace and skill. Before long Ulrich popped his head in to tell the boys the bell had rung, but TJ stayed playing. Jake left and returned a few minutes later with Aly and the twins in tow since Aysté had gone to the library with Sami.

"Eat something TJ," Aly ordered as she tossed an apple at his head. He barely caught it in his hand holding the bow.

"Thanks," he smiled and Jake placed a carton of chocolate milk by his feet as Evan pushed one of his sandwiches toward him. TJ smiled appreciating his friends more than ever.

***

TJ lounged on the steps of the main entrance to school after the last bell rang reading. He was glad for being a fast reader since that half hour was the only time he ever allowed himself to read a book for fun. Otherwise, he would spend too much time reading and not enough time doing homework and getting other things done.

Small arms wrapped themselves around his shoulders and he felt knees push slightly against his back, "Hey dear."

TJ leaned back setting his head against Hayle's shoulder and got a face full of her abundantly curly hair, "Hey. How was your day?"

She laughed and wrapped her arms tighter around him, "Better now. Frayten's are my favorite."

"Why is that?" He asked closing his book.

In answer, Hayle leaned down and kissed his angular cheek, "No one stays long so I can do this in public and spend more time with you. I must ask though, how are you able to just close a book and know exactly where you were?"

TJ shrugged, "You ready to go?"

"Yep. Are you staying to eat dinner with us?"

"Ummm, sure. Yeah, that's fine," he nodded and gracefully rose to his feet, taking her hand in one of his own callused ones; he scooped up his bag and led her down the stairs toward the Mercante District. Since it was barely three in the afternoon the streets were nearly empty, but as a mass of people gathered around a street corner listening to a preacher of Atropos, he couldn't help but recall the riot from a year ago. He took this same walk then and one of his sisters got ripped from his hand. Hayle helped find her again. He owed her more than he would ever be able to express, but he refused to tell her those three words.

I can't, TJ thought as she led him up the stairs to her elegant brick house with vines creeping up the sides. *Everything I have ever cared about has left me. The only constant I have is music. Even she doesn't truly care,* he looked at her through his thick eyelashes. *At least not enough. She won't admit it to anyone.*

The inside of her home was pristine and elegant just like the outside. Her mother Lily spent hours cleaning and tidying the home and Marques, her father, made enough to afford the latest products to keep it that way. Hayle's room was tidy, but it at least looked lived in and her desk was stacked with papers and notes.

TJ set his bag down on the floor. Hayle copied him and sat down, "So, where do you want to start?"

"What don't you understand?" He questioned sitting on the floor across from her as he pulled out his math book, followed by his sheet music.

Hayle looked quickly through her homework returned that day, "I didn't get the first one, or fourteen, and fifteen right."

"Okay. Let's see what you did," he took it from her hand and quickly scanned the problems and noticed the same thing done wrong in each, "Easy mistake to make." He pointed to a double negative, "This makes it positive. That's it."

Hayle gave him a frown, "Easy mistake? You make me feel so dumb sometimes."

TJ's voice wavered, "Sorry. I-I didn't- don't mean to. But you're better at alchemy."

She watched him tense up, "I didn't mean that as a bad thing." She smiled at him slightly and set her hand on his ankle, "I actually appreciate it quite a bit."

TJ visibly tried to relax by taking a deep breath, "Thanks. So, let's see… How about you redo those problems and then the examples in the book?"

The young woman tied her hair back and TJ smiled as she bit her rosy lips and her collar bone became more distinct, "Okay. Fine."

She pulled her yellow notebook over and got to work as TJ scribbled notes to himself over the violin staff, marking rhythms, hard notes, and breaks. He went through it a few times before Hayle finished and then he corrected it.

"Do you want to play?" Hayle asked her voice sounding loud in the silence. TJ looked up from the sheet music and his tapping, "What?"

"Do you want to play my violin?" Hayle asked again. "She needs a little attention. I haven't been able to play her in a while."

The half-elf smiled, "As long as it won't distract you too much." She shook her head as she stood to retrieve her violin in its black case.

It was a beautiful instrument made by elven hands. TJ had sold it to her parents almost three years ago. A darker wood than normal with shining silver colored strings and a matching bow, TJ smiled as he lifted it out of the velvet.

The half-elf tightened the bow and pulled the rosin across the horse hair before tuning. Hayle moved to her bed to lean against her lilac pillows and cover her lap with a deep purple blanket. TJ placed the sheet music on a stand in the corner of her room. He played over and over again. Yet every time there was a difference. Softer, louder, staccato, legato, quicker, slower, and a mixture of all. Eventually, he seemed to find a happy medium between the different styles and combined them to something which brought a look of peace on his face.

Hayle finished and snapped the math book shut and began her literature homework, "TJ come on. You have lit homework too."

He stopped, "What's that?"

"You left, but we got literature homework. Finish up *Sonoretta* and answer these questions. I grabbed one of the sheets for you."

TJ sat next to her on the bed along with a pen. "I already finished it. And thanks for grabbing the worksheet." She smiled and he wrapped an arm around her waist as he set his notebook on his knees.

2

Chapter 2

Erinn wrapped skinny legs around her brother's shoulders and he gripped her knees tightly as he reprimanded her for bouncing all the while, "Erinn! Stop that or you will fall." He looked down to where Kali attempted to tie a bow into her hair, "Come here. Erinn hold on. Kali give me the bow."

The little girl obeyed and her big brother tied a blue bow into her hair, matching the color of her eyes. It was Kali's favorite color and a surprise present to the girls. Erinn's was an emerald green he braided into her long blonde hair that morning. Erinn squeaked as he stood back up and clutched at his forehead.

"Alright. Now we have to hurry or I am going to be late," he looked down at Kali while Erinn gripped the top of his head. Kali clung to his hand with her tiny one and smiled widely at him.

He smiled back and wished he didn't have to leave them again. *I feel like I am always leaving them for something. I just wish the world would stop for one minute and give me more time. I love them so much, but I wonder if they realize it?* Kali squeaked and swatted at a bug. "Stop that. He didn't do anything to you."

"But Tam, it's icky," she whined.

TJ laughed, "Maybe it thinks you are icky. We don't kill things just because they look different Kali."

Erinn laughed, "You are icky."

Kali pouted and TJ squeezed the other girl's knee, "If she is icky then so are you missy."

"No I'm not!" Erinn exclaimed in apparent horror.

"Yes," he told her. "You are identical in appearance."

"But you can tell us apart," Kali added in her innocent manner.

"I have known you two since you were born. I would be a poor excuse of a brother if I couldn't." He quickly pulled Kali out of the way of a dock worker and waved to an Orc hauling a net of fish over to a scale. He had been a friend of his older sisters and had helped them out a few times when he was younger, but TJ tried to stay in contact with him. "This way girls. To Colette's remember?"

The orc took two of his long strides over, his blue tinted dark skin shining in the sunlight, "Doing alright?"

TJ nodded and shook his hand, "Currently. Nice to see you Jerico."

Jerico handed a sack of fish to TJ with a broad white toothed smile, "For your help fixing those nets last week. Gotta get back to work." He patted TJ gently on the shoulder and strode back to the dock leaving TJ with the dripping fish.

"Colette's. This way," TJ nodded his head to his left, hoping Colette would have room in her cold box.

The girls frowned, "TJ are you coming back?"

Those words hit a chord in TJ and his throat thickened, "I will always come back. Promise."

Kali's hand circled around his thumb and she looked up with her heavily lashed eyes, "Good, because I don't want you to leave."

"I won't ever leave you and, I promise, I will always protect you. I won't let anything harm you while I am around," he swore and once again pulled Kali out of someone's way, then picked her up in one arm and set her down on the other side of a puddle. She giggled gleefully as Erinn squeaked at the sudden movements from her perch on his shoulders. "This way Kali."

She hopped over a bundle of fish and the girls made noises and complaints at the smell. TJ laughed and steered them down a back alley which was the shortcut to the Shop District and Colette's herbal remedies store. A few minutes later, they walked up the brick steps and tapped on her front door.

Colette came from around the back with a trowel and pail filled with leafy plants spilling out of it, "Good afternoon my dears! Oooo such pretty ribbons you have!"

They smiled, "TJ got them for us!"

Colette looked up at him, "How nice of him. Get yourselves inside and take those back packs off." She watched as the twins dashed inside and strode over to TJ, "And might I say not something you would usually pick out. Aly help you?"

"Nope. Did it all on my own. Aren't you proud of me?" He laughed and Colette nodded in approval. "Can you put this in your cold box? Jerico ran into me on the way here and just handed them to me and walked away."

"Of course. I have room. What was the occasion?" She set the pail and trowel down by the steps and began dusting herself off as TJ inhaled the mix of scents from her garden.

"They got their tests back and both had all A's on them," he sighed. "I wanted to reward them for it. Positive reinforcement. You know."

"Someday you are going to make a great father," she smiled and then frowned as he snorted, handing her the bag of fish. Colette rolled her cat like yellow green eyes at his snort. "No, I am serious and, in a way, you already are to those two. They are very lucky to have you."

"I rarely get time to see them and actually play with them or anything though. I wish I had the time, but between everything... I feel like I am constantly ditching them with either you or Grama," TJ sighed and fiddled with the cuff of his sweatshirt sleeve.

"Oh, never mind that. They know you are there if ever they need anything. And have you talked to Gary about bringing them around the shop?" TJ shook his head as the girls came pounding out of the little house. "Well, I did. He said that on the weekends it would be just fine."

TJ laughed and opened his arms out to Kali who launched herself off the top step and into his expectant arms. He wrapped her up tightly and kissed her forehead, "Are my aida's going to be good tonight?"

"Yes," they said in a chorus.

"Promise?" He set Kali down and kissed Erinn on the forehead as well.

"Promise," they repeated.

"Good," he looked at both in turn, "Now, I will be back later tonight and even though it is a Festival, I want you to get some good rest. Tomorrow I get some time off and I want you awake so we can go to the park. Understood?"

They smiled gleefully and Colette laughed at their enthusiasm, "I will make sure they get to sleep at a decent hour. When are you coming back? You are staying the night here too, right?"

TJ nodded, "If that's alright. It's closer to Mercante District than the Dead Lands."

"Always alright TJ," she gently laid a hand to his angular cheek, "Now go and get to work before you are late and good luck tonight at the Festival!"

He shuddered and hugged both girls before turning and calling over his shoulder, "Thanks for reminding me Colette! Thanks again!"

The woman shook her head as he leapt over her iron gate instead of opening it and careened back down the alley. She turned to the little girls with mischief in her cat like yellow-green eyes, "Now little one's what mess do we want to make tonight?"

"Rhubarb pie!" Kali yelled while Erinn yelled, "Strawberry!"

Colette sighed in laughter, "Erinn, I think we will go with Kali's suggestion since you are both allergic to strawberries."

Erinn frowned as she struggled to understand Colette's Layendrian, but finally figured it out, "Okay." She replied in the same language. Kali took her twin's hand, *"Tam is taking us to the park tomorrow?"*

"Yes. He said so. Will he keep his promise?" Erinn questioned back in their silent way.

Kali nodded, *"He always does."*

"No, he doesn't," Erinn pouted.

Kali looked defiantly at her sister, *"Almost always. He will."*

"I hope so," Erinn finally stated as Colette got out the ingredients to make the pie and ordered the girls to wash their hands and Kali agreed.

***

"No more!" Jake and the other band members yelled at TJ who had drilled them with the challenging parts of their songs for the past hour. "And we are on in fifteen minutes let us just breath for a few. Alright?"

TJ conceded, but didn't look pleased about it. He was nervous as usual and the crowd seemed larger than normal as word spread about the Festival through VeeCee's surrounding cities.

"Lightin' up will you?" Jake asked putting his arm around TJ's shoulder and shaking him slightly. "Everything will be fine."

TJ questioningly looked up and his voice was high pitched and cracking when he spoke, "Yeah. Sure it will be. I think I-" he stopped as a glass of water was shoved into his hands by the bands' drummer, David, "Thanks."

"Stop hyperventilating," they advised as TJ's breathing became more and more irregular.

"How is it that we have been performing for about two years now and you still get so worked up over it?" Jake questioned.

TJ shrugged trying to seem nonchalant, but failed as his face took on a tint of green. He sipped the water instead of attempting speech.

A stage hand poked his head around a red curtain and looked at a sheet of paper, "Andronicus is up next! Five minutes! Get ready to go on!"

The green in TJ's normally golden face darkened and he sprinted to the edge of the platform and vomited over the side into the bushes. He wiped his mouth on the back of his hand as Jake and the other two band members came over and apologized to the girl TJ almost knocked over.

"Come on. Get your guitar," Jake coaxed as TJ looked ready to run away. "You will be fine. You always are."

"Andronicus!" The stage hand yelled as a storm of applause sounded from the other side of the gently wafting curtain.

Jake shoved TJ's guitar into his hand and the other two pushed him out onto the stage behind Jake.

The broad-shouldered young man stood relaxed and comfortably spoke to the thundering crowd gathered on the green hills of the park at the city center, as TJ adjusted the power to his guitar making sure the sound would be properly amplified. "We're Andronicus for those of you who don't know. Presented to you by Make A Noise from the Shop District," Jake explained as the crowd began to grow larger. "We first would like to introduce ourselves. My name is Jake and I'll be playing bass and lead vocals. On the drums is David. Over there is Chris playing back up guitar and piano. Last is TJ who is singing back-up vocals, lead guitar, and- well, everything else." A rumble of laughter sputtered from the crowd and TJ hit the power button as he strummed a chord followed by David rolling out a rhythm, "Guess we're ready. First song is *Fire The Water.* Hope you like it."

They began the song nice and easy, but as they started the second time through Jake and the others put their plan into action and Jake stepped away from the microphone and closed his mouth. TJ didn't notice at first, until a confused silence threatened the crowd for a brief moment, only to break into a huge applause.

TJ looked over at Jake to figure out what was going on and froze at the realization of being the only one singing. His voice caught in his throat and his nimble fingers stumbled to a stop on the neck of his guitar as he backed up, but Jake stepped behind him and pushed TJ to the microphone again and didn't let him go, "You're fine. Just sing."

The half-elf shook his head as David and Chris looped the song back around. TJ took a deep breath of air and, fingers stumbling, began to play again, but he couldn't calm down enough to sing. The others began looping again and TJ attempted to stutter out the lyrics, and the crowd began singing with him. It reassured him immensely and his voice grew stronger as the second verse began again.

The conclusion of the song ended in thunderous applause and once again Jake walked up to the microphone, a huge smile on his face, "So as you can tell, we have a confession to make. TJ is, in fact, the lead singer and, also as you can see, incredibly angry at us for letting you all find out." TJ gave him a murderous look as the crowd laughed good naturedly. "How about we give him another applause for encouragement?" The audience exploded into applause, louder than the first as the band started up the next song.

***

TJ collapsed on the stairs leading down to the back of the Shop District's stone buildings, "I am going to kill you, once I can move."

Jake shrugged, "You needed to get over it eventually. The audience loved you."

"They were being kind. I messed up," TJ said taking large gulps of air like an asthmatic.

"You were scared shitless," David consoled. "Don't worry about it."

"Seriously, you have a great voice. You don't need to worry," Jake stood and walked down a few of the stone steps until he could see TJ's face better in the moonlight.

Applause once again sounded behind them as Sound System started their first song. TJ stood on shaky legs, "Don't you ever do that to me again."

"Won't. They would know it was you. It would be pointless," Jake grinned evilly.

"Run," David advised, as he saw the half-elf take a deep breath and shift his legs preparing to move. Chris and Jake took off running down the stairs as David, smartly, ran the opposite way. TJ jumped the last five steps and agilely sprinted around the few people separating him from his band members. It didn't take him long to catch up and tackle one to the ground, "I should kill you for that."

"Come on. You deserve the recognition," Jake spluttered, mouth filled with dirt.

Chris tackled TJ off Jake and the two boys attempted to pin him, but TJ spun away and kicked out catching Chris in the stomach, "I didn't want it."

"No, you were scared to have it," Chris chocked out.

Jake, finally, got TJ pinned with the help of Chris and David began creeping back over, "Get over it TJ. They applauded louder than ever."

"Polite…that's all… it was," he squeaked as air abandoned his lungs from the pressure of the boys.

David laughed as he sat by TJ's head, "There is no such thing as a polite crowd except at a school concert or a recital and, even then, sometimes it doesn't exist."

"You forgot about when King Nor-Ten speaks; people are generally nice, because it's punishable by death otherwise," Chris added.

TJ snorted and began sneezing as dirt went up his nose, "Okay, okay. Let me up."

"You won't hurt us if we do?"

"No," TJ coughed. "I won't."

The boys slowly removed themselves and stood, "Anyone for the ports or a bonfire?" Jake questioned.

TJ put his hand up and Jake gripped it, pulling him to his feet, "I need to drop my instruments off and get to The Bakery. My shift is up soon."

"It's cold," David said, thoughtfully for once. "And I signed up to work with TJ."

"Bonfire then and we can have it at my place. My mother would love to make us food and you can bring your sisters if you want," Jake said looking at TJ.

***

David and TJ took off, running out of The Bakery at the end of their shift to Jake's home. It seemed like a relatively short amount of time, but they were on their feet the whole three hours as the two boys ran between the different tables and rooms.

"Sorry I ditched you with the drunks," David called to TJ as they leapt over a stand of tomatoes.

TJ glanced quickly to David and skipped around a little boy, "No worries. They weren't so bad. Just boisterous. Got a huge tip too."

"How much?" David stumbled on the curb as they entered the Mercante District and the crowds thinned.

The half-elf grinned, "Two Gold Pieces. I think they got them confused with Coppers."

The two boys laughed as they sprinted around Jake's house to the backyard devoid of fallen leaves despite the fall. Already a bonfire was lit, the flames dancing in the night. Shadows framed the outskirts of the field of light the fire put out and a small hum of noise issued above the popping and crackling of the logs. David and TJ slowed as they neared the fire and their friends came into view along with the table of food with a cake placed on it reading "Happy 16th Birthday" written in blue frosting.

"Tam!" A high-pitched voice squeaked and ran over on tiny legs with her duplicate on her heels. The young girls latched onto him and hugged him around the waist.

"Hello aida's," TJ smiled as he patted them on their heads. "How has your evening been? Late for you to be up."

"Great! We got to color and make your birthday cake and rhubarb pie!" Erinn gleefully exclaimed to her brother ignoring his last comment. "Jake's mom came and got us. She wanted to surprise you."

TJ smiled and moved to sit down on the grass, "That's great. I'm glad you two had fun. Jake did – thanks."

Jake patted TJ on the shoulder as he handed him his cherry colored acoustic guitar. "Colette said to enjoy and to just stay here tonight," TJ nodded in response. With one little blonde girl in his lap and the other sitting next to him clutching his arm, TJ tuned his instrument and began to play. It was a folk song everyone in Astèndre knew. All of the Dead Landers sang and danced to the music, including Kali and Erinn, as the night wore on.

After a time, they ate the birthday cake and, eventually, TJ and David carried the twin girls into the house and set them down to sleep in the guest bedroom before returning outside for more dancing – and in TJ's case playing. It was one of those rare nights that felt calm and peaceful. TJ smiled to himself as his fingers flew across the strings with barely any thought.

***

"TJ!" Jake snapped his fingers in front of his face for the second time and he shook his head, pulled from the trance.

"What?" He questioned.

"What is so interesting over there?" Jake craned his neck looking down the alley, but only a cement wall painted his view.

TJ shrugged, "Nothing. What did you want?"

It was Jake's turn to shrug, "Just didn't want you thinking about whatever it was you were thinking of."

The half-elf looked confused, "Why's-that?"

"Please don't slur your words together like a slum kid. It doesn't become you. You are better than that," Jake sighed.

"Sorry charté," TJ bowed to Jake as he used the Layendrian term for lord. "I didn't mean to offend you with the language of my backing."

Jake sighed, louder this time. TJ was being really touchy today, but it was obvious why. His lip was split and a discoloration colored on his right cheek bone as well as cuts on his back from where his stepfather whipped him. The only reason Jake knew was because Aysté had heard from James and Evan that shattering glass and yelling went on for hours the night before. She came into Make A Noise earlier and made him peel his shirt off his shredded back so she could clean it and properly bandage it. "Sorry Tam."

The young man shrugged again, "No matter." Jake caught the vacant unemotional tone in his voice, but before he could say anything TJ jumped off the wall and began patting the pockets on his jeans and then ran inside and began dumping the contents out of his bag.

Apparently, he didn't find what he was looking for. He stood quickly and with a new anxious expression spreading across his face, he wrung his hands and turned to his best friend, "Could you tell Gary I had to run to Colette's?"

"Yes. Sure. Will you be coming back?" Jake questioned as he realized what it was TJ was missing. His best friend nodded before running out. Jake followed, but went up to the counter where Gary stood talking to a customer.

He paused seeing Jake stride up, "Was that TJ running out?" Jake nodded. "Everything alright? He usually doesn't just run out like that."

"He'll be fine. He forgot to take his medicine this morning. He ran to Colette's. He said he would be back soon."

The owner nodded, "At least he went to get it. He's had a rough morning so far."

Again, Jake nodded as Aly slipped into the shop. He wrapped his arm around her, "And how are you this morning beautiful?"

Gary shook his head smiling and turned back to the customer. One thing Gary wouldn't trade for the world was the sense of kinship his employees had. Gary had not grown up in a safe and loving home, but promised himself if he ever made a home of his own, he would give people what he didn't have. He succeeded in doing that and it warmed his heart in a way nothing else ever could and, besides that, they all worked hard and, most of the time, their friends would help.

Aly hopped up to the counter and once the customer left, she smiled brightly at the middle-aged owner, "Hi Aly. You look like you want something."

She shifted from side to side, "Perhaps." He leaned under the counter and pulled out his accounting book to go through, then raised an inquiring eyebrow. "Okay, well, since we had the Festival last month I was wondering if we were going to have the staff party sometime soon. I had an idea for a masquerade theme! And it would be just before the Festival of Lights – so fitting!"

He couldn't help, but smile at her enthusiasm and not wanting to see the sparkle die from her blue eyes he nodded, "But Aly... you aren't even a staff member."

She laughed, "No, but I basically live here along with your staff. So, I can set up for it?"

"Yes, my dear," he popped open the register and pulled a gold piece and a few silvers out and held them out for her. She took them with slight hesitation, "To cover any costs, including food. I want an exact list of any charges, you hear?"

She nodded, "I will."

"That's a good girl," he marked the expense in the ledger and waved as she scampered out.

Aly's bright mood didn't last long as she ran out of Make A Noise and turned the corner to smack into a small brunette. The other girl looked up and bit her lip in apprehension, "Sorry Aly."

She glared, "Watch where you are walking. You don't own this place."

Hayle entered into the fight knowing it would come bidden or not, "Stop right there. I know you hate me and I know you only put up with me because of TJ, but why? Why do you hate me so much?"

Aly smiled bitterly, "Really? You want to know Mercant?"

Hayle flinched at the slander of the district she lived in, "Yes, I do."

"Because I see you as no better than the scum you slink around with. You profess you care for TJ and you may be dating him and have done a lot for him, but I see one big flaw that has cut him deeply already and it is only a matter of time before I will step in and take care of it. I know I won't be alone. So, you had better watch yourself you...you-you," Aly was lost for words in her anger.

Looking at the other girl, tears came into her eyes, "What are you talking about? I slink around? When did I hurt him?"

"Don't you dare cry," Aly fumed, "You hurt him with your stupidity. With your nobility. By ignoring him in public and through your deceit to the people you call friends. Have you not noticed that all of his friends know? Besides Sabella who knows?"

Hayle bit her lip, "No one."

"Exactly," Aly said triumphantly.

"But-But how could I tell them without getting him put in prison for it or turning on my own family?"

"Two solutions come to mind," Aly paused "You at least admit you are friends, because that would help or the other option is you figure out what is more important to you. Him or your stupid nobility. There are plenty who have made that choice before you. Now it is your turn. Figure it out before we make the choice for you Mercant."

Aly stalked past her leaving the girl clutching her paper to her pounding chest. Her eyes spilled over and she brushed them away angrily. *It isn't like you didn't see that coming and you know it is true. All of it. Eventually you will have to decide.* Hayle told herself and she knew exactly which path she wanted to take, but for some reason she felt like something pulled her away from that end with an iron grip.

She sucked in her breath and calmed herself before continuing down the block to TJ's work. Gary looked up from the counter as she pushed open the door and the bell jangled above her. "Morning Hayle. Are you alright?"

Hayle tossed her abundant curls over her shoulder and smiled, "Rough morning. I'm alright. I actually wanted to show you something I found." She spread the paper out on the counter and gave him the chance to read it. When he looked up, she asked, "What do you think?"

He grinned, "You are thinking of this for Andronicus? TJ's band?"

She nodded, "I know they have the potential to be great. Each one is so individually talented and together they are incredible. But they can't apply for the scholarship themselves."

Gary went back and read the final part of the paper and paused, "Hayle, it costs forty silver pieces per person to enter as reassurance for the scouts. I would support them and put their names in, but I just don't have the money to get the whole band in just now." He sighed, "I know if they were able to get the scholarship and get into the Academy of Music they would make it too."

Hayle smiled and placed a large pouch of coins on the counter, "Eighty sp. If you can fund the other two."

His eyes widened, "That has to be all of your savings!"

"Not quite," her smile grew bigger, "My family will pay for me when I go to university. TJ doesn't have that and he has his sisters to worry about as well. Jake is the only one who won't have to pay on his own." Her face fell, "Please Gary. This may be the only thing I can really do for him. Do you understand?"

Gary frowned wishing the world was less judgmental, "I do my dear. I can fund the other two. Let me just write this up. How did you get your hands on this anyway?"

"I have a cousin who lives in the capital and, when I visited her last weekend, I went to see the academy since TJ had been talking of wishing he could go one day. I just happened on this and picked it up." She ran her fingers over the porcelain keys of the piano. "Thank you, Gary. I appreciate your help."

He smiled broadly, "No problem." The bell to the shop rang and TJ strode back in out of breath from running, "You alright?" Gary asked as he put the application onto his ledger book and took the pouch of silver Hayle gave him into his arms to let TJ take over at the front.

The half-elf smiled and nodded, "Yes. Sorry I ran out."

"That's alright. I need you to run the register and it's tuning day," Gary said walking to the back and pushing open the door with his shoulder. "Try not to make too much noise and if you do, open the front door."

TJ grinned. He loved tuning day. It meant he had the excuse to play all the expensive instruments in the store. Hayle laughed at the boyish look of excitement spreading across his face. She slipped her hand into his and squeezed. He looked down at her and gripped her other hand, "Hi."

She smiled, "Hi. How are you?"

He took a deep breath, "Better. Your eyes are a little red. Everything alright?"

Her smile faltered as she thought back to Aly, but knew she wouldn't tell TJ what happened, "Just a long morning. I'm better now. Do you mind if I hang out here for a bit?"

TJ looked at her in slight surprise, "Are you sure you want to? A whole manner of people will be coming in and out."

She shook her head and looked straight into his lavender tinted eyes, "Doesn't matter. I don't get to be with you very often." She smiled up at him, "Plus, I get to hear you play. Lovely background music for doing homework."

He laughed, "Maybe." He let go of her hands and walked over to the back door and leaned in, "Jake! Tuning day. Get your butt out here and help!"

A whoop of excitement echoed out, followed by Jake. Hayle laughed and pulled a book out of her purse and perched herself on a piano bench as the two boys began to tune the mass of instruments in the shop.

***

It came to the point where he needed to talk to Hayle. He didn't know what he could do to make her understand, but he at least needed to try. He didn't care what happened after. He'd been disappointed before; he would get over it.

They started dating in Greenmoon and it was now Duskmoon. If she didn't know exactly how she felt now, then maybe he needed to rethink. It seemed worth the risk to him, but he didn't know if she thought the same. He planned exactly what to say when they met up that night. They were going to stargaze. It wasn't exactly the best plan and he knew it, but he couldn't think of anything else.

At first, he took her to dinner just outside of the Shop District. She was wary at first since it was a place known to collect members from the gang called the Lightning's, but TJ was friends with most of them. The gang members even accepted her right from the start. Many came over to meet her and chat, but soon, with the meal finished, he led her to the sandy shore by the ports.

"You're really quiet tonight," Hayle muttered as she looked up at his angular face.

TJ bit his lip, "I'm always quiet."

"Not like this. At least you aren't with me," she eyed him and he took a deep breath and let it out slowly not realizing he admitted to her something was on his mind. She sighed, feeling nervous, "What is it?"

"You don't want to hear it," he paused. She sat up to better look at him and he copied her.

Hayle eyed him nervously, "Just tell me TJ. I can handle it."

"Okay," he grimaced and tried to figure out a way to explain his thoughts despite all of his careful planning, "I have to explain something first. Alright?" She nodded and he continued, "My father loved me, but he left because of me; Heather – my older sister – died 'cause I – I," TJ's eyes filled and his voice stuck. He didn't realize how hard it would be to say this.

Hayle raised her eyebrow and tilted her head to the side as her heart began to race. *He never talks about his past. So why is he now?* She watched his eyes and her entire body suddenly felt like it had been dumped into a freezing cold river and, immediately, her heart rate picked up. She felt it thumping in her throat. She looked into his eyes, which from the dim moonlight were a clear blue, almost transparent in color.

He swallowed and tried again, "I was stupid. She came after me. That's how she died. My mother blamed me. One of the reasons she hurts me. Oreal – my twin – I never see, and Roger is a dick. I have nothing Hayle, and no one. No one is ever willing to stick their neck out for me, even though I always do for them," he shifted and took another deep breath to attempt to stop his shaking. "It's just that – well, it's like I am always on the back burner. I feel like it's the same with you. I'm there only when you want me to be." He stopped and looked straight at her and, for a brief moment, she felt as if he looked at her soul, "It comes to this: I need to know you care enough. That I am worth the risk. Otherwise this needs to stop."

Hayle sat stunned, surprised he said this. It was unlike him and she didn't know what to say. Her thoughts began to drift to when they first met in the hallway. Their hands touched and she knew he was right for her. She knew she would say yes. That she would do anything and everything for him. Then almost as if someone else controlled her thoughts, they shifted. *How can he ask this of me? There is no way I could give up everything to be with him. I wouldn't be able to show my face in public ever again and he could get thrown in jail.* She pushed the thoughts away. *But I would give up everything for him. I love him.* Her thoughts were dragged away from that path immediately, *but he could die. And if you love him so much, why have you never told him?* She shook her head.

TJ bit his lip and nodded. His once passionate voice suddenly became devoid of emotion, "I can still tutor you if you want."

"Thanks. I would like that," her response was devoid of emotion as she clung to the only way they could still see one another. She didn't want to lose him completely and something just didn't feel right about giving up on their relationship, but try as she might to grasp it, she felt like she was being pulled that much harder in the other direction. "Where are you going?" Hayle asked as he stood up and looked ready to leave.

"No point sticking around. I'll see you after school tomorrow," he mumbled and disappeared into the dark, feeling an emptiness he hadn't in a while. *Something just doesn't feel right.*

***

Home is definitely a place I should have avoided, TJ thought as he dodged a plate being thrown at his head. *Especially after finding out I mean nothing to the girl who means the world to me.* Preoccupied by his thoughts, he didn't notice Roger, his stepfather, come up from behind until it was too late. Roger quickly, for such a large man, gripped TJ around his small waist and pinned him against the cupboard with the door knobs stabbing into him in uncomfortable places.

"P-please. Duh-don't," TJ gasped out. He knew what was coming and tried with all his might to escape. Roger took hold of his wrists; his mother lashed them together with rope, and proceeded to tie him to the top cupboard. TJ bit back the plea of mercy on his lips knowing it wouldn't do him any good. *At least the girls aren't here,* he reminded himself and gulped at the sound of the polished leather belt whistling through the air before burying into the scarred flesh of his back.

He gasped in pain and a small yelp issued from his mouth – the only sound he let escape – before he sighed minutes later as he fell into the blissful black of unconsciousness.

***

He plagued Hayle's thoughts all day, but he didn't show up to his first classes and that was never a good sign. Hayle hoped it didn't have to do with her. Last night, as she lay on the quilt and felt the warmth of where his body had been, she realized suddenly, like walking out of a fog, they were meant to be together. There was a rightness to it. The stars began smiling down upon her and the spheres of heaven sang. *I need him,* she realized, *and he needs me.* As she stood gazing around the locker banks in the middle of the day, she knew she needed to speak with him. Hayle's mind wandered through the different possibilities and then stopped her thoughts in their tracks.

TJ, finally, appeared across the hallway walking toward his locker, but something about his steps were off; he didn't walk with his usual grace. When Jake gripped his shoulder, TJ bit his lip as his face contorted in pain. He backed up from his best friend as if frightened. *That's never good. Usually means he has been beaten badly to have him forget his friends would never hurt him.* She watched the two talk and saw Jake run off to class. Hayle hurried to catch up.

"Jake!" Hayle called and watched the tall young man turn and stop. He didn't look pleased, but a look of surprise altered his features that she would call after him in the crowded hallway.

"What do you want?" He asked in a flat voice.

Hayle bit her lip, "I'm sorry. I'm going to fix it I swear. I didn't know. I wasn't thinking."

"You never seem to. You do understand he loves you right?" Jake's voice suddenly grew in his annoyance at the small woman in front of him and ignored the people beginning to stare. "TJ may not ever say it or understand, but to those who know him, it's obvious. He's scared of love and you proved he has a reason to be."

"I know! I know," tears began streaming down her face and Jake helplessly looked around for some way to stop it, but Hayle began speaking again. "He's supposed to tutor me today. I'll tell him I was stupid. Jake, I love him. I know I do. Every little thing about him. I didn't mean for this to happen. It's like – I had no control. Please understand."

Jake sighed and wrapped an arm around her shoulder in the now almost empty hallway, "As long as you set things right. Be careful though. His stepfather and mother whipped him pretty bad last night. Apparently, there was a spoon in the sink."

"Can't he just live with you or me?" She wiped her hazel eyes, turned glassy from her tears.

He shook his head, "He won't leave his sister's. You know that."

"I know," she frowned. "I'll make things right."

Jake rubbed her shoulder, "Come on. We're going to be late to choir."

The last two hours of the day seemed to be on fast forward for Hayle and she soon stood on the steps waiting for TJ, which was a change as he usually waited for her. She saw him jumping down the stairs looking annoyed and upset, "TJ!" She yelled stepping into his path.

"Hayle, I have to go," he tried to step around her and she could tell his mind was on something totally different than their plans, but she tried to take his hand anyway.

"I need to talk to you," she said desperately as he pulled his hand away from her like it was made of thorns.

TJ rolled his eyes as he recognized the emotion on her face, "That's great for you, but I really have to go. Erinn and Kali got in trouble at school and their teacher sent a letter over here for me to come and get them."

"I understand, but I really need to talk to you. Could you bring them over? My Mom won't mind," Hayle almost pleaded.

TJ shifted and looked around at the people beginning to stop and watch, "That's fine. I'll be over in about an hour."

She nodded in understanding and tenderly touched the back of his hand as he took off down the steps.

It took her less than five minutes after he left to realize he would, more than likely, not come to her house. It wouldn't be a punishment for the little twins, since they loved coming to visit and, in an effort to make them realize they did wrong, TJ would take his sister's home and ground them to their room all night. She struggled for a moment, feeling pulled in two directions. Following him won out. She took off at a jog to his sister's school hoping she remembered the correct way.

She didn't remember and the alley she turned down wasn't a short cut anyone would ever want to take.

3

Chapter 3

I've always heard stories of girls being crazy and sending mixed signals, but they really weren't kidding, TJ thought as he quickly strode through all the back alleys and short cuts possible. He kept fiddling with his frayed backpack straps in confusion over Hayle's actions and resolved to go and see her tonight after dropping the girls off at Colette's as planned.

As he walked through a doorway and onto the blinding street it happened again, the visions of people dying and mutilated corpses put together with red waterfalls and dying trees, but that wasn't what shocked him. After the death visions another death followed, one of a clock tower reading five minutes to 2:45, a sign reading Everclear, three boys with a look of an insatiable hunger on their faces, and Hayle – back pressed against a brick wall at the end of an alley. Whatever the boys said to her gave her an uncomfortable and terrified expression. TJ watched the boys close in on her and she tried to beat them off, but she was too little. TJ's mind tried to pull away from the vision, but he couldn't. As the boys pulled away, they laughed and stabbed her before running.

TJ began violently sneezing as a little boy tugged on his arm trying to make him move from the doorway. He wiped his streaming eyes and, immediately, took off running to Everclear and to Hayle, praying he could get there in time. He rounded the corner and into the alley knowing he missed the boys, her blood seeped onto the dirt covered ground. He skidded to a halt and kneeled next to her. His jeans began to soak in her blood, but he ignored it, "Hayle. Hayle, please don't be dead. Sweetie, come on open your eyes for me."

Her eyelids fluttered open, "TJ? Wha-what are you doing here?"

"Don't worry about that," he took his shirt off revealing a lean stomach blemished only with a bruise on his sternum. The half-elf pushed his shirt against her stomach and she gasped, but he needed to stem the flow of her fleeing life.

She grimaced in pain, "I need to-to tell… you something."

TJ shook his head, "Tell me later. Need to get you some place that can help you." He pulled her onto his lap and began to look for a place to take her.

"No TJ… You know… it's too late," Hayle began shaking violently as she placed her small hand against his face forcing him to meet her eyes just like the day they searched for Erinn in the riot. "Just listen. Can you… do… that?" He nodded listening intently to her fading voice. "I- I messed up… big time and… I was… wrong. You are… worth… the… risk. More than… worth it. TJ," she smiled tiredly as TJ pulled her hair out of her porcelain face, his hand shaking. She was losing strength fast and he could tell she was struggling to say the last part, "I…"

Even TJ's elven ears couldn't catch what she said as she died. He felt her body go limp as her hand slipped off his cheek. Something in TJ broke as blood dripped out the side of her mouth. He felt the tears start and he didn't bother stopping them, because at that moment it seemed the universe cried too. Nothing made sense and he didn't know what to do. He went numb as he picked up her vacant body and carried it into Everclear and sat waiting as the police came to figure out what to do.

***

The store manager froze as a half-elf walked in with the lifeless body of a teenage girl cradled in his arms dripping blood onto his normally spotless floor. His eyes were vacant and yet creepily beautiful as he stared at the manager as if waiting for him to tell the young man what to do. He floundered for a moment in shock and confusion, but this wasn't the first time he had seen a dead body or even someone killed.

"Lay her down here. Come on, over here," the older man, finally, walked over and sat the tall half-elf down by the counter. He laid her down and slid to the floor. As the half-elf curled his legs into his chest the manager noticed his jeans were dark with her spilled blood along with his hands and stomach stained red. The manager turned to his store clerk, "Run and get the police. Hurry now." The younger man faltered for a moment, his face pale, but the manager didn't have time for him to get his act together, so banged his fist on the counter, "Now. Police." The man scurried out.

He kneeled down by the half-elf, "Are you alright? You're not hurt?" No response came. He just sat staring. No matter what the manager did he couldn't get the half-elf to react.

Finally, three police came running into the shop followed by the clerk. One went to the girl and the other two went to the half-elf and store manager.

"What's your name son?" The bulky police questioned. But he still didn't reply. The police turned to the manager, "What happened?"

"He walked in from the alley carrying her. I think he's in shock, but I don't know who they are or what happened," the manager said.

"Go find the scene where this happened and get it cleaned up," he told his partners and turned back to the half-elf. "Son, we need you to talk to us. Alright? We can help." No response. The police gripped his shoulder causing pain to flare up and burn through his shock.

TJ turned his head, "I-my sisters-school-Hayle-raped-gone-need-I didn't... they..."

"Deep breaths. Start with your name," the police man advised.

His mind went into automatic and almost too quiet to hear answered, "Tamynaen Jacob Christiansin Zyrqrouise-berĭta."

"Well, Tamy-"

"TJ."

"TJ," the police man false smiled. "Now, who are *they*?"

"The three boys. Did terrible..." TJ's voice trailed off.

The police man didn't push it, "Do you know this girl?" TJ nodded. "Who is she?"

"She's not there anymore."

The police man exchanged a look with the manager, "Okay. Well, who was she? And do you... know what happened?"

TJ nodded again, "Hayle Mae Carico. She got trapped... in that alley... they - terrible... her. Stabbed her... left her... alone."

"You weren't with her then?" He asked.

TJ shook his head before answering vacantly, "I saw it."

"Why didn't you stop it?"

"Visions. I saw it," his face contorted in pain not physical, but felt much worse. "I would have- I couldn't stop it – never would let that happen. I tried to get to her. I loved her-" he froze at his final admission and spoke no more on the subject no matter what they said.

"I need to get my sisters," TJ mumbled after he had been silent for a time and Hayle's parents were sent for.

The police man looked at him, "Where are they?"

"School. Port Primary. I need to pick them up. Should have a long time ago."

At that moment, Hayle's parents came into the shop and froze. Marques gulped in air like a fish out of water while Lily cried hysterically muttering, "My baby," all the while.

"TJ, were you with her?" Marques asked and he nodded. "Good. I'm glad. Are you hurt at all?"

"His back is torn up, but it doesn't appear to have been from this," the police said as TJ shook his head.

Marques pulled TJ to his feet as Lily's breathing calmed, "Can you come with us back to the house?"

"My sister's. They're at school. I need to get them."

The older man began shaking as he took on TJ's appearance and it broke through the natural calm that came with being a doctor of high merit, "We can take them, but TJ you- you are covered in blood and you- you aren't wearing a shirt."

TJ looked down at his body as if just realizing that. Lily gazed up at the two men, her eyes streaming with tears, "It's going on three thirty dear. When were you supposed to get them?"

"I got the message at two fifteen," he began shaking again as he realized all of this came to pass within an hour. *Life changes so quickly.*

The manager chewed his lip in thought, "I have a spare set of work pants in the back. You can take them. Wash up in the bathroom as best you can. Don't know what to do about a shirt though."

TJ pulled his sweatshirt out of his bag one of the police brought to him. He didn't feel like ever talking again.

***

He didn't show up to school on Mierten and he didn't come in to work that weekend or show up for band practice. Aly eventually broke down and went to his house to see if he was there, but if he was, he didn't answer the door. Grama, finally, came out from next door and explained in her crackly old voice, "Hayle died in his arms. He isn't quite right. I fear for him."

"What? No wonder Sabella has been acting strange," Aly swallowed hard, feeling uncomfortable. She didn't really like Hayle, but TJ loved her and Hayle loved him back. It was that stupid law that kept them apart. "What can we do?"

"About TJ?" Grama asked and Aly nodded, her normally tanned and freckled face turned pale. "This isn't the first time someone died that he loved. He isn't taking it well."

"How are his sisters?" She absentmindedly began running her hand through her curly blonde hair. "There has to be something Grama."

Grama placed a wrinkly liver spotted hand against the girl's cheek, "Calm. You need to stay strong for him. Colette and I will take care of his sisters, but Jake, you, and Aysté need to keep him off those drugs. Help him to realize he isn't all alone."

Aly shivered as she remembered last year when he had been addicted to opium. It wasn't the first time either. His mother, Annah, gave it to him. He resisted for a while, but the drug quickly became too much and he fell under. He became shaky and thin. He didn't sleep and she could tell he hated the drug and himself. She, nor Jake, nor Aysté could get him off. Aly frowned remembering who finally did – Hayle. "I'll try," she answered in a choked voice.

***

Lily and Marques always suspected their daughter had feelings for the tall half-elf and the fact he had been present at her murder cemented it. His eyes were vacant and his face showed no emotion, but the way he held his sisters when they retrieved them from school screamed of the amount of pain he was in. He was just as bad off as them, but in a different way. In thanks and sorrow, a week later, they sent her violin to him at Make A Noise with a small note attached reading:

We will always remember what you did for our baby girl and we thank you for it. I hope you will accept her violin and remember the good times. We know you did everything you could for her. If ever you need anything, we are there for you. Never hesitate to ask.

Our love,

Lily and Marques

TJ couldn't even smile as he picked the beautiful dark violin out of the case and tuned it. He played without thought in the back of Make A Noise, but the haunting melody spread through the door to the front and it reduced everyone to tears.

***

He didn't get better, even though he began coming to school again. Instead, he reverted back to when Jake first met him four years ago. TJ wouldn't talk and when he did his voice was hollow and his eyes, vacant, took on a color of murky green brown. Sabella, in an attempt to help him, finally, chose between the Mercante kids and the Dead Landers. She told everyone Hayle and TJ dated before she died and began to hang out with them instead. It warmed him a little, but only for a time. He was lucky no one did anything about them breaking the law, but he also didn't care.

All his friends tried to help. They would drag him to their homes and force him to eat for fear of him starving himself unintentionally. Aysté, in particular, put out her hand to save him and it kept him off the drugs, but they all realized the only thing keeping him alive was his little sisters and the letters he began to receive weekly from his twin sister, Oreal, who lived with his aunt in the country.

For a time, it seemed to help. He loved hearing from Oreal and about everything she did. It gave him a distraction and he resolved to go and see them this summer if he got the chance. He hadn't been to Loui in over a year.

But things tend to come in pairs and not long after he began to get better, the next tragedy struck. Aysté became sick with a deadly virus. The elven woman knew she couldn't possibly overcome the disease and, with her failing health, she took TJ aside in her hospital room.

Aysté pushed herself up in bed and TJ tried to get her to lay back down, but she refused, "No. You will listen to me. Understand?" TJ didn't respond out loud, just nodded and she continued in Layendrian. "Good. I want you to promise me something. Can you do that?"

He shook his head, "Stop. Stop that now. No promises."

"Tammy… don't you make this harder for me," she sighed wearily and rubbed her eyes with the back of her hand. "Promise me something, please." He shook his head. "You know I am dying. So, stop acting like a child."

"I am a child Aysté! I am sixteen years old!"

"You may be sixteen, but you have not been a child since you were ten."

TJ's eyes welled up, but he refused to let the hot tears spill over, "Only because my sister died. It isn't fair."

"Life isn't fair and you of all people have experienced that," she looked sadly at him despite the stern voice.

"Doesn't mean I have to like it," his voice caught in his throat. "I certainly have an angel watching over me," he laughed in a cruel manner. "Angels. Fuck them and fuck Atropos."

Her eyes widened, "Don't you curse a god." She said nothing about the angels though. They both knew angels didn't exist. They were used to refer to unlucky people and situations. She couldn't count the number of times she had used the common phrase 'I have an angel watching over me' when she failed a test or tripped over something.

"That's a joke Aysté. Angels aren't real and neither are gods. If gods were real, I don't think they would let anyone's life suck as much as mine. They couldn't live with themselves. And if angels were, well, they would have done something to help me by now."

Aysté closed her eyes, "You don't mean that."

"Yes," TJ sighed, "I do."

"Tammy…"

"What?" He moved and sat down next to the girl he knew was dying.

"Do you really not believe in a god?"

"Yes… wait no. I don't know. Why does it matter?"

"Just answer the question."

"Yes, I do believe in a god, but I think he has a cruel sense of humor and laughs at the joke of a life I have and is just waiting for me to break."

"Well," she breathed shakily, "At least you believe in a god, but are you breaking?"

His voice was strained when he answered and he wouldn't look at her, "I already am. Aysté you can't die. Please hold on. Don't leave me here without you. When Heather died, it was you who took care of me in her place and you were only twelve. What am I supposed to do without you? I can't do this." He paused and his voice became thick with unshed tears, "I can't do this on my own. Please. Please don't leave me here in this hell."

She bit her lower lip and closed her eyes, "You can. I am dying TJ. You know that. I can't control it and, if I could, you know I would stay. You can do this. You have to."

"I don't have to do anything."

"Don't be difficult."

"I could die right after you. There is nothing that says I couldn't."

She glared at him, "If it is by your own hand, I swear I will… I guess I couldn't do anything, but Atropos have mercy on your soul because when I catch you in the afterlife I won't leave you alone for centuries."

"Promise?" He met her eyes and she witnessed a tinge of lime green blossom in his irises.

"Tamynaen Jacob. Do not push me," she sighed and took his hand. "I know this is hard for you, especially after losing Hayle. I know…"

"Stop. Please don't," he began shaking.

"Don't what?" She looked confused.

"Don't talk about her. It hurts too much. I don't want to even think about it. Please," a strangled sob came out at the end, but he kept his tears in check.

Aysté reached over and took his other hand, "You have to in order to let go."

"I can't let go. It was my fault," a tear slid out the corner of his eye, but he just let it slide as if it were condensation on a glass.

"Don't let this consume you. You can't let it destroy your life because without you the girls will surely be lost too. You need to think of them as well."

"Aysté, do you think I am stupid?" He shook his head angrily, "They are *all* I think about. They are the only reason I haven't killed myself already."

She froze, "What?"

"You heard me. What other reason do I have to live?"

"Plenty. You are incredibly talented and have your whole life ahead of you. Not to mention you have friends who love you."

"What is that in comparison to a family who treats you like shit and reminds you every hour of the day you were a mistake and they wish you had never been born. Ribs constantly broken or bruised and a back torn all to hell. That no matter how much you work it is never enough and you watch your sisters being half starved and know that your parents are wasting their money on beer and drugs to shoot you up with and then laugh as you come down. Where is the comparison? Tell me because I can't see it."

Tears fell out of her eyes and she pulled him down to her and wrapped her thin arms around him, "There isn't Tammy. There isn't. But promise me you will stick it out. Just two more years and you can take the twins with you when you get in to the Academy of Music and be on your own. Promise me you will let your friends help you."

He wrapped his arms around her waist and knew that he was losing the last person he would ever let hold him like this, but even though he shook, no more tears would come. He had nothing left, "I will try."

"You must. Let someone take care of you for once."

"I can't promise that, but I will promise you I won't kill myself. Only because of my sisters. I can't leave them alone. Is that enough?" He mumbled into her shoulder.

She stroked his soft black hair, "Yes. That's enough, but do try love."

They sat there holding each other for a long time before the nurse came in to check on Aystè and make sure she was comfortable. The nurse had no idea what occurred and neither did anyone else when they came a few hours later. Her health failed quickly after that and within the week she too had passed on. The Dead Landers crowded into her small room and, clutching TJ's callused hand in her own, she willed him to see he was loved, but knew he didn't.

He placed her cold hand gently on the white hospital sheet and with a face of stone turned and walked out. His life became a pattern and he listened to no one. Day after day passed seamlessly with work, school, and his little sisters – the only thing – he lived for. His angels in a world where angels didn't exist.

***

Just after the long night celebration TJ, finally, did the one thing he hated most. He hated it as much as it gave him a sense of peace. Never once did he intentionally walk there, but his feet always led him at least once a year. Knowing his sisters were safe, he began to walk around the Dead Lands. He passed the run-down streets with garbage piled high in the hopes someone would come and take care of it, passed by homes people tried to take care of and homes others gave up on long ago. TJ saw with unseeing eyes; it was just a normal part of his existence and he no longer cared. He knew he fit in there and even if he did have friends from each district, he alone stood out. Someone dumped a bucket of dirty water off a balcony and it steamed in an arc against the cold. TJ dodged it as it splashed into the dirty street. Striding quick in the cold, he hopped the wrought iron gate, rubbing the rust onto his jeans, turning them a red brown. When he landed, the slush from the snow splashed up leaving droplets on his pant legs and soaked into his worn shoes.

He walked through the one-track road silently, almost as if he was too loud he might wake the sleepers. Row after row passed by. Some headstones – big and gaudy – showed the dead's family possessed money, while others were smaller and insignificant. TJ knew some of these people were loved more than any epigraph could ever express. Pausing for a moment he rubbed his hand across the freezing marble of a young man's tomb. It read, 'William Mantague' with no dates attached to it, but TJ remembered his death quite well. Will was the first death TJ had witnessed.

He had been seven years old at the time, yet, could clearly remember the night. A sweaty summer night, but he still held Heather's hand until a shout and shrill whistle rang out in the late night. A single boy ran straight past them followed by a group of tough looking young men. TJ saw the moonlight shine off the silver blade of a dagger and looked up at Heather in fear, but she told him nothing would happen to him. The young boy gazed up into her face and knew she didn't know what to do, but quickly came to a decision. She tucked him away in a corner beside a dumpster and made him swear not to come out or make any noise and then ran off to get help, but help almost always came too late in the Dead Lands.

Will tried running away, but tripped at the mouth of the alley directly in front of TJ's hiding spot and the ones following him pounced like large cats. Like cats, they played with him until they heard help arriving, then slit his throat. With wide eyes, no longer innocent, TJ watched in fear. He didn't answer when Heather called him to come out. Instead, he made her come to him where he sat huddled in the corner with his small arms wrapped around his bony knees. Her boyfriend carried him home to his house.

TJ shivered in the cold and wished he could have done something other than watch, but it seemed he was fated to never be able to do anything to save anyone – just sit back and watch them die. He cleaned the snow off the tombstone and walked on until he got to a large rose bush, scraggly barren wooden arms creeping to the black sky, and turned left.

He continued down the rows, until he passed a young sapling, stopped, and kneeled. He felt his throat close and his eyes suddenly felt warm as salty tears slipped out and turned cold on his cheeks. Reaching up he wiped this tombstone clean like the other, but this one held the name of a young girl on it with a birth and death under. It took all his savings and a loan from a few close friends, but TJ still wished he could have done more for Heather Airéanna Zyrqrouise-berĭta. "Why did you have to go?" He asked of the cold stone knowing it wouldn't answer. "Why did I have to be so stupid? But you promised! You promised you wouldn't leave me!" Anger suddenly over-rode his sadness and he began to yell.

"A promise is a promise! Isn't that what you taught me?" TJ wiped his tears away and sniffed as more pooled over and spilled out. "You taught me to keep them, but you can break promises?

What are you a damn hypocrite? Fuckin' 'ell. It ain't fair. It aint fair. Why'd I gotta be left alone? I'm not old enough. I can't take care of myself lettalone two girls..." TJ began sobbing as he slipped into the port dialect he grew up with. "I can't do this. Not 'n my own. Heather why'd you go? Why did I haf-ta be so stupid? Mama's right. I'm stupid. I deserve it. Iss all ma fault. All ma fault." He wiped his streaming nose and eyes with the back of his hand and suddenly wished he brought something to color her bleak resting place, but he only found a dried-up twig sticking out of the ground.

Picking it up, he moved it to the middle of the snow pile in front of the headstone and tucked it into the frozen ground. In his imagination, it was her favorite flower, a poppy – bright and red-orange. *It isn't much of anythin', but ya never woulda cared. Ya woulda played along wit yer idiotic kid brother. Ya woulda acted like I'd given ya the crown jewels of the missin' princess.* TJ thought as he closed his eyes and fixed an image of her laughing face in his mind as he held out the single poppy to her. He pulled his hand back and went to stand, but froze in shock as a single poppy sat in the twigs place. He rocked back on his heels and gazed in horrified wonder. *I can't've done that. There's no possible way. I must be on something.* He rubbed his eyes, but it was still there. In fear, he stood and hurriedly walked away. By the time he made it back to the gates, he convinced himself it was due to lack of sleep and hurried on to Jake's house in the Mercante District.

***

Spring poked through the light dusting of snow which still hung around the streets of VeeCee. Puddles of snow melt lay around under the swings and at the bottom of the slides in the park. TJ caught Erinn as she went flying down the metal slide and spun her around in a circle before setting her down away from the cold water just in time to catch Kali and do the same. Upon setting her back on her feet, Kali and Erinn jumped up on him until he fell to the ground and began tickling the two girls, "Give up you know I'll win." He said joining them in laughter.

"No!" Erinn and Kali shouted and sat on his chest.

"Oh come on. No! No! Let me up! Trantepa! Kaymentra! Da! Da!"

The girls laughed hearing him call them monsters and saying he was trapped. They let him up and ran to the swings. He stood and dusted himself off as he walked after them. The girls bounced up and down waiting for him to put them on, so they wouldn't get their feet wet. He joined them facing the opposite way with a slight smile on his nearly emotionless face, but his eyes had a lilac star surrounded by lime green. He made faces at them as they began to swing back and forth. They giggled and made faces in return. "Tammy, can we do crafts now?" The twins asked in unison after a time.

"Craft extravaganza? Is that what you two want?"

"What is eggstravgah…?" They started.

"Extravaganza. It's a fun time that's what it is."

"Oh. Let's do it!" Erinn shouted as Kali laughed in glee.

TJ jumped off the swing and turned around to get the girls off their swings. They each slipped one of their hands into one of his callused hands as they left the park to Colette's. "How is school going?"

"It stinks!" Erinn pouted.

"Boring," Kali added. "You already told it to us."

TJ laughed, "I taught it to you. Not told it to you. Sorry aida's. I wanted you to have a head start, but pay attention and think of it as a game."

"A game?" They asked simultaneously.

"Yes. A game," TJ eyed them, "Whoever can pick up on something you haven't learned before and the most, new knowledge at the end of the day wins."

They looked confused, "How is that fun?"

TJ suddenly bent down and released their hands. He waved to the girls and they bent next to him. Pushing back a few spring flowers, he revealed a tiny fairy and whispered something in elven to the small creature. The fairy flew up and landed on his finger and the girls looked on in amazement, "Don't you want to understand more about the fairy's? How they fly and make and tend such beautiful flowers?"

The small fairy flew over and tied a spring flower in each girl's hair. TJ thanked her as she flew back to her garden.

"I want to, but we-" Kali began and Erinn finished, "Don't learn anything about *that*." Both girls sighed dramatically and they stood and resumed control of his hands.

TJ laughed and continued walking, "No. Not yet, but you will and if you don't pay attention and learn *everything* you might not understand later. And that would be sad, wouldn't it?"

The girls nodded as they turned a corner into the Shop District and the crowds became larger. TJ weaved expertly in and out, taking back alleys and side streets to get to Colette's quicker. He pulled the girls away from a muddy puddle and around another corner.

"Colette! Colette!" They yelled to the elf bending over a sweet pea plant. She straightened and smiled brightly at them and her yellowish eyes traveled up and down TJ's body immediately. Her smile disappeared as she ushered them inside.

"Hello girls. Go on inside. There are some snacks on the table," the girls ran into the living room and attacked the celery and raisins. Colette rounded on TJ, "Clearly you used some of the cream, but let me see your back."

TJ followed her into her work room just off the main hall. He set his backpack down by the counter and gently pulled off his t-shirt. He felt the scab's on his back tighten and pull. Colette sighed as she poured a minty smelling liquid into cold water. "It's going to be cold, but it will help," Colette said.

TJ nodded and Colette dunked a cloth into the water and placed it on his back. TJ tensed and then sighed as the minty something she put in the water relaxed his back. It felt good. "What is this stuff?"

"Loosening up the skin. It will speed up the process of healing. It won't itch or scar now, but I want you to come back tomorrow and Wisterten if you can," she dunked the cloth in again and applied it to his back once more. "You have work at three?"

TJ nodded, "Yeah, but we had a half day so I was going to run home and grab some lunch."

"Have some lunch here. I was going to make some soon," Colette tossed the cloth into the bucket and TJ put his shirt back on.

He switched into elven, "Are you sure it's alright for the girls to stay here and craft? You really don't mind?"

"Tamynaen Jacob it is perfectly alright. I love the twins and they deserve to have a good place to stay and they can learn a lot here. You shouldn't have to raise these girls on your own at sixteen."

"But what about your customers?"

"That's why I am going to send you to the workshop," she smiled and they walked to where the girls sat. "Come on girls we're going to the back." TJ helped to set them up with paints, paper, and ink pens as they sat down in chairs to begin crafting.

***

"TJ, go get the boxes from the back and start tagging them!" Gary called throughout the store. Not knowing exactly where the young man was.

The half-elf looked up from the history book he was reading with a sigh. Classes just started up again after the summer break and he was already worried about falling behind. He stood up straight and set the book back on the counter before turning and pulling the boxes down off the shelves and began tagging the items inside. Gary walked into the back an hour later, "You're not here tomorrow, right?" TJ shook his head as he wrote another number down on a price tag before looking up at his boss. "Good you deserve a day off. Here's your pay. Enjoy yourself tomorrow, okay?"

TJ looked up and took the pouch of money, "Thanks Gary. And I will."

"What do you plan on doing?" The older man inquired.

"Ummm," TJ shuffled from foot to foot and shoved his hands in his pockets, "I was thinking about taking my sisters to the park or something like that."

"Good, good," Gary nodded thoughtfully. "Well, it's past ten kid. You should get back to those girls."

Yawning, TJ nodded in agreement, "Let me finish this one and then I will." He picked up a pen and quickly scribbled a number down before shoving the pouch filled with money into his backpack along with the text book, "See you in a couple of days."

He left out the back door and turned onto the alley leading to the Dead Lands, but even though it was late he didn't worry about anyone harming him. Especially since the first person he saw hovering in the dark was an old friend. He waved.

"Hey Tammy! How's it going?" The young man asked. He was a few years older than TJ and the second in charge of the most prominent and noble of the gangs in VeeCee, The Lightning's.

A slight smile brightened TJ's normally blank face, "Ced! Not too terrible. What are ya doin' down this way?"

"The Skully Gang was givin' people troub. We came over ta take care of the problem. Where ya headed? I can escort ya Tam," he waved him to walk by his side.

"Home," TJ strode quicker to catch up to Ced and slipped into the port dialect. "How've ya been?"

"Great. Got money back ta this old couple livin' few doors down from ya ta other day. Took it from thee Reaps. Then got money off a couple a scoundrels," he smiled widely.

TJ laughed, "That's great. Ya'll are the best."

"So what 'bout ya?" Ced questioned.

"Been better. Kina sucks sometimes, but my friends're great. Help outta lot," he smirked as they turned onto his street. "Feel like ya already knew that though."

Ced shrugged, "Heather made me promise ta look after ya. So I do."

"I know. Doesn't mean ya had ta," they stopped a few doors down and TJ glanced at his home and breathed a sigh of relief as he saw the lights were off. No one was home.

"I loved yer sister Tammy. I would never break a promise ta her," Ced smiled and clapped the younger man he considered a little brother on the shoulder, "Get yerself home and get some sleep. You look like ya need it."

"Thanks Ced. I appreciate it," he turned and walked away to his home and up the creaky porch steps. As he opened the door of his house his mind wandered off since he still had school tomorrow and was supposed to meet up with Jake tonight at Grama's still. Then a glass connected with his head. A woman of incredible beauty sat hidden in the shadows. She began swearing at him like one of the sailors who worked on the docks.

"Where have you been?" She screamed.

TJ rubbed his head and tried edging by, but she grabbed him by the hair and jerked him around to face her so he would have to answer, "W-w-work."

"W-w-work," she mocked cruelly and slammed the side of his head against the cupboard door with surprising strength. "Why didn't you tell me before you lazy shit?"

"I-I did," he stuttered as she slammed his head against it again, "Mama, please!"

"Oh, you poor thing," she laughed. "You're just a scared little wimp. That's what you are. But don't worry. I can fix that." She slammed her knee up into his groin and he collapsed as he groaned and hit the ground hard. Annah pounced on her son like a cat on a mouse and pulled a syringe and bottle of opium seemingly out of nowhere.

TJ's throat went suddenly dry and he could barely breathe from fear. She laughed again, a light sound, as she watched his eyes turn black with panic. He thrashed around under her as he tried to escape, but she put the needle to his throat threateningly. He froze and she gripped his arm after systematically pulling the drug into the syringe and tapping it to cause the bubbles to rise. She squirted a bit out before smiling pleasantly at him and stabbed the object into his arm. It easily pierced his flesh right in the crook and he felt it being pulled out again. She didn't bother to cover up the tiny hole. Instead, she watched his eyes shift between colors before landing on blue-green. She smirked, "That should fix you."

Annah tossed the syringe on the counter and walked out of the dilapidated house. TJ lay on the floor for a few minutes before pushing himself to his feet feeling dizzy and nauseous. *This isn't normal. I've been shot up with opium before, but this is new. Why is this so wrong... abnormal... I need help... shit.* He stumbled to the trash can in the corner and threw up. He continued for a few minutes before everything expelled itself from his stomach and then he began to dry heave until a hot iron taste filled his mouth. *Blood. Oh shit. Not good. Help? Somebody... help me...* Then he passed out.

TJ awoke with a damp cloth pressed to his forehead, shaking. It felt like a thousand needles pushing their way into his skin over and over again. Brown eyes, faded from age, watched him and sudden anger hit him from nowhere and he started yelling in broken Astyreian and Layendrian.

Grama looked down at him and tried to calm him as she pinned him to the sofa while he yelled and she said something to someone he couldn't see. He heard a door open and close.

"Calm down honey. We're trying to take care of you. Jake went to get your medication. Had to give you detox to get that opium your mama gave you out of your system. You shouldn't be given that stuff when you are on your meds. Not that you should take it anyway. I know you didn't give it to yourself though. You wouldn't do that. You are much smarter than all of that. Ahhh here he is. So, don't you worry, everything will be just fine. Good thing you called me to you. No idea how you did it, but you did. I heard you calling and I came. You were passed out by the time I got there," She took the bottle of medicine and pulled out two pills, "Take them sweetie. It will help."

TJ reached out a hand shakily and popped them into his mouth. It took fifteen minutes before he calmed down enough to be left alone. It was the first time Jake had seen TJ that angry.

Grama left the living room of her home and went into the kitchen leaving the boys in an awkward silence, only to be broken by TJ moving into a huddled sitting position and Jake coughing. They wouldn't meet each other's eyes. "Sandwiches and lemonade," she said coming back into the room and setting a tray out on the table. She handed TJ and Jake a plate each and then poured three glasses of the cool liquid. "Why the silence? You two are best friend's aren't you? Or was this just too much for you?" She questioned Jake. "I thought you had seen him like this before." She turned on TJ, "And as for you, why are you ashamed or embarrassed?" TJ blushed and took a sip of lemonade. "I take that as a yes," Grama turned on him, "You have nothing to be embarrassed or ashamed of." She said noting the yellow tint to his blue-green eyes. "You cannot help that you are bi-polar and can't control your emotions when you haven't taken your meds TJ. And you," she returned to Jake, "Shouldn't judge him because of it."

Jake jumped at being addressed, "No! No, no, that's not it at all. It's just I – I wasn't expecting that. I never thought I would see my best friend almost dead and then nearly hit someone. Hit you." Jake faced TJ, "I don't care if you are bi-polar Tam, and never have. Just next time a forewarning would be nice if you might just randomly flip out."

TJ, finally, met his eyes and chuckled slightly, "You don't care even knowing now what I could do?"

"No," Jake smiled, "Why would I?"

"I – I will. I will try and let you know next time," TJ smiled shyly back at his best friend. "I'm really sorry."

"Don't be. I'm just glad you are alright," Jake looked at the sandwich and carefully balanced the plate on his knees before taking a bite.

***

"Medíc is threatening war again," James – the freckled blonde twin – explained to the gathered Dead Landers.

Evan rubbed Aly's shoulders and kissed her neck and continued his twin's explanation, "We aren't the type to just sit and watch."

"We need to be in the thick of it," he blew a long breath of air into the silence following their words.

Aly bit back a small sob, "So, you're both joining the military. James the cavalry division and you," she leaned back to see Evan's dark features, "the ocean division."

"That's right," they said in unison after giving a practiced speech explaining their decision to join King Nor-Ten's forces against Emperor Medíc's invading armies.

Another moment of silence plagued them before a large dark skinned Orcana commented, "That doesn't really surprise me. I have known you all since you were youngsters. Always knew you two would go in that area. Knew it. Thrill seekers. That's what you love."

TJ smashed his fist into the miniature sand castle he built and looked up at the Orcana whose tint of blue skin was emphasized by the ocean they sat next to, "It's true. We all knew it would happen. Just stay in contact."

The two boys nodded and once again Jerico spoke, "And Evan, if you go to the islands where my kind live, will you send a message to my relatives? Tell them I am alright?"

Evan nodded in understanding. Jerico had been attempting to buy himself – like all Orcana who worked at the ports – out of slavery since he appeared fourteen years ago.

"Still don't have to like it," Aly complained.

TJ stood up and pulled his shirt over his head and climbed up to the edge of the docks and dove the twelve feet into the water. He was sick of listening to their thoughts and watching Evan hold Aly. He wanted his own girl and they didn't seem to understand they weren't losing each other. They would get leave and come back and training came first anyway, not war. No real harm would come there.

The cool salt water caressed his skin as he popped back up to the surface wishing, desperately, he could stay under in the dark waters which cared not where you came from or what would come to pass. His back stung, but that too would end in time as the salt cleansed his shredded back. He was used to it by now. Roger loved tormenting him in that way since no matter what happened, TJ would always have the scars.

The half-elf closed his eyes, letting the water take him into the shore. He tried to ignore the image floating to the front of his mind. It was his sisters being smacked, the ultimate punishment for him. He pushed his mother in response and because of this she – with the help of Roger – threw him to the ground. She shot him up with opium and, hallucinating, beat him. He couldn't move much – just stumble around – when on the drug due to his elven heritage reacting strangely to it. She would only laugh at his misery, then tied him to a table and left him to come down.

A splash made his eyes fly open and he saw Jake and Aly swimming over, "Are you," she spit water out of her mouth as a wave hit her face, "going to the Festival of Lights?"

"The elven festival might not happen this year," TJ said sadly. It was one of the most beautiful festivals in his mind. The park was lit up with soft lanterns and the lake filled with flower petals. Even the tiny fairies came out to celebrate with them. "The Empire's ban on elven travel has grown worse. Even the elven king, Keldar, isn't allowed to cross the borders and that's where the Forest of Lights is located."

Jake frowned, "I just can't imagine someone would be that cruel."

"That's Medíc for you," TJ sprayed water into the air in exasperation. "Have either of you heard mention of an apartment for rent?"

Jake shook his head as he looked up at the brilliant sun, but Aly only looked thoughtful and asked, "Why?"

"My eighteenth birthday is in a few months. I can leave and legally adopt my sisters. I just need a place to live," he explained.

"Just live with me," Jake said.

TJ shook his head, "I have to be in a place of my own for it to be legal. Trust me. I checked."

"We'll keep our eyes open," she said as the rest of the Dead Lander's began to dive into the ocean and come toward them.

Just like in the old days they played in the waters for a time and enjoyed the company of one another. It all seemed to be ending so quickly since it seemed like it had only been a few days since they began attending high school. TJ sighed in satisfaction as they crawled back up onto the beach when the sky began to darken.

***

Sprinting into the house, TJ tossed his backpack on the floor by the couch before scooting back out of the door to Grama's. He tapped on the door and it opened quickly, "Hello TJ dear. Come in."

"Can't. I was actually wondering if you could watch the girls for another hour or so?" He questioned as he shifted from foot to foot as he hovered in the door way.

She watched him with her faded eyes, "Of course I can, but is everything alright? You seem... antsy."

Sucking in his lower lip, he looked down the street in a paranoid way, "The house is a disaster. I just want to get it cleaned up and that is much easier without the twins under foot."

"Of course," she sighed. "Just come and get them when you are done."

"Thanks, Grama," he flashed a half smile. "I owe you."

"You owe me nothing dear. In fact, if you come back over when you finish, I will feed you all some dinner."

"Really? You are the best," in an odd moment of compassion he kissed her wrinkled cheek.

The old woman blushed pink and pushed him over to his home nestled in ivy, "Get going." As he left, she raised an eyebrow in confusion and slight fear. He hadn't done anything like that in over a year.

TJ pulled open the battered screen door and entered into his run-down house. He quickly looked around to take in the damage.

A shattered glass lay on the floor and a ceramic plate lay chipped next to it with a knife buried into the cupboard above, the sink filled with dirty dishes, and the stove with a burned mass of something his mother tried to make stuck to it. The light filtering in from the windows was a sickly yellow from the grime and the living room wasn't much better. Plates filled with crusty food lay about on the tables and flies buzzed around it. Moth eaten blankets lay in piles and a few clothes and smelly shoes were tucked in corners. TJ picked up one of the plates and nearly vomited.

Suddenly, a feeling of shame filled him for letting his house get so disgusting. He threw open the windows and made a promise to never let it get that bad again. With sea air blowing through the house, it quickly began to smell better and he smiled to himself, loving the salty smell. He pulled a few rags out of a cupboard and put water to boil on the wood stove after cleaning out the ashes and lighting it. Once the water boiled, he cleaned the windows and then the plates, dusted and swept up. He washed the blankets and set them to dry in the backyard and then straightened up all the rooms before going into the bathroom and scrubbing that down, followed by the kitchen. By the time he finished, it was growing dark. He closed the windows and put the now dry dishes away, but just as he closed the last cupboard he heard footsteps on the stairs leading into the house. He swore. The screen door opened and closed and two pairs of shoes left dirt on his clean floor. He gulped and quickly ducked his head and tried to leave the kitchen, but a long-nailed hand gripped his wrist and dug in pulling him back.

"Don't even get a hello?" The musical voice muttered in a mocking tone. "Did you see that Roger?"

TJ was forcibly turned to view the beautiful face of his mother. He didn't respond.

His stepfather smiled smugly, "I did see that. I think he should be taught a lesson Annah. Don't you?"

"You always know best," Annah gripped his chin and forced TJ to meet her eyes, "Now why did you not say hello? Huh? Do you think you are too good for us? Is that it? Don't you look away from me. Don't you dare look away! I asked you a question?"

TJ didn't answer. He just gulped and tried to wait out the course of her anger. He felt, rather than saw, Roger scoot behind him and scrunched up his eyes in anticipation, but the blow didn't come. Paranoia set in as he waited.

Annah glared at him and her deep red lips parted in a sneer, "Huh? I asked you a question! Does the fucking mistake think he is too good for us? Does he? DOES HE? Or possibly you can't hear?"

"I-I… I- he-he-hear. Sss-ssorr-rry," he stammered out in a mumble. He began shaking in fear. Then the first blow came from behind into the base of his spine. His knees gave, but he caught himself before falling. He managed not to whimper. He despised giving them that satisfaction.

"What was that?" She growled at him. "I hate it when you stutter. I hate it when you mumble. How many fucking times have I told you not to do that? Huh? How many? Tell me!"

She began twisting his wrist and her perfect nails bit into his flesh leaving ruby lines of blood in their wake. He watched transfixed and didn't answer. He couldn't, because this time Roger hit him in the kidney and he dropped to the ground as his mother made him bleed. A drop of blood fell onto his cheek. Roger pulled him up by the scruff of his shirt. TJ struggled to stand.

"ANSWER! NOW!" Roger spat in his face.

The half-elf felt the warm spit drip off his cheek, "A-a lo-lot."

"Never listens!" Annah screeched. "I JUST SAID NO STUTTER-ING!" She gripped her son's hair and slammed his face into the hard wood of the counter top. He felt his lip split and tasted the iron of his blood. His head began throbbing as she repeated the action again and he slid to the floor as Roger kicked the back of his knees. Annah pounced on top of him and flipped him over before sitting on his chest and gripping his neck with both hands, "I'll teach you a lesson you vermin. You disgusting creature. You ruined my life. Do you see what you are making me do? You make me do this. You did it to yourself."

His eyes wouldn't focus from the throbbing in his head, but he could feel the tips of her nails digging into his neck and he felt hot blood running into his hair. He began to get dizzy as his vision unfocused slightly. Black spots danced in front of his eyes and he thrashed a bit and tried to push the small woman off, but Roger came at him with a knife. He held the tip just above his eye in warning. TJ froze and whimpered as the blackness took him.

A few minutes later he came to, but he didn't move. He stayed still and listened to the voices as he tried to place them. They sat in the living room. TJ rubbed his throat and felt the need to cough, but he suppressed it as he slowly rolled onto his hands and knees. He wished he had left his backpack at Grama's, but he couldn't risk retrieving it from the living room. He crawled to the screen and silently pushed it open and made his escape.

The cold air hit him and he breathed it in and began coughing as he ran around to Grama's. She threw the door open as she saw him coming, "What happened?" She froze at the bright red mark on his neck already turning a deep purple and the lump on his head. "Oh my. Come in. Get in and drink some tea. Are you alright?"

"I'm fine. Not dead," he said in a flat voice.

Grama raised a silver eyebrow, "That's good at least. Aly came over. She is playing with your sisters." She reached over to the stove and pulled out a plate with food on it. "This is yours. I saved it for you."

"Thanks, but I don't think I can eat much," TJ sat down and struggled to swallow the tea. He winced as the hot liquid seared his swollen throat.

"Oh dear," Grama frowned as she watched the boy. "You should go and see Colette tonight. She could help."

TJ shook his head, "It should be fine in the morning. Swelling should go down," his voice sounded ruff and dry. He coughed again. TJ stood and leaned against the counter and ran his fingers through his hair. He pulled his hand away and looked at the red covering his fingertips. He had forgotten about that. "Shit." Aly walked into the kitchen followed by Kali and Erinn. The twins looked up at him with wide eyes, "Hi aida's. Sorry I missed dinner."

Aly raised an eyebrow. His voice was still flat, "Girls, how about you go play with your dolls in the living room? I want to ask your brother something." He watched them go without a word, "Why don't you come and stay with my family for a little while TJ? This is getting out of hand."

"No."

"Why not? What is your reasoning? The girls shouldn't have to see this," Aly said in frustration.

TJ's eyes flashed and Aly immediately knew something wasn't right, "Why do I have to justify anything with you? It isn't your place and they aren't your sisters."

"Do not yell at me!" She countered back in shock and it immediately occurred to her what was wrong. Grama took a step forward as she felt the tension between them. "Where are they?" Aly demanded.

"What are you talking about?" TJ growled.

"Where are your pills?" She demanded again as she heard the girls enter the room. "Girls leave. Please."

TJ picked a vase up off the table and chucked it at Aly. Luckily, Grama saw it coming and hit his arm just as he let go and the vase shattered against the wall dripping water mixing with the crystals and flower petals. The twin's eyes widened in fear. They had never seen their brother like this. TJ's eyes widened as well and his manic high flipped. He froze to the spot and gulped. Looking around wildly his eyes found what he looked for and groped for the sharp weapon. Aly fought him for the knife as he put it to his already damaged wrist, but not before the sharpened knife bit into his flesh. He tried to kick her away, but Grama gripped him around the waist and pinned his arms to his side, "Stop it aida. Stop. Calm now. Breath. Not in front of the little ones. Don't let them see."

This finally got to him and his legs gave out. He slumped to the ground shaking, "I'm sorry. So sorry." TJ sobbed out, tears streaming down his face.

Aly grabbed a hand towel and pushed it against his bleeding wrist and held it there, "Your medicine Tam. Do you have it with you?" He shook his head. She looked up at Grama, "What do we do?"

"I have some here. Colette gave me some," Grama pushed the twins out of the room. They began to cry.

"Are you going to be okay?" Aly asked as she watched him shaking and rubbed his arm.

"No. I am falling apart," he coughed and winced. "But that doesn't matter."

Grama came back in and handed him an opened bottle of pills and filled a glass with water. He popped two of the small pills into his mouth and drank the water. It took a little while for the medicine to take effect, but Grama didn't wait for it, "Why didn't you take your medicine this morning?"

TJ flushed, "I ran out."

"And you let that happen because?" She condemned him.

The flush grew deeper, "I didn't have the money to get more."

"You know Colette doesn't care about that. TJ think of what could have happened! The consequences are too large for you to be doing something like that. Never again. You go to Colette and... I don't know fix something in her house in payment if you are too proud to just ask for it."

He couldn't meet her eyes. He just nodded as Aly rubbed his arm. Kali scooted into the room followed by Erinn. She crawled silently into his lap as Erinn wormed her way under his arm. He buried his head in their shining hair and wanted to cry; he felt so guilty. *I don't need them to tell me what could have happened. I have the two reasons right here. I am stupid. I could have lost everything.* He wrapped his arms around both of them and would have fallen asleep right there, if Aly hadn't began rubbing the dried blood at the back of his neck with cold water.

***

TJ knew they had been talking about him. For the past year and a half, it had happened and it didn't help that somewhere along the lines he learned how to speak through his mind to others and read their thoughts as well and couldn't always stop it. *Whatever. They can talk about me all they want. As long as they let me play and we get that scholarship to The Academy of Music and I can bring my sisters, I could care less what they say.* He set his battered guitar and violin cases on Jake's bed and began tuning, knowing Jake watched him.

They practiced well into the night, as they were playing the main set at the Festival the following weekend. TJ, now over singing in front of people – for the most part – still hated talking, so he let Jake do that. They filled an hour and a half worth of music and were pleased with the selections they chose to play. Finally, TJ's fingers red and raw, they stopped for the night.

Chris and David sighed in relief and went downstairs in search of food and drink. Jake walked up to TJ, "Come to the party after. Gary isn't making us work that night once we play and David said your shift is in the morning at The Bakery."

"I have to work at the liquor store on the corner of Maple and Karion," he answered putting his precious guitar away.

Jake grabbed TJ by the shoulder and forcibly turned TJ to face him, "You need a break and I am not going to stand by and watch my best friend lose his mind. I didn't even know you were working at the liquor store. When did you get a job there?"

"Last week," TJ tried to turn, but Jake wouldn't let go. "And I already have lost it. Didn't you hear?" He bit his lip and shifted uncomfortably as Jake watched a star of yellow blossom in his eyes.

Jake knew he was ashamed just by seeing the color, but he also could tell from the purple coloring under his eyes he hadn't been sleeping, "You forgot to take your medicine and lost it on Aly. Calm one second and the other you threw a vase across the room. Then frantically began searching for a knife." He watched TJ's features shift in torment and noticed the mottled bruises on his face and neck. One of his parents had attempted to strangle him again. "Don't worry about it. Aly knows you're bi-polar and that it's different for elves. We all know."

"It was my fault though. I didn't take my medicine," he turned his face from Jake as he took a deep calming breath and laid his hand on Hayle's violin.

"Stop blaming yourself for everything. It is not all your fault. When do you start work?"

He thought for a moment, "Three in the morning."

"Party should start at eleven. You could come. In fact, you should," Jake smiled at the young man in front of him who shifted uncomfortably and yet with a grace Jake would never possess.

"Fine. Not promising I will be much fun though."

"We all will be tired."

"It's not that. I never sleep anymore," TJ ran his long fingers through his dark hair as Jake let go of his wiry arm and raised an eyebrow in question. "I just... I don't know. Too much death."

Jake's muscles clenched and shock spread across his face, "What?"

TJ sneezed, "I keep seeing death. Visions. They don't make any sense, but with all this talk of war with The Empire, I guess it doesn't really matter. It will happen eventually."

"What kind of death?" Jake asked hesitantly.

TJ's eyes clouded over in a grey like fog, "Hayle's was the first full vision, but since then it has been hundreds or more. Sometimes of plains filled with the dead. Holes with legions filling them. Rivers red and the ground turning brown with decay, all the trees and flowers dying. I think I'm going insane sometimes and when I sleep that's all I see. It's like the world is going to end."

Again, Jake shifted uncomfortably, "That's really not good," Chris and David interrupted him by entering the room and tossing apples at them. "Talk to Colette or Grama. Maybe they can do something about it."

TJ shrugged and out of habit took the violin out of the case and began wiping a soft cloth over it. Even though the cases were battered and old, in comparison, his instruments looked pristine in condition. The only taint was where the common chords were played. The acid from his fingers had worn away at the neck of the violin and guitars, but he didn't mind. It added character.

The other band members lay down as Jake blew out the multitudes of lamps and the one electric light bulb in his room. Since his family were one of the wealthier ones in the Mercante Distric, they could afford electricity and an electric carriage, but they only used it on the weekends and the carriage only three times a year.

The half-elf sat down on the window seat and stared at the sliver of moon. It cast an eerie glow across his features and caused his normally golden face to pale throwing his bruises in stark contrast and his dark hair turned silvery. Jake turned over and gazed up at his best friend and sighed. He looked like a music god as he moved the bow of the violin smoothly across the strings. It was sad – the music, but he could hear how different TJ was from the tiny ten year old boy he first met all those years ago. He even changed from the boy he was just over a year ago. TJ grew quickly and had an almost stretched appearance for a while – long and lanky, his hands seemed too big, and his legs too long, but all that changed. He filled out, his shoulders got broader, and he had gained weight. His face was still angular, but more defined. He was handsome and Jake came to realize he wasn't the only one who noticed anymore.

The running must have helped strengthen some of his muscles and obviously lifting the crates at Make A Noise helps, Jake surmised. He saw a tear slide down TJ's smooth cheek leaving a silver streak like a shooting star in the black night. He wished he could do something but knew if he offered TJ would just close off even more.

***

The wind blew the vacant swings in a motion suggesting a person already sat in them as TJ approached, a small hand holding each of his. It was the first full day off work since Mid-Moon and he decided to spend it with his sisters.

They gazed up at him, innocent smiles spread wide across their faces, large blue eyes reflecting the towering grey-white clouds as their golden hair captured the fleeting light in its long stands. "What do you want to do?" He questioned letting go of their hands.

"Swing!" One exclaimed as the other squeaked, "Monkey bars!"

TJ smiled, "Well, go on then."

The one took off to the monkey bars and soon hung upside down by her knees trying in vain to keep her green dress from covering her face. The other looked up at TJ, "What're you gonna do?"

He smiled lovingly at the nine year-old, "I don't know what I am going to do… want me to push you?"

She nodded enthusiastically and skipped to the swing. He pushed her and kept one eye on the other girl making sure the more daring of the twins didn't get herself into trouble. It was silent except for the whistling of the wind and TJ's quite humming until he saw the other girl grip the bar next to her and swing one leg off. "Erinn… please be careful," he called.

She smiled innocently as her little arms clung to it, "I'm being careful."

He didn't believe her and ran over just as her arms slipped. She screamed and he caught her before she hit the ground, "How about you come swing with Kali and me?"

Wide eyed, Erinn nodded and he set her in the wooden swing facing the same direction as her sister and began to push her. Then he climbed into the swing facing the other way, so he could make silly expressions causing them to giggle hysterically like he always did when they swung.

He gazed out into the distance and saw Jake, Aly, Sami, and David sit down by the pavilion with a basket of food. Sabella followed not far behind with Chris. He let go of the rope with one hand and waved. Jake waved back and motioned for him to join them and TJ jumped off the swing, "Are you girls hungry?"

They nodded and he caught the swings and slowed them enough for the girls to hop off. Climbing the grassy hill, they entered the pavilion. It was windier up there and brought goose bumps to his skin along with the smell of the sea, "What are you guys doing here?"

"We thought you might be here with the girls," Aly smiled. "We brought food for you three too."

TJ blinked in surprise, "Oh. Thanks. I was just going to say hi and head to The Bakery."

"No sense in that, but you should start a fire. It's cold with this wind."

"Why me?" TJ asked as the twins hopped up onto the picnic table to watch Aly set out the food.

Sami strode over on her long legs and fluttered her overly long eyelashes at him, "You love fire."

TJ shrugged, guessing she most likely meant something sexual by the way she moved her curvy hips. He went to the hearth and began stacking the wood up properly before the storm hit. He pulled out his matchbook and frowned.

"What's the problem?" Jake asked as he sat down next to him by the fireplace.

"Only two matches left. Do you have any?" TJ questioned and Jake shook his head as the first drops began to fall from the rain clouds. "David, do you have matches?"

He checked his pockets and shook his head, "I can run and get some if you need me too." Chris was already shaking his head and Sabella shrugged, unhelpfully.

TJ frowned, "No big deal. I should be able to start it."

He struck the match, but nothing caught. Frowning, TJ placed more tinder on and struck the last match, but it too quickly went out causing only a thin stream of smoke which quickly died. "You spoke too soon," Jake patted him on the back. "Maybe you should order it to start Master of the Flames."

Mockingly, TJ spread his fingers over the logs, breathed deeply, and letting it out said, "Burn." Then leapt back as brilliant blue flames sprung out of the logs and tried licking his face. Jake yelled in shock and David stared wide eyed.

TJ gaped at the blue flames which died down to a merry crackling and popping.

"What just happened?" Jake asked after finding his voice. "You realize I was kidding about you being Fire Master?"

TJ nodded.

"Did you know you could do that?" David questioned in shock.

He shook his head and tucked a dark lock of hair behind a pointed ear, "How would I have?"

"I don't know," David muttered. "Still, that's pretty cool."

Aly looked over, "Good you – why is the fire blue?"

"It's pretty! We like it!" The twins exclaimed in their high-pitched voices as the boys pointed to TJ who looked completely bewildered, "Don't ask. I have no clue how I did it."

She rolled her eyes as Sami brought food over to the boys and sat as close to TJ as she possibly could, before the twins, seeing the look on their brothers' face came and squeezed onto his lap and in between the two teenagers. He smiled broadly – the first time in a long while – and began playing with Erinn's long blonde hair.

They went home not long after with TJ's mind a mess of confusion. *How did that happen? That has never happened before. Why now? I don't understand. Will this happen to the girls too? I mean, I remember Oreal talking about the wind picking up when she got angry and the water slowing when she wanted to cross the river, but that stuff never happens with me. I can just communicate with anyone through the mind and read their thoughts and memories. Guess I can control fire now too.*

Wrapped up in his thoughts, he didn't hear his stepfather until almost too late. He quickly pulled his little sisters back out the door as Roger snatched up a walking stick. He attempted to grab Kali, but TJ wrapped his arms around her, his back to the large man and Kali out of reach. He felt the stick tear his flesh and pushed the little girls toward James and Evan's parents' house across the street. Roger struck TJ again as he turned and TJ felt a rib crack and he pulled his fist back and let loose in fury. *No one hurts my girls. No one threatens them.* His fist connected with Rogers jaw and he felt it give. His stepfather froze in pain and his face turned red in rage. He gripped TJ's shoulders and pushed him down onto his knee coming up. It struck him in the lungs knocking the air out of him. He gasped for breath that wouldn't come.

His eyes opened to colors swirling about him in odd shapes and patterns. His ribs ached, but he didn't mind. He felt good and nothing mattered. None of his sorrow or loss. TJ's mind was in euphoria and he wanted to go outside. He had no idea where he was. It made him laugh. No one was around, he left quickly and stumbled down the stairs to the alley's connecting the Shop District with the Dead Lands. It was getting late and no one could be seen, but he went in search of his dead sisters' old boyfriend. For some reason, he felt like he should speak with the guy who once meant so much to him.

Awhile later, TJ's thoughts were very different. *Never again. Just never again. Let me die. Please let me die. I almost did once, but for some reason I came so close, but I couldn't. This time for sure. Let me die.* TJ lay curled in a ball at the end of an alley having never found Ced. Night time for most people meant you stayed off the streets since the Dead Lands weren't a place anyone wanted to walk around at night, especially past midnight. That is, unless, they lived there and although TJ never found his dead sister's boyfriend, he did have the protection of his gang.

A shadow fell across the mouth of the alley where TJ lay clutching his stomach and shaking. He watched the two figures come closer, trying to discern if they were real or hallucination. *I've been having a lot of those lately. I wonder, if I hallucinate death, if I will die...* The taller one of the two saw him first, looked at the girl, and they both sprinted to him.

"TJ! TJ!" The girl's hand hovered just above his shoulder. "What happened?"

"What do you think happened Sami?" Jake asked sarcastically. "Please tell me you didn't give it to yourself."

TJ felt ready to puke and responded by putting his head between his knees. Sami pulled his straight black hair behind a pointed ear and looked at the normally golden skin tinted bright red and purple, "It wasn't him Jake. As usual."

"She shot me up with something," TJ muttered trying to focus his eyes. "I think I would appreciate death at the moment. Can one of you perform the task?"

"Haha, real funny Tam. No one here is going to kill you," Sami answered kissing him on the forehead in the usual gesture of kinship and blessing.

Jake put his arm around his best friend's shoulders while he put his other under his knees and stood, easily cradling the tall boy in his arms as TJ wished Sami would act normal all the time. "Let's get you out of here. My mom's home and she would love to see you. You are way too thin by the way."

"Isn't he always?" Sami inquired following Jake as he walked out of the alley and onto the run-down streets of the slums of Veecee.

"Well, yes," Jake mumbled as they turned another corner and onto the other side of the darkened street headed to the better part of the Dead Lands.

***

They dragged him to the party. TJ didn't want to go. He felt like his time could be better spent. The party was at one of the gang's hideouts. Although in the Dead Lands, it wasn't dirty or even hidden. It was The Lightning's territory and no one messed with them. Food and drink littered one corner while live music took up the other side of the large room. Tables and chairs had been set up and people lounged talking about the new school year or where they would be working. The balconies were crowded with people getting fresh air and watching summer turn into fall. He determined and convinced himself, he would have a good time – if only all the girls would leave him alone.

One girl clung to his arm as another fawned over the bruise not realizing it was a track mark from his mother shooting him up with opium last weekend. TJ wasn't the only one with girls clinging to him though and he soon realized the reason. Andronicus' popularity grew considerably over the summer with Sound System, finally, having moved away. Girls also clung to Chris and David, but, unlike TJ, they enjoyed the attention. He sighed and looked over at Jake who sat talking with Aly un-harmed by women. Suddenly, TJ envied his best friend.

I wonder, TJ thought and smiled. He shook the girls off him and strode up to Jake and said into Jake's mind, *"Please just go along with this. These girls are scaring me. Will you pretend to date me? For just a night?"*

Jake smirked and hugged TJ close. "Sure, but you know I really do like you," he whispered.

TJ nodded enable to meet Jakes eyes in his guilt. *"I'm sorry,"* he said into his friends mind.

With an unconcerned shrugged, Jake said, "Should be entertaining. This party was starting to get dull."

The half-elf leaned back and placed his hands on Jake's cheeks – his thumb's covering the taller man's lips – and leaned in just close enough to make it seem as if they were kissing. Aly drew in a sharp breath as the other girls looked on with eyes wide in disbelief and bitter disappointment while TJ and Jake grinned mischievously. TJ's followers left quickly in different states of sadness and shock.

"What just happened?" Aly asked.

Jake laughed, "He wanted them to leave him alone. And what better way than to pretend you are gay with someone who is?"

Aly looked slightly repulsed that Jake would let TJ use him like that, but shook her head in amazement, "I can't believe you two sometimes."

"I just wanted to be left alone," TJ shrugged. "It worked, didn't it?"

Aly nodded, "I'm going to get some punch. Would the lovely new couple like some?"

Jake took TJ's arm, a ridiculous grin on his face as he held back laughter, "Of course."

TJ laughed and followed his friends to the tables and chairs in the other corner of the dark room. He, finally, was enjoying the summer. Unfortunately, it was the last weekend before his final year of school began.

4

Chapter 4

"We got it TJ! The letters," Chris and David waved paper in front of his face and Jake slapped one into TJ's hand. He looked at the expensive paper with a wax seal in royal blue.

His eyes turned aquamarine as he slit open the paper and read the contents, "We – I can't – Oh wow."

Aly and Sami came up and snatched the letter out of his hand and scanned it, "Congratulations! I can't believe the full tuition scholarship came through!"

"And to the Academy of Music!" Sami added smiling broadly.

"What's going on here?" The assistant principal asked striding over to the group standing in the vacant hallway. "Class started a few minutes ago."

Jake handed the older man his acceptance and scholarship letter. The man took it and glanced through, "Good job, but just because you four are going to be famous doesn't mean you can go in and out of class as you please. Come along now." He shuffled them off to their classrooms.

Everything began to get better once school started up again. Although much harder than the previous year, TJ put all he had into school to make up for being absent in mind the year before. All the Dead Landers helped him catch up in classes because he didn't have time for school with the ridiculous amount of hours he was putting in at his three jobs. His grades only dropped a letter grade the previous year, but from having perfect grades all through school until now, it made him disappointed.

Just like in middle school, TJ and the others began to get together at The Bakery to study and go over notes. To TJ it felt like the old days when everything seemed simple. He still worked the three jobs and barely slept, but it helped him ignore all the pain of losing the ones he loved and not feeling loved by the ones who should.

By the end of Fellmoon, he was almost back to normal – at least as normal as TJ had ever been. His grades went back to where he expected them to be – except alchemy, but without Aysté or Hayle, he expected that. His band attracted many followers and he now managed Make A Noise – which also came with a substantial pay raise. Things seemed to be changing and for once in a good way.

The beginning of Bloodmoon, he even felt things would turn out alright. With luck, the extra job, and a loan from Gary, TJ secured a small house for his sisters to live in until they would all move to the capital, Portico, for his schooling.

***

"TJ?" Aly called. He didn't look up. Instead, she saw his head slump. Aly stepped quickly up to where he sat on the edge of the dock. His hair, misty from the sea spray, looked knotted. She sat down next to him, "TJ, you alright? Grama said she heard yelling and you never came over."

He looked up at her with red eyes, "Fightin'. Yellin'. Who gives a fuck whatcha call it. Fuck it. Sick of it all."

"Stop talking like a port kid," Aly reprimanded.

"We're port kids Aly. I'll talk how I please," he lay his head in his long-fingered hands and sighed as he rubbed his temples. Trying to remind himself he didn't have to put up with it for much longer, but the previous night he just couldn't stomach without some external aids. It was the first time in a while, but he only slightly regretted it.

"Sweetie, come back to my place. Please," she began running her hands through her curly hair, "Have you been smoking?"

"Yep. Life's bliss when you're fuckin' high. The come down reeks like piss," he laughed to himself and looked up at her, "You're mad, right?"

"Yes, but I'll get over it. Are you hurt?" She set her hand on his shoulder.

"Not too terribly. I'm alright," they lapsed into silence then. The sun rose up over the blue horizon of the ocean before TJ, finally, sobered up, "Sorry Aly."

"I know honey. Let's get some food into you and get you cleaned up. Alright?" She stood and reached her hand down not expecting him to take it, but he did and after a few steps he put his arm around her, "What hurts?"

"My knee," he gasped. "I'm sorry. It's why I smoked. Hurt a lot."

"Don't worry. I've got you. Relax," she took his arm and pulled it tighter around her shoulders, "Can I put my arm around you? I can support you better that way."

TJ grimaced, not liking the contact, "That's fine."

Very carefully she wrapped her arm around his waist and then pulled it back in shock, "You're bleeding!"

"Was. Sorry. Thought it would be dry," he grimaced again as she wrapped her arm around him once more. They made slow progress back to Aly's home a few blocks from his own.

Aly's younger sister waited for them with the door open. Her parents set breakfast on the table as she shouted, "Found him!"

"Finally," her mother added to her oldest daughter's comment. "We were about to send a search party after you." She stood and quickly pulled chairs out for the two and sat TJ down. Aly washed her hands of his blood and tossed a cloth to him. He ate as if half starved, but when finished, Aly pulled rags out and a pail of warm water.

"Off with it," TJ gave her a blank look and she waved her hand at his shirt, "Come now. You know what I mean."

Slowly, TJ removed his sweatshirt. Her mothers' hand flew to her mouth. His shirt was stained a dark red. He gasped as he peeled it off his back, tearing open the fresh wounds. "I'll go get the alcohol to properly clean that and some bandages."

"You don't have to Aly," TJ muttered.

Aly looked at him with a raised eyebrow, "Because you can clean it yourself? You can barely move. Now sit still."

The half-elf muttered something in Layendrian, but did as told while she cleaned the blood off his back. Aly bit her lip. His back was a mess. Whip marks crisscrossed over each other. Some new and other's old. "TJ, this is horrible and some of it looks infected. You should go see Colette."

"She is busy without me taking up her time. Salty ocean. That cleanses just fine," he smiled at her before flinching from the wet cloth she used.

Aly turned to her mother who came back in with a bottle of cleaning alcohol, "Thanks mom. And TJ... no. Not really. Deep breath this is going to be cold and sting." She poured a bit of the alcohol onto a clean cloth and pressed it onto the first cut. She watched him bite his lip, but otherwise there was no change. That cut cleaned, she did the same with the rest, then she rinsed off the cloth in the red water and began wrapping bandages onto it, careful not to make them too tight since his ribs looked bruised again.

A knock sounded on the door, followed by excited voices and thundering steps. TJ sighed as Aly cut the last bandage and tied it off. A little girl appeared at his elbow and he patted her head, "Hello aida."

"Tam, where-"

Another head popped up, "-did you go?"

"I needed a walk. I'm sorry I left you two," he stood and stretched, wincing slightly, he bent to pick up the second girl, "Kali dear, what have you done to your hair?"

Erinn frowned, "I braided it for her."

"You knotted it sweetie," he smiled, "I'll fix it."

The one girl stepped up onto his feet and gripped him around his middle in a hug before saying into his stomach, "Why are you all wrapped up?"

Frowning, TJ looked between the two girls, still very small for their age, "You should know why. You know I got hurt yesterday. Aly just patched me up, but have you two eaten?"

"Yes. Grama fed us," they said in unison.

Their brother smiled and shifted his weight off his bad knee, "Good. Now, Erinn, if you get off my feet and borrow Aly's brush, I will redo your hair and then I need to get ready for school."

Aly smiled and walked into her bedroom she shared with her two sisters and came back to see TJ sitting cross legged on the ground untangling Kali's hair with Erinn humming next to him. "Here, this should help."

TJ took the brush and Aly spun around and scooped up Erinn who whooped gleefully and began giggling as Aly danced around the kitchen with her. She set Erinn back down as TJ finished Kali's hair, "All done little one," TJ kissed the top of her head and stood. "Grama brought my backpack over, right?"

"Over there," Kali pointed and TJ retrieved it with a heavy limp and pulled a t-shirt out followed by his toothbrush, toothpaste, and medicine.

Quickly, he got ready as Aly did her hair next to them and, soon, they walked out the door to catch the cart out of the Dead Lands to EsCe for school.

***

"Where is your head boy?" Gary asked as he came up behind TJ who stared vacantly at the ceiling.

"Huh?" He looked over.

Gary laughed although he looked closely at him for signs that he hadn't taken his medication, "Day-dreaming?"

"No, just tired," TJ rubbed his hands against his eyes as he yawned. "Sorry. Did you need something?"

"There is a guitar in the back that still needs fixing. Fairly simple job and a few others could use a polish," the owner opened the register and pulled out a slip of paper, "Think you can do that?" TJ nodded and Gary smiled, "Go ahead and bring it out here. David is working in the back today and I fear he would just be a distraction."

Flashing him a smile, TJ responded, "He always is."

"Oh and one more thing," Gary looked down at the paper, reading the note left for him about an order, "You got a package today. Looks like it's from Louí."

His eyes widened happily as he realized it must be from his sister if it came from his aunt's town, "Really?" Gary nodded and TJ smiled and scurried away to the back.

The employee door swung closed behind him and David looked up, "Package from your twin over there."

"Thanks," TJ walked to the counter where a random assortment of strings and guitar picks lay about with a paper and a package. He smiled and pulled out a knife and opened the lid. Inside sat a few shirts, a pair of jeans, and socks. TJ ignored them at first and lay them aside, looking for something more important. Under those, lay a few packages of some of TJ's favorite food and some of Aunt Poliana's best baking lay hidden, but what TJ really searched for was on the very bottom. Letters. There were four letters in all. One from his female cousins: Meg and Thalia, one from his male cousins: Ash and Tony, one from his Aunt Poliana, and the final one from his twin sister Oreal – which he tore open first. The last two were incredibly thick, but Oreal's the thickest of them all. He turned around and leaned on the counter, one foot propped up on the cupboard to read her letter.

David looked up from fixing a drum set when TJ began laughing out loud as he read the letters from his family. TJ got a package from them with letters every month or so. In some ways, David believed it was one of the few things that kept TJ from completely falling apart. The half-elf read through the letters then pulled out a chunk of homemade bread and popped some in his mouth before offering some to David – which he took with glee. Aunt Poliana was an amazing cook. As lunch time came around, TJ moved the guitar to the front of the shop and began pulling strings off as he hummed to himself – a bouncing, happy tune.

***

Their final test was coming up. Andronicus would play the main set for the Festival, the third weekend in Bloodmoon with the trustees from the Academy in attendance. It didn't help to calm TJ's nerves, but they had time to widen the variety of music from folk to modern metal.

The old men stood in a roped off section of the crowd near the middle – a perfect place to hear the music in balance. With their black jackets neatly buttoned and ties knotted into perfection, the men closed their eyes to listen. One by one as they young men played through their set, the trustees lips tilted up into smiles. If the trustee's loved anything it was variety and style. These boys had it all and held the crowd captive. It was clear to the trustee's the crowd loved the young men. As Andronicus ended their performance, they went to the back to invite the boys out for drinks to talk and see what manner of people they decided to accept into their renowned school.

As they watched, the older men's eyes widened in surprise at the boys who truly seemed to care about one another – unlike many bands they saw. The lead singer, especially, always seemed to be of the self-centered variety always searching for praise, but this one praised the others for a job well done and helped the next band set up giving them encouragement and trying to calm the younger kids. Finally, the tall broad-shouldered bass player saw them and came over.

"Sorry," he shook the hands of the trustees. "We didn't see that you were here yet."

The drummer and back up guitarist came over and shook their hands, while thanking them for coming out. They turned to look for their last member with a sigh. He stood talking to someone, oblivious of the trustee members. "TJ, get over here. The trustees of the Academy traveled all this way just to see us! Don't be rude!"

"Sorry!" TJ dipped his head in acknowledgement, "I hope you enjoyed yourselves."

They eyed the young man, surprised, he appeared timid as he fidgeted with a loose string on his faded t-shirt and shifted from foot to foot, "That's alright. You were not expecting us so quickly. You sounded wonderful. Of course, we sent scouts to listen, but we wanted to hear for ourselves."

The dark-haired half-elf looked up and smiled brilliantly, his eyes and skin shining in the lamplight. The trustees couldn't help but smile back. However, the bass player spoke for them, "Thank you. We appreciate it. He near worked us to death practicing for it."

TJ blushed, still not saying anything, "But if it wasn't for him, we may never have gotten this far."

The other two band members laughed, "Of course not." They waved at a few people walking by carrying copious amounts of equipment to the stage.

"You all work hard on your own. It's not just me," TJ expressed, staring uncomfortably at the ground.

A girl called his name and he looked over, "TJ! Take your demons! They are driving me insane." She held out two little girl's hands who pulled at her and jumped about.

He laughed, "I'll take them." She let go and the identical girls came running over. They giggled as he caught them in his strong arms, "Did you enjoy yourselves?"

"Yes!" They squeaked in unison, smiling into his face.

The trustees looked on in surprise, "And who are these little ones?"

"Erinn and Kali. My sisters," TJ explained as Erinn bounced up and down trying to get a good view of the man with the fluffy white face as Kali buried her face against TJ's side and clutched at his back pocket with one hand and his belt buckle with the other. "Kali's shy and Erinn-"

"What's that on his eye? It looks funny," the little girl began giggling as she interrupted her big brother.

TJ quickly put his hand over her mouth and pulled her into him, "Stop that." She immediately stopped and gazed up at him innocently. "She likes new people." He smiled at the little girls indulgently.

"We wanted to take you all out for a drink, but," the trustee with the monocle paused and looked around at the others who all nodded, "Is there a place we could go where they can come along?"

TJ nodded, "There is a backroom in The Bakery that's almost never used." He picked up Kali and put her on his shoulders and without being asked David did the same with Erinn.

"Sounds excellent. Lead the way."

***

"I was not expecting that," Jake smiled as they made their way to the ports.

"Me either," TJ grinned as he shifted Erinn on his back. "What do you think girls? Are you excited to get away from here?"

Erinn bounced up and down and Kali gripped his shirt, "Yes! We wish we could go sooner."

"I liked eye man. He was funny," Erinn added and the boys all laughed. The man with the monocle kindly performed little tricks for the past hour to entertain the girls while the other trustees talked to each band member individually.

"You're in luck then," TJ ruffled Kali's hair and looked at Erinn, "We are moving in a week and a half."

"Really?" They exclaimed and Jake, Chris, and David looked up.

TJ grinned, "Yes. Not the best place – a studio apartment, but it has a bathroom and small kitchen – but it's better than nothing. We can move in on the thirty first."

"That's in eleven days!" They exclaimed and TJ laughed.

"You can –" he froze suddenly then began to sneeze violently. Jake raised an eyebrow in a silent question. "Shanah, by the ports. Skulley's she," he sneezed again, "Get's stabbed."

"What?" David asked as he began sprinting toward the ports.

"Skulley's and Lightning's get into a gang fight and Shanah and Aly get sucked into it. Shanah gets stabbed," TJ set Erinn down and Jake set down her twin, "You two hide here. We will come back for you, promise." He kissed them both on the forehead in a blessing of kinship.

"Don't leave us here," Kali pleaded.

TJ smiled, "I will be right back. I would never leave you two for good. But someone is going to get hurt and I don't want it to be one of you. Will you stay here? Keep quiet?"

They nodded and TJ sprinted off. The four boys showed up at the climax of the fight. TJ scanned the darkened ports looking for Shanah – Aly's younger sister – and ducked a fist and jabbed his shoulder into the smaller man's stomach. He saw her closer to the piers and ran off in that direction. A glint of the thin moon on metal caught his attention and he moved faster, ducking around the bodies, not knowing who was who. He gripped Shanah's shoulder and pulled her toward him but the knife sliced into her skin and stuck. He glared at the boy in rage and a wind picked up. The other man stumbled back, looking from his bloody hand to where the young half-elf, hair billowing around him like a black halo, glared. He turned and ran. The other Skulley's soon realized what happened and retreated as well, not wanting to be around a body. TJ picked up Shanah and ran to Colette's, everyone else following a half step behind.

He passed the light form of the girl to Jake as they neared where his sister's hid and waved them out picking one up in his arms as Chris picked up the other and they ran.

A while later, they sat on the four steps leading up to Colette's home talking and wasting time until she told them whether or not they got Shanah to her on time. The Lightning's felt horrible for being the cause, but the Dead Landers all knew they would do just about anything to change her fate. They were the only gang in town who defended others and only stole from the merchants and rich. They were the elite and friends with all the Dead Landers and asked all of them at one time or another to join their gang, but all had refused.

TJ bounced as the wind blew the scent of Colette's herb garden past his nose and he put an arm around Kali. The sound of soft steps came up to the open door and he looked back. Aly stood in the doorway shaking and pale, her freckles dark splotches on her face with her yellow hair a tangled mess. TJ pulled Kali closer in a hug before going to Aly, "How is she?"

She choked back a sob and TJ took his oldest friend in his arms, completely unsure what he was doing, but Aly stuttered out, "She's okay. She's gonna be okay," and buried her face against his dark hooded sweatshirt in relief.

He sighed, "Thank Atropos. This nigh's bin way ta hectic."

Aly laughed at his port dialect mixed with his education and stepped out of the circle of his arms. She wiped her hand across his chest, "I got your sweatshirt wet."

"It's 'kay," he shrugged. "Not any worse than what those two've done." Kali peered between his legs and smiled brilliantly as Erinn looked out from under a bench where she pestered a toad. "I should get 'em back home. It's getting' really late."

Aly nodded, "Thanks for sticking around and, well, I guess seeing it."

"No problem. See you on Mierten. Everything will be fine. Isn't that what you all are always telling me?" He asked taking a step down.

She smiled, "And it is, see? Things are getting better."

TJ rolled his eyes and steered the girls through the mass of people to the rusting gate.

***

"This is possibly the most boring lecture I have ever heard," TJ sighed and Jake and Aly snorted from different areas in the classroom.

TJ kept the link up, connecting the three in their minds and Aly said back, *"You are being so distracting,"* but he could hear laughter in her mind and smiled broadly at her.

She turned back to the teacher and tried to take notes. TJ's voice in her mind was harmonic and almost liquid, but overlying a pain so intense it felt like gripping a pine tree and someone strangling her simultaneously.

"When is this going to end?" TJ bounced his feet up and down impatiently.

Jake laughed. Their favorite class was coming up soon – orchestra with Ulrich. *"Five minutes TJ. Calm down."*

"What's going on?" The teacher fumed as she turned from the board for the third time to see Aly, TJ, and Jake laughing. "Well, who's going to answer?"

"We didn't say anything," Jake spluttered out through his laughter.

The teachers face turned red in anger, "Kelsee," she looked at the girl next to TJ – her star pupil, "What did they do?"

Kelsee shook her head and shrugged, "Honestly, I didn't see them do anything."

Her nostrils flared and the bell rang. Her students quickly gathered their items and scurried out the door. The three burst out laughing and made their way to orchestra, "You almost just got us into so much trouble!" Aly exclaimed, but TJ gave her such a genuine smile she couldn't even pretend to be upset with him.

"So? It would have been worth it," Jake chuckled pushing open the doors to the music room.

They separated, each going to their instrument: TJ the violin, Jake the bass, and Aly the clarinet. They began tuning and practicing immediately as the last of the class came in. It was a class which always seemed to go by quickly though and soon the boys walked to Make A Noise for work with Aly following.

The afternoon flew by in a whirl as Aly rambled off test questions at the boys for their mid-term exams. In between her rapid firing of information, the boys took care of the trickle of customers. Eventually, as the sky began to darken, Aly left for home and the boys were left alone to talk about the coming concert.

"I can't believe our first concert is in two weeks," TJ admitted as he checked the tag on a set of strings.

Jake nodded, "I know what you mean and then we both have our show in Darkmoon. I don't want to even think about that."

"Have you decided what pieces you are going to play yet?" TJ asked as the bell rang and a customer walked in.

Jake waved at the regular, "Not yet. I don't even know if I am going to sing and play or one of the two."

"Do both," TJ said. "Why not?"

"So much work," Jake complained dusting the neck of a violin.

"No, it's not."

"For *you* maybe. What are you doing?"

TJ sighed, "Machiaventae's *Into the Forest* and Strenchen's *Ninth Symphony.*"

"Let me guess, Machiaventae's is in Layendrian and a cappella?" TJ nodded. "And are you playing the entire symphony?"

TJ went around to the counter to check the customer out and shook his head, "Ulrich wouldn't let me. I had to choose only two. I'm doing the first and third movements.

"But the third movement is so hard," Jake said shaking his head

"It's wicked fun to play though," TJ smiled as his eyes glazed over while he went over his favorite parts in his mind.

Jake rolled his eyes, "I know it's probably awesome to play, but still hard."

"It's not that bad," the employee door opened and Gary stuck his head out. TJ waved. "What's up?"

"You boys realize it's almost seven, right?" Gary inquired.

They laughed, "Nope."

"Get yourselves home. You probably have better things to be doing than hanging out here," Gary smiled and came to take over the front as they left through the back door for home.

"Thanks Gary," TJ smiled. "See you tomorrow."

Gary nodded and Jake walked out the back door with TJ and down the alley. Jake clasped TJ's hand and pulled him into a loose hug impulsively. Like his body knew something his brain couldn't comprehend – or simply didn't want to, "See you tomorrow morning."

"I just can't wait for school," TJ said sarcastically, his lime green eyes glinting in laughter.

Jake laughed, "Sure. Have a good night." He turned away and paused, then turned back, "You sure you don't want to come over?"

"I would love to, but the girls…" TJ bit his lip.

"Bring them."

"I couldn't."

"Why not?"

TJ took a deep breath considering, "I – well… I might."

Jake smiled, "Then hopefully I will see you later."

The half-elf came home to a miniature disaster. Pots and pans lay across the kitchen floor and glasses were shattered. Apparently, his mother had another tantrum sometime throughout the day. *At least she isn't here now.* TJ thought as he carefully walked around the debris and to the back of the house. He found his sisters in their room sitting on the bed playing a hand clap game, "Come on you two. Pack up."

"I thought we were leaving –" Kali said and Erinn finished, "In eight days. It's only the twenty-third."

TJ smiled and kissed them both on the forehead, "We are going to Jake's for the night."

The door snapped shut from the front of the house and TJ swore, "Hurry up."

He quickly left the room to see which parent it was. A beautiful woman with a small frame and piercing golden brown eyes glared at him from the kitchen. He breathed deep and stepped into the living room. His stepfather then came into view and began shouting. He ignored them and strode into the kitchen to clean up. He knew they wouldn't hear him if he spoke. They never did and there were only a few more days left.

He ducked as Roger struck out with his fist, but didn't expect the ceramic plate his mother swung up. It hit him in the forehead and he stumbled back. Roger took him by the shoulders and picked the young man up off the floor, his arm around TJ's neck constricting his air supply. The beautiful woman tied her dark hair up with long fingers and picked up a knife.

She smiled dangerously and caressed the blade, eyeing the son she despised. She wanted him out of her life, but not the little girls. If she killed him though the girls would hate her forever. *Better to just take them all away.* Her twisted mind stumbled along, coming to a conclusion at seeing the little blonde heads peer around the corner. *I will punish him for his insolence. Take my girls from me? I will send them to a place you will never reach... Eternity in the sky, but you will go to hell with Lucvoyeur.* She said to herself, naming Atropos' opposite.

Annah came in close to TJ and whispered in his delicate ear, "I will send you to hell and your precious sisters will never see you again." She licked dark rosy lips and dragged the knife slowly across his angular cheek, a trail of blood blossoming and dripping like tears down his face.

She set the knife on the worn counter and gracefully walked to where the girls hid and, in a sickeningly sweet voice, called to them, "Girls come out and play with me."

TJ screamed to them in Layendrian, "Don't! Run! Climb out –" Roger smacked his head against the counter.

Annah gripped the girls by their hair and dragged them into the kitchen. TJ began to fight against the larger man who held him, but it did nothing, "Tie him up."

Roger did as instructed. He tied TJ's arms above his head to the cupboards handles and, laughing, punched him in the stomach. His mother glared at him angrily, "This one too." She kicked Kali toward Roger and he obeyed, not sure what the woman was doing. Kali squirmed against her bonds and both girls began to cry. TJ fought even harder, finally catching on to the woman's twisted thoughts.

"Don't you dare," he growled thrashing about. "Leave them alone!"

"Shut up!" She screamed.

"Take me. Kill me instead!" He gasped in a strangled sob. "They haven't done –" She smacked him into silence.

"That's not enough. They would still hate me. You have poisoned them. Don't you get it you idiot? You fucking mistake?"

Annah caressed Erinn's face and the girl whimpered, not understanding what was happening. She gazed at TJ, her sapphire blue eyes begging for his protection. He kicked at the cupboard and put all of his weight on the rope, but it did nothing except rub his wrists raw and bloody. His mother slapped the girl, "He can't save you. He isn't an angel. There is no such thing." She took the knife in her hand and Erinn screamed and backed up, but Roger gripped her by her tiny arms.

"Tam!" She screamed as the knife slipped into her tiny chest piercing her heart.

"Cut down the other," she yelled to Roger over TJ's sobbing curses.

Kali's eyes, wet and wide in horror, looked to her brother and TJ felt the pain from the death of the girl who completed her. He fought hard and finally pulled an arm free. His mother smiled wickedly and he saw the insane look in her face. He fought violently trying to get to Kali, but the other rope wouldn't loosen. She swiped the knife across Kali's throat cutting her windpipe. Blood spilled out and she gasped clutching her neck before falling still.

TJ's world crumbled in and broke apart. He didn't understand what he had done to deserve all this. Everything was getting better and now every reason to continue living disappeared. He felt Roger pull him down and smash his head against the wood, but the added pain didn't make any difference. Roger beat him till almost every inch of his skin was red and his wrist and two ribs were broken. He lay face down amongst the shattered dishes and waited for the final blow, but it didn't come. He just heard shrill insane laughter filling the emptiness inside him.

Please, don't leave me here. Just end it, TJ pleaded though he knew she couldn't hear him.

"Flip the bastard over," Annah commanded and Roger obeyed. TJ felt himself roughly being turned over and opened his swollen eyes to see the woman who should love him with a bloody knife.

Thank Atropos, TJ sighed, happy it would all be over as she leaned down and set the knife close to his skin.

She cut his shirt and smiled, pulling the shredded thing off, "Drag him to the sycamore. After all, isn't that your sanctuary?"

TJ couldn't help it; he whimpered just like his little sisters and froze. His twin sister entered his mind in a vision. Calendar marked Bloodmoon, thirtieth, two thousand and eleven. She played in the hayloft and fell to the ground below – a thirty-five-foot fall. She didn't move and he knew she died a day before their eighteenth birthday. He had no way to warn her. *That is all I needed. Just pile it on before I die.* He sneezed once as Roger dropped his body by the tall tree which reminded him of Heather and all the good times in his life.

Roger dropped him to the ground and Annah grinned as she unzipped his jeans and slid them down his body. TJ's eyes widened in confusion and shock until she set the tip of the knife on his pelvic bone. He tried to move, but couldn't. Roger gripped him too tightly.

Annah began to dig the knife into his skin in a complicated pattern as TJ's mouth opened in a silent scream. Finally, she stopped and leaning down she gazed into her son's unnerving brilliantly pale blue eyes, "Because you were such a great guardian. Such the angel, aren't you?"

She stood and gracefully walked out of the clearing as her son's blood dyed the moss under the sycamore red. He lay unmoving and uncaring. He welcomed death. It was the kindest thing that could happen now.

Darkness crept into his sight and he felt his pulse flutter, his breathing stopped and for a moment he felt suspended outside of space and time, then a bright golden light pushed against his eyelids and he woke up gasping.

5

Chapter 5

TJ's eyes snapped open, only to be blinded by a golden light. He blinked tears from his eyes and closed them again, unable to look into the light. Suddenly, he felt pressure against his eyelids and the light dimmed.

"Tamynaen, get up," said a voice.

The half-elf could barely raise his head as he opened his eyes and saw a beautiful being standing in front of him. His features looked like the work of an artist. He appeared tall, but then again TJ was laying on the ground, "I ca-can't." He coughed, "and it's Tamynaen *Jacob*."

He didn't look amused at being corrected as he appraised TJ from his great height, "Do you not know who I am?"

The dying boy tried to recall who this being could possibly be, but he could barely think and then it dawned on him and he gasped. It set off a spasm in his lungs and he began hacking up blood. Finally, his coughing subsided and anger conquered his mind. He growled, "Atropos."

"Watch the way you speak to me boy," the god warned.

"Why?" TJ questioned as rage consumed him. "I am neither alive nor dead. There is no worse punishment I could have other than being stuck here with the memory of what happened to all those I loved. The ones you condemned."

"I condemned?" Atropos shook his head. "No. No, my son. I didn't condemn them. I couldn't save them."

"You are a god!" TJ shouted in anger, before another spasm of coughs racked through his body. More blood trickled out of his mouth in a red froth. Atropos knelt next to the moss dyed red with TJ's blood.

"Calm. Peace," Atropos commanded. "I always did like that spirit of yours. Through all you have been through it has stuck with you," he smiled at him like a father would his favorite son. "I cannot step in once a being has been born. Lucvoyeur does that. I can only watch and sometimes take the being out of their pain and suffering."

"So-so you're going to let me die?" TJ asked and, realizing it sounded like he didn't want to die, he added, "Please. I don't want to live anymore."

The god sighed, "That's a pity. I was hoping that spirit of yours would keep fighting. I would make you my first angel."

"What?" TJ began coughing again and more blood trickled out the side of his mouth in a thin stream. "Why?"

Atropos knew he was running out of time. His brother was coming to take Tamynaen, "If you became my angel then you could step in to help save those I could not."

"You mean... I could... stop what happened... to me from... happening... to... others?" TJ asked between bloody coughs.

Atropos nodded elegantly and felt a presence behind him, "Do you accept?"

TJ thought for a moment and felt blood drip out of his nose, "Yes."

A victorious smile spread across the god's sculpted face and he placed his large hand across the half-elf's brow and just as darkness encompassed TJ's vision, he heard someone yell in a voice like silver bells. His broken body already relaxed though and peace encompassed him.

***

When he finally opened his eyes again, it was to a room covered with white and for a moment he thought he was in a hospital. He turned his face and surprise filled him to see his guitars and violins propped in a corner and a beautiful piano next to them. Then everything came rushing back. Tears pressed on the back of his eyes, but that wasn't the only thing pressing against him.

A wait pushed on his back and he felt behind him and heard a rustling and soft hum fill the room. New muscles flexed and shifted as he turned his head to look at the new addition to his body. He tried to sit up, but couldn't figure out how with the monstrosities behind him. Finally he gave up and rolled off the bed to his knees, just as his door opened. He tried to stand, but the added weight of his wings caused him to stumble into the golden man.

"Careful. Give yourself time to adjust," Atropos smiled kindly at him and TJ bowed his head in recognition and began to kneel, but he pulled him up, "Never shall you bow to me. You are my first and always shall be my right hand. Understand?"

TJ gazed at him in confusion *Why me? Of all people why would he pick a broken boy?* "Of course," he answered aloud.

Atropos waved a hand at the nightstand and food appeared, "You must be hungry. After all you have been asleep for quite some time. Eat and I will explain what I can."

He helped TJ over to the bench, "Thank you. How much time has passed?"

"Almost a week of our time. Your body was found the night after you died by Jake Weston and Aly Matriske. Because you died in that world, you will always be this age in appearance. Jake worried when you did not go to his home or to school the next day and went in search of you."

Letting the news wash over him, TJ pushed the food around his plate briefly before locking the emotions away, deep inside only to be let out when he was alone, "What do you mean after I died? I'm living, aren't I?" He asked between bites of the pasta and vegetables. It was the best food he had ever tasted.

Atropos smiled, "You have quite the appetite," TJ blushed and the god went on as he slowed down his bites, "For food as well as knowledge." Atropos smiled indulgently, "You had to die in order to come to my sanctuary."

"This is basically like a secret haven then? Since no one can reach it?" TJ questioned.

"Yes. Time, however, passes differently here than on Astyreian. You still have much to learn. Later, I will show you the rest of my sanctuary, but for now calm your mind. Find your peace. I feel the pain you are trying to conceal from me."

TJ bit his lip and turned away. Atropos gently took hold of TJ's face with one shining hand to make him meet his deep knowing eyes, "I will always know, but in time the pain will pass. I will know what you feel even if you hide it from all the others and even yourself. For now, I will leave you. I have a guest." Atropos stood with a flourish of his crimson robe and left TJ's room, closing the door with a snap.

Well that was unhelpful, TJ thought, fiddling with the white pants he had on. *He barely explained a single thing. And what is this obsession he has with white? Stupid. It stains...* He sat down on the piano bench, thoughts beginning to drift back to his friends who found his mutilated body and family who had passed on before him in such violent ways. He frowned, running his long fingers across the porcelain keys. It was a beautiful instrument. He plunked one of them down and smiled. Perfectly in tune, it set off a harmony inside his torn heart. He began to play in earnest letting his feelings wash over and through him. For how long he played, he didn't know, but it felt good to be free.

***

"What are you doing here?" Atropos growled in fury at the shadow in his private garden.

The shadow shivered and a man of the exact same appearance, but with a silvery glow, stepped into the light, "Calm down, brother. Always that temper of yours."

"You are disobeying the rules of our game. Is this forfeit?" Atropos questioned, after reigning in his initial anger at seeing his twin appear.

"No, Atropos," Lucvoyeur laughed and his silver sheen rippled. "We never agreed that you could take angels. I came to clarify and take what is rightfully mine. The Gala is not pleased you disrupted the chain."

"Rightfully yours? You only want him because he is a demi and could be more," Atropos grinned maniacally. "And The Gala has never cared for what we do."

"What *you* do brother. I only care for those you have cast off into the hell realm. The Gala – the council of the gods – they create the chain that must be unbroken from the orders of the Empyrean. You broke it."

Atropos shrugged, "What chain did I break?"

"Hayle and Tamynaen Jacob were supposed to be together. She will be reincarnated whether you like it or not since he still lives.

Along with a multitude of other things," Lucvoyeur sighed. "And I care not that he is a demi-god. I have his sisters. *All* of them."

"What good are they? He is the most powerful," Atropos sneered.

Lucvoyeur smiled, "You never could understand what it means to care for others. Only power. You could care less about his well-being, only that his power is intact. Heather can map out the futures – all of them. She is The Knowing. Oreal – his own twin – is The Elementalist. The twin girls are chaos and order – The Division."

"It doesn't matter. The Division can do nothing. They are too young," Atropos said in a fury.

"You can't control him. He came too close to his coming of age," Lucvoyeur retorted and tilted his head listening to the glorious music in the background. "So beautiful and heart wrenching." He paused for another moment to listen and it even captured Atropos' attention for a few brief seconds.

"I can control him and I will prove it to you," he said pulling his attention back.

Lucvoyeur laughed again, "For a time, possibly, but this is a game you can never win. He doesn't like being controlled and The Gala chose him."

"He is The Infinite," Atropos said, acknowledging why they wanted him.

"Nothing will stop him once he accepts what he is. Once he finds out," his brother warned.

Atropos leered, "He never will. Even if he did, with all he has been through, I highly doubt he would believe it or even use the power he potentially could have."

"All he's been through?" Lucvoyeur shivered and sneered. It turned his beautiful face ugly, "You mean, all you have put him through. You are sick. You play with their lives and find joy in it."

"What else should we do with the power we have? Not use it?"

"I use it to care for them when they die – or rather, when you get bored of them."

"But if you were to trick them into eating the fruit, you would just sit and watch them kill each other. That is so much better than what I do?" Atropos questioned.

"I like to think so. I give them the choice. The blood isn't on my hands."

"It just makes it easier for you to feel better about their deaths. Be honest brother."

Lucvoyeur shook his head. It was an argument continuing on for eons and neither of the twin gods ever got the upper hand, "At least I don't condemn them from the start." He sighed and it sounded like a miniature wind chime, "I will let you have your angels, but keep in mind, eventually, you will lose control of The Infinite. His path isn't a path at all. And least of all, can you control what The Gala commands? They hold the five in the palm of their hands and they are still collecting." He turned and stepped back into the shadows of the vibrant garden. "Take care Atropos."

Atropos just sneered in response, "Thank you for the unnecessary warning, Lucvoyeur."

"Farewell," he said and departed in a flash of silver.

The golden one growled into the abandoned garden he so carefully erected thousands of years ago, "Why did he have to come and ruin my perfect victory? Why does he always have to do that?" He questioned of himself aloud, used to being alone. "And why did The Gala talk to him instead of me? Unless, of course, he was lying… that has to be it. Lucvoyeur was just trying to frighten me. He wants The Infinite, Tamynaen." He gazed around at the colorful plants and shimmering fountains listening to the changing music.

He misses his sisters and that girl who almost messed up all my plans, Atropos thought reading the music like a book. *He is healing though, but he will keep his scarred wings so I forever will have a hold of him.* He left the garden with a satisfied smile on his face to see his first of many.

***

"One day – once you gain control of your powers – you can go back to Astyreian. I will need your help soon for a war is coming. Hopefully, you will be able to help stop it, or at least help those who just want peace," Atropos explained to the half-elf as he showed him around the grounds. He walked at a stately pace which irritated TJ, whom just wanted to walk around and discover his new home alone at the pace he chose.

TJ stared in awe at everything. The sky colored a brilliant blue-green with clouds the purest golden white he ever saw making everything seem serene and peaceful. The grass, soft underfoot, a bright green and the trees, spread everywhere in the distance, seemed tall and strong. In the valley between two hills a large lake sprawled out looking like a silver mirror. Lily pads scattered around its edge painted yellow, white, and peach specks where they blossomed. He wondered how cold the water felt and how deep.

"What powers?" He questioned confused, pulling his attention back - with difficulty - to the god.

Atropos put his hand on the young man who stood only a hand shorter than him and smirked at the slight tremble he felt underneath, "I know you are able to speak to others through their minds and read their thoughts, we call that telepathy, and you can control fire and sometimes air, can't you?"

TJ looked thoughtful, "Well, yes, but can't most elves use power of some form?"

"No. Only a few have a little of the sight or visions. You are special and, because of that, you must learn how to control your power. And, above all, you must learn how to fly," he smiled encouragingly at the boy who looked frightened. "Come. I will show you more of where you will be living from now on."

He, finally, led TJ over the rolling green hills and through the large red wood doors of the castle where Atropos lived. The walls were a blue-white stone with no seams in it which made it appear carved into the shape of the castle instead of pieced together. Brilliantly colored tapestries of every fabric lined the walls and soft rugs lay underfoot. Atropos pushed open a door near the back of the castle and watched as TJ walked through the door and gazed into the center pool which reflected his image perfectly.

He was no longer bruised or scarred everywhere and, already, he looked healthier. He had filled out and the sleep helped him lose the gaunt dead appearance. Knowing, almost immediately, what the pools were for, TJ knelt on the thick moss and trailed his fingers across the surface of the water and watched the ripples bounce off the edge of the pool and stop. The surface turned glassy smooth and then clear, he watched his friends faces appear and disappear as they went about their lives reaching age like he never would.

"You are more skilled at the sight than I thought. When watching these pools, time here slows to that of what it is on Astyreian," Atropos praised before explaining. "Can you tell the future or past?"

"The future, but all it is, is death," TJ sighed wishing the visions of death would stop or he could learn to control it.

Atropos pointed, "Come. Let us see."

TJ obeyed and dipped his fingers in the smooth water. This time, incomplete images of the dead and dying passed across the surface. Bloody and rotting ground and three figures stood together. TJ pulled his fingers out and shook them dry. He walked to the first pool and hesitated before dipping his fingers in. He saw his mother clothed in a bronze silk dress with a small tiara of topaz gemstones sitting atop her waist length dark hair. She was at a ball of some sort, dancing with what appeared to be nobles. *What? We were poor. Why is my mother at a noble's ball?* The image faded and a young Jake stood talking to the tiny TJ, convincing the quiet boy to hang out after school, then followed an image of TJ running around a corner directly into the new girl, Hayle. Their books went flying and TJ picked them up, bent down and took her hand. He remembered it felt like electric when their hands met and he heard the stars singing. He pulled his fingers out of the water and looked away.

"I've never seen the past before," TJ muttered.

Atropos helped him to stand, "Not surprising that you can with the pools. They help concentrate your abilities. This last place I show you, only you are allowed to enter without permission." He pushed open the dark doors and led TJ into his beautiful garden. The floor was tiled in golden colors and a balcony went around the outside with only one other door. A large fountain stood in the center by a small table with two chairs. The fountain drained into a pond near the center of the garden.

"It's beautiful," TJ said stunned.

Atropos smiled and steered TJ toward the table and chairs, but his angel couldn't sit. His large wings wouldn't allow it. Atropos laughed and changed the chair into a bench, "Sit. You should eat. Get your strength back."

***

He stared at his reflection in wonder. Wings so large and white they almost glowed, showed in stark contrast to his golden skin and straight black hair that needed to be cut. He wore loose black pants and out of them, in a pinkish white scar, angel wings crept up his taut abdomen mocking him in remembrance. He struggled to pull his teary clear blue eyes away from the mutilation.

TJ climbed up to the rock peering over the silvery lake and told himself he needed to get this flying thing right the first try or he would end up drowning from the weight of his wings. He took a deep breath and shuffled himself closer to the edge. Atropos told him to wait until he fully healed, but he couldn't. He threw himself off the rock. TJ worked his new muscles, but his mind couldn't understand what to do. The water came closer and then he felt the wind sing by and the feathers of his wings hummed discordantly. *It's like music. Smooth and flowing. Wrap it around, carry me up like clouds. That's what the wind is telling me.* He flapped his wings and realized how powerful they felt. He banked on an air current he heard singing by and sighed as his toes skimmed the water, then flapped harder and rose steadily into the air. He laughed and felt proud. He closed his eyes for a few seconds and opened, trying to turn away from the tree in front of him, but smacked straight into it. He grabbed a branch before falling and pulled himself up, completely out of breath, ears ringing. Then tried again.

His control of air helped him the most. He could tell it to bear him up and redirect it around his body and his large wings made it easy to carry his weight. What he had trouble with most was controlling the fire.

He could control his body and learned how to repress his memories, but the fire kept burning him in a brilliant blue light.

"Fire is rebellious, just like your spirit. If you can control that, fire should be easy," Atropos told him.

It was the link TJ missed and he reminded himself that music sang in everything – it was the harmony of the universe. He controlled it through the movements and the crackles and the pops, the snaps, and the sparks. He felt ready.

"Learn to defend yourself against people and beings. There is a master of the arts waiting for you. Be honest and she will train you," Atropos told him.

TJ looked worried, "How do I make my wings disappear though? Everyone will know what I am."

Atropos smiled at him indulgently, "Here in my sanctuary you will be in your true form almost all the time, but anywhere else you may grow them and make them disappear at your will."

"How do I get there and back?" TJ questioned, knowing Atropos would make him figure it out for himself.

"You fall," a grin spread across the gods face. "I know. It's poetic. The back of the castle is a cliff face leading to the clouds. Fall through them. When you wish to return you will know which one to fly through."

"So, your sanctuary is in the clouds?"

"No," he laughed. "But the clouds hide the only way to get here. Go now and learn all you can from the Dragons. You are ready."

TJ followed Atropos to the back of the castle and through the last door on the right. A balcony overlooked a sheer cliff with clouds at the bottom. He felt nervous about going back. He knew years had passed in the months he spent with Atropos. The Dead Landers had all moved on or passed away. His mother and Roger were dead. Annah went insane and killed herself. His Aunt Poliana still lived, though very old, and the King of Astèndre – Nor-Ten – also lived along with his two youngest daughters and son.

"There is a genocide going on," Atropos told him. "When Medicée killed Medíc – her father – she began it. If you go to The Empire, be careful. They don't like elves of any kind or fairy creatures."

"I know. Even the dragons left to the islands of the Orcana. I know what is going to happen in about thirty years. A war. I understand why all I have ever seen is death. That's all that is in our future. I will train hard to fight and save those I can. Learn all I can of Astyreian."

"Be listening for my call. I will need you back here." Atropos gazed out into the obscurity of boiling clouds as TJ nodded and pulled himself up to the balcony. Standing perfectly balanced as he spread his magnificent wings, TJ didn't look back. Atropos muttered a phrase to allow TJ to come and go as he pleased before watching his angel fall.

TJ let his body plummet through the clouds until he could see the ground below and gasped. *It looks so small from here, like a patchwork quilt.* He opened his wings and gracefully soared down until he could determine his position in Astyreian and smiled.

Atropos placed him an hour south of Louí. TJ knew he would be there by sunset. TJ had not seen the place where he was born since he was fourteen years old. He knew the way to his Aunt Poliana's only because he forced himself to commit the maps of all Astyreian to memory.

The world he grew up in looked changed already. More people used electricity, that before only the nobles could afford and now it appeared all the merchants drove the motor carriages. However, only the carts and horses traveled out of the big cities. Tall brick and stone buildings, like in his time, had grown taller and the roads looked smoother cut with stone, but his Aunt's hadn't changed. The farm house made of wooden planks was still the same color blue and though none of the same people lived there, it still gave him peace.

TJ landed with ease and shrugged his wings, a soft hum filling the empty front yard. He bit his lip and felt his throat tighten as he nervously strode to the door. Unsure of what greeting he would receive, he knocked quietly, almost hoping she wouldn't hear. He heard a shuffle and the door opened a crack as she peered out and froze.

"Hi- Aun-Aunt Pol-Poliana-na. I-" TJ stuttered and swallowed in a dry throat. He didn't know what to tell her.

She opened the door a little wider and raised a gray eyebrow on her wrinkled and sagging face, "Tamynaen Jacob?" She questioned by using her nephew's full first name. It certainly looked like him, but he died forty-six years ago. The young man nodded and fidgeted nervously. She heard a rustling of feathers and a soft hum filled the night air, "Boy did you bring birds with you?" Poliana threw the door open and shock filled her once more. Her all seeing eyes widened at his appearance.

"Aunt Poliana… I don't really know how to explain. I know it will sound crazy…" He fidgeted again, shifting from foot to foot and played with the belt buckle holding up his faded jeans. He wasn't wearing shoes she noticed.

She shook her head, "You always did get yourself into the oddest situations. Come on in. There's a new group of orphans here now. All asleep though. I'll whip you up something to eat. Go and wash up and meet me in the kitchen."

TJ smiled at the small old woman. *I knew out of everyone she would just take it in stride. You can always count on Aunt Poliana.* The half-elf walked silently into the bathroom and turned on the faucet. Cool water ran into the porcelain basin and he washed his hands off and splashed his face. Snatching up a towel he dried off and looked in the mirror. *I look just the same except for those wings and that scar.* His eyes filled with tears, but he refused to cry. He had refused to for a long time. *I still miss them. I miss them so much. And I am branded because of what happened.* He sighed and went into the immaculately clean kitchen. His Aunt's back was to him, so he pulled out a stool and sat at the counter playing with a spoon.

"Stop that," Poliana scolded the angel. "Now are you going to explain why you haven't come to visit me all these years? And where you got those wings from?"

TJ took the food she set before him and shoved a bite of the sandwich filled with sprouts, his favorite cheese, tomato, and hot mustard into his mouth. A smile filled his face, "As much as the food in The Sanctuary tastes god-like it is nothing compared to yours, Aunt Poliana." He swallowed the mouthful, "To answer what happened, well, I died."

"They said your body had, basically, been mutilated," she cringed remembering the vivid description.

He frowned, "Well, it was. The scarred wings are all that's left. Atropos saved me. Said he liked my spirit and gave me the choice to be his first angel. I agreed."

"That's blasphemous Tammy," she said using his childhood nickname.

Her nephew laughed, "I know. It sounds crazy Auntie, but look at me! I have wings. I can fly and I'm living."

"I saw you buried. So, of course I believe you, but was it really Atropos?" He could hear her unshed tears constricting her throat at the memory and would not meet his eyes.

TJ nodded taking another bite of the sandwich as the tea kettle whistled.

"So where have you been all this time?" She asked pouring the tea and placing it in front of him and reaching for the honey pot.

"In a secret haven," he laughed. "I should call it that Haven. Sounds so much better than 'Atropos' Sanctuary.' I was training and learning."

"Learning what?" She questioned, still unsure of what was going on. She believed him, but it seemed too surreal to be true.

"How to fly. How to control my power. Learning about Astyreian and coping."

"Power? And coping with what?" She asked worried.

TJ smiled sadistically. He knew he had become a master at hiding his emotions if Aunt Poliana didn't notice he felt torn apart, "I watched the twins die Auntie and Oreal too. That's too much for anyone to bear."

She wanted to hug him, to hold him to her like when he was young, but she knew from the look in his eyes it would be a bad idea, "I'm sorry."

"That doesn't change anything," he said bluntly and spooned honey into his tea.

Poliana watched him closely, "No. It doesn't, but I can still be sorry you had to go through it all alone. So, what is this power of yours? I know your twin was able to control most elements, although fire was a little tricky for her."

TJ frowned and sipped his tea, "I can control fire and enough air to make flying the easiest thing ever, a bit of water, and I can make things grow. I have a little of the sight and I don't know. It's hard to explain. I can do lots of things when I want to. It just comes to me. Like I can multiply things that are man-made and can amplify my voice. Little things really."

She looked amazed, "I have a feeling it isn't all that little."

He yawned, "Doesn't seem that impressive to me."

"If it has to do with you, you never think it is," she smiled warmly at him, her voice crackling with age. "Can you make those wings disappear?"

He thought about it for a moment before answering, "I was told I can, but never tried before." He rolled his shoulders and imagined them becoming invisible and trans-missive. No matter what came near his wings it would just pass right through and they would never be able to tell, "You wouldn't happen to have an extra shirt lying around would you?"

***

"Auntie, who's that?" A little girl asked as dawn rolled in over the ranch house.

The old woman smiled, "That's my nephew dearie. He came to visit for a little while."

"Oh," she turned her doe eyes on the figure of the young man, "What's his name?"

"TJ." She walked over and shook him. No response came other than him grumbling in Layendrian. "Get up, TJ!" He still didn't respond, so she pulled the sheet out from under him, unceremoniously depositing the half-elf on the floor.

He sat bolt upright, "What? What's going on?"

The old woman cackled at him, "Just like you were, when last I saw you at fourteen. You feel safe when you sleep and the world is basically dead to you, but if you feel threatened the slightest breeze will wake you."

TJ rubbed sleep out of his eyes and looked about, "What time is it?"

"Morning," the little girl said dancing about the room on tiny feet.

"It's eight," Poliana elaborated. "Why don't you get up and take the horses out to pasture?" She asked in a commanding voice.

He stood and folded the sheet and blanket, "Can I have food first?"

"No," she took him by the arm. "You know the rules. We take care of our charges first. Go on now."

TJ sighed and left as his stomach growled in protest. He walked out of the old home and into the pale sunlight of morning, looking around. It all appeared to be the same with the tall white gate guarding the pasture and the potholed dirt road leading from the main road to the barn. The field was flecked with the brilliant colors of the early wildflowers and the lake sparkled a deep blue in the distance, the rotting dock at one end. An apple orchard filled one side by the barn while a large garden spread itself between the house and the tall wooden structure. Behind the lake was a dense forested area that TJ still remembered every path in.

He threw open the barn doors and stepped into the dark and looked around. Each stall held a horse just waking up. The half-elf pulled the locks out two at a time and led the beautiful horses into the pasture, learning their names as he went. There were dappled grays, chestnuts, paints, all white, all black, mares, ponies, and stallions. Aunt Poliana was the best trainer and breeder in Astĕndre. The reason she could afford to take in all the orphans she did.

I still wonder how my parents met her though, since she is of the Old Blood line. The descendants chosen by the dragon guardians to rule Astĕndre and Layendria. They were given the gift of long life and she sure has had one. TJ sighed in thought and led a beautiful mare, just caught, out of the stall. He could tell she wasn't broken yet by the way she pranced. The mare didn't even wear a halter. He stroked the horse's dark mane and looked for its name, but she wasn't named yet – wild and untamed. TJ stepped around and gazed into her eyes. She calmed slightly, "Come on girl. Let's get you out to pasture." He led the mare out into the morning before gracefully hopping the tall wooden fence.

Happy he came for a visit, TJ strolled up to the light blue house, but he knew he couldn't stay long. He still needed to find the dragons who would train him. They were the masters of the fighting arts and kept the secrets of the ages that would prepare him for everything to come.

"How long will you be here?" Poliana asked over breakfast.

TJ shrugged, "I was thinking about a week. I have things to do."

"I know," she smiled. "You were never good at staying in one place for too long. Your destiny I fear is to travel."

"There is no such thing as destiny, Auntie. Destiny doesn't exist," he bit into the toast. "But yes, I am a wanderer."

She smiled as if she knew something he did not, "Well, I wish you all the best and you know, as long as I live, you are welcome in my home."

TJ nodded feeling emotions he wanted desperately to never feel again. He choked out, "Thank you."

***

It took much longer to reach VeeCee by horse, since the stallion was slower than flying, but TJ cringed at the thought of walking the whole distance. It was night when he left and the shadows painted the road in the color of nightmares. TJ fought them back and re-pressed the horrid memories taunting his consciousness and con-centrated instead on the hypnotic rhythm of the horse's stride. He battled with his eyes to keep them open and refrain from drifting. By early morning, the road widened and smoothed as it led into the old capital city; his home town.

The roads, in the past fifty odd years, seemed to have been re-paired – except for in the Dead Lands which had grown worse due to the wars, but TJ didn't need to go there. Instead, he went to the Mercante District where people were just beginning to leave for work. They got into their motor carriages and onto their horses. Some walked and others road bicycles. TJ nodded politely to a few people as he made his way to the house of the Red Dragon.

They were all called that – the leaders of their Guild of the fight-ing arts. Each a master of their own style: metal weaponry, silver; archery, green; tyela, red; and martial, blue. TJ would be learning tyela, a style of hand to hand combat that taught you how to use your weight against others. It helped teach flips and turns, how to hit correctly, kick correctly, speed, agility, and the best pressure points.

TJ jumped off his horse and stopped in front of the door to the simple home and knocked. A woman with radiant flaming hair, a pale round face, and a small girlish appearance opened the door. "What?" She asked in a voice as rough as sandpaper.

"Training," TJ answered simply.

The woman looked him up and down appraising the lean half-elf, "You had better talk to the Red Dragon."

He followed her through the front door and into the building with polished wooden floors and sliding doors. After she took him into the main training room he stopped and questioned her quietly, "You are the Red Dragon. So how are you to lead me to her?"

She smiled wickedly, "Why do you want training? You seem strong enough already."

"But I am not trained. And I want to be able to defend others."

"Not yourself?"

TJ shrugged, "I want to give others a chance in this struggling world."

"Good answer. I will train you," she reached into a wooden chest and tossed a pair of loose-fitting cotton pants with a tie at him and a white cotton shirt. "Your training begins with the others. Go and eat with them. Down the hall and to your right."

The training was hard. They would wake at four every morning to scrub the place down and care for the garden and grounds. Then they would eat a simple breakfast of oatmeal and fruit. Next came the real training. TJ progressed fast since he had been a Dead Lander and already knew a lot about fighting and things every kid needed in the slums to survive. He spent the better part of six years training until he could defeat the Red Dragon, who had become a great friend.

"You are always welcome here and if ever you need my assistance, all you need do is ask," she handed him the reigns to his young stallion. TJ leaned down and kissed her on the forehead, speaking a

Layendrian blessing meaning, 'May the winds watch over you, and the moon guide you.' He spun his horse and headed for Portico, the capital city, where the Blue and Silver Dragon's lived.

Their trainings were drastically different and took longer than the tyela training. Martial training focused around discipline of the spirit. He would balance on a pole for hours and then hop from one to the other and hope it didn't fall or get knocked over. Then hang by his legs from a vertical pole for long stretches of time. He learned how to control his emotions to a pinpoint and how to be completely expressionless – to give nothing away in battle. He learned how to defend himself, where tyela concentrated more on the attack and defending others.

The Silver Dragon spent hours training TJ on the positions and forms to use in every style of fighting until he could move between all of them like liquid. It became impossible to tell which style he drew from. He wasn't even allowed to touch a weapon until he could properly forge his own. After three years of training, the Silver Dragon began his real training.

Fifteen years later, TJ became a master. His weapon of choice was his favorite to make and created by him: two thin knives the length of his forearm attached by a chain. He knew, when he flew, he could throw them with deadly accuracy.

Training completed, TJ said farewell to the Blue Dragon and then the Silver Dragon. The weapons master didn't really like farewells so he just shook the angel's hand and slammed the door in his face.

The half-elf's next master, the Green Dragon taught him archery. His elven heritage helped him drastically because of his perfect vision. He mastered it quickly in three years with his excellent muscle memory aiding him. That was when he learned of one last master. The Gold Dragon who dwelled on the cliff edges of the

Orcana Islands. The only way to get there by boat or, in TJ's case, flight.

***

It was a long flight. Two days and nights of no sleep. When alive, the farthest he ever traveled was to the capital city Portico one time with Aunt Poliana. The expanse of water he flew over now seemed dark and mysterious. It fascinated him in a way nothing else ever had. As he flew, he watched the waves crash against one another in an ongoing battle. A few times, he saw a whale surface in the distance and expel water in a burst of shining droplets. Even from the distance, TJ could smell the whale's breath if he dropped too low. They reeked. The dolphins, however, never smelled and they played in the sparkling water with abandon. Finally, they led him to the cliffs of the islands.

TJ swooped down and froze, hovering in the air. Lurking right at the edge was the most shocking and miraculous sight he had ever beheld. The Green Dragon failed to mention the final master was an actual dragon. The dragons' scales gave him his name. They gleamed golden bronze in the sunlight of the early morning. TJ landed hesitantly on a tall rock to properly see the giant creature.

"What a lovely sound," growled the dragon turning his plate sized milky eyes on the half-elf angel perched on the boulder. He sniffed TJ and raised himself up on his legs as large as an ancient tree. "What species are you? I smell some pine and blue bells, fresh cloud and sea salt… dirt. You need a bath whatever you are."

TJ laughed nervously, "I am a half-elf and an angel."

"Finally, you have arrived. Atropos told me one with wings would seek me. And here you are. I warn you, Atropos likes to play games and you are one of them. When you decide you have played enough, take the fall. You block his vision. You are guarded," he seemed to be speaking to himself as he clicked his claws and TJ realized the dragon just made a prophecy about him. "You are going to be here many more years."

TJ shifted uncomfortably as the dragon moved his head slightly and stood fully up, stretching his wings wide. The gold dragons' wings spanned the entire cliff face and TJ, suddenly, felt small and insignificant. The ancient one opened his muzzle and boomed out laughter, his pointed teeth inches from TJ's body, "Fly with me. We have much to discuss and I have much to teach you."

TJ spread his wings, which always seemed so large before, in confusion. *How can a blind dragon fly?*

***

The gold dragon, Herokinareshta, had been correct when he said he had much to teach. He helped TJ learn to stand on his own and formulate his own ideas and interpretations. Herok, mostly, spent his time in silence while TJ would explain different things he saw around the islands where Herok would send him, many times he would send him on long trips to the mainland as well. Herok wanted TJ to experience the cultures which would be destroyed and wanted TJ to understand not everyone was like his parents and, most importantly, that life goes on. TJ, finally, decided he wanted to write the histories of Astyreian because he knew his world would end.

***

Twenty years after first meeting the dragon, TJ was called back to Atropos' Sanctuary. He said farewell, knowing he would see him again before it all ended. TJ returned through the clouds to meet with Atropos. Over the years, he learned so much, it almost surprised him to see nothing changed in the place he called Haven.

In the last few year's he spent with Herok, TJ met Caladria and Ruby, the youngest princesses of Astèndre. The women decided they no longer wanted to be a part of the fighting since their brother, Rupert, took over at the death of Nor-Ten, five years before, with the help of the Regent. In truth, the Regent was now the one who ruled. Their brother only wanted to continue fighting and the princesses wanted no part in it any longer.

The two women helped teach TJ about the nobles and more about the Old Blood lines. He learned there were two lines which stretched back to the beginning of Astyreian. The elven royalty: the chosen line picked to rule the elves for their wisdom of nature, and given long life and the gift of sight. The other blood line, the human royalty: the chosen line picked to rule their race in wisdom and granted long life and knowledge of peace and serenity. Each line had a number of people in it, but over time, through multiple marriages to closely related family, the blood lines began to run thin. Neither line lived as long as in the past and some began to lose their sanity.

The princesses' oldest sister, Annahbelle, always easy to anger, frequently believed she was being followed and assassinated. They never suspected she would leave and never come back.

TJ was fascinated about this and wondered what happened to Crown Princess Annahbelle. He pushed open the door to his room and threw his bag filled with books into it, then went to the Garden to meet Atropos.

The dark doors closed, TJ leaned against them to force them to open. From the balcony, he saw the sparkling fountain and his Maker sitting on the ledge watching a fish swim in and out of the roots of the lily pad. TJ jumped down and floated to the tile floor.

Atropos looked up and smiled, "I have a mission for you."

6

Chapter 6

Medicée craned her elegant neck over her subjects who cringed every time her eyes swept their way. She was looking for someone, but they didn't seem to be there. Her fierce angular face snapped to the tall man at her side, "Governor, where is Gabriel?"

The Governor licked his lips and flared his thin nostrils, "Empress, I – I'm not sure."

"He was told to be here, was he not?" She snarled, eyes narrowing on her subject as she drummed her fingers against her thrown impatiently.

"Yes," he stuttered. "Yes, he was."

Medicée turned her attention back to the subjects in front of her. The hall of the throne room was filled with dark décor: the candle holders in black iron, the rug a deep blood red, and in each window a black velvet curtain. A tapestry depicting a vicious battle scene was pushed back as a medium sized man with corded muscle and an angelic face entered the throne room. He quickly approached Medicée as one of the guards shouted a belated announcement, "Empress Medicée of The Empire, Reverend Gabriel has come."

The man called Gabriel knelt and bowed his golden blonde head, "My Empress, forgive me for being late, but duties called."

Medicée smiled, but it looked more like a smirk, "Gabie, I forgive you. Rise." He did as instructed, striding up to her while keeping his face impassive despite being called by a nickname that made his stomach churn.

He bowed his head close to one of her small ears, "You should perhaps consider changing the name of your empire. It would make your title sound less redundant."

She laughed cruelly and watched the handsome man turn and gaze over the crowd of people scurrying about and trying to look busy, "Gabie, are you to join me for dinner? It is roasted turkey tonight."

Gabriel carefully monitored his face to show no sign of annoyance; *I hate it when she calls me that. It's not like we are lovers. In fact, I hate her more than anything or anyone.* He faked a smile and turned his tanned face toward her, refraining from chewing on his lip, "I won't be able to, majesty. There are midnight ceremonies tonight since it is leading up to the summer solstice. I must prepare for it."

Medicée pouted and her dark features glowed as the lights were turned on and a black candle was lit by her throne. She liked candle light, knowing it made her look softer – fooling her enemies. "Atropos will understand if the ceremony isn't perfect," she wheedled.

The man gave her a smile, "I don't think Atropos cares much for the trials of man. He only cares that we serve him and pay our homage. Only then will he help us in turn."

"You must be right, Reverend," Medicée bit her dusty red lip seductively. "Well, then I guess you should begin setting up for your service."

Dismissed, Gabriel bowed and slowly walked out of the hall through the battle tapestry. He sighed and shook his head as he walked away. The castle's walls were undecorated and lit by bulbs hanging from the chains. Leaving it cold and unwelcoming to better confuse unwanted visitors. He skipped down the steps two at a time and looked down the passage leading to the church. Turning his head from side to side, he saw no one and proceeded to run his wide hand along the wall and pushed the rough ice-cold stone. It slid in and he pulled a handle as he shoved his body against the hidden door. It slowly swung inward on invisible hinges. He slipped through and it closed silently on its own. He fumbled in his pants pocket for his matches and lit a lantern. Walking quickly down the tunnel toward the counsel room, Gabriel tried to remember how he had made it to this point as he chewed his lower lip.

Gabriel laughed mutedly, *Because I witnessed what the Empress does to those who disobey her. I saw her cruelty and yet know that even though many of my country men are damned to hell for following her, I know that I can help. I always knew I could help and so joined the Rebellion and became a priest of Atropos. I teach of his kindness that helped save me, while plotting to murder the Empire's ruler.* Gabriel smiled as he remembered the caring family who took him in as a lost young boy and taught him the ways of his god. He paused momentarily in front of the thick wooden door and collected his thoughts before pushing it open, "Good evening all. Thank you for joining us."

"Gabriel," a thick man nodded in greeting, "What did the nuisance want?"

"Dinner. I said no. I have a ceremony to set up for after all," he laughed and it sounded like deep bells. "We have a lot to discuss and in a short amount of time. So, if everyone could take a seat." Gabriel and the dark haired man took a roll of paper out of a stand and spread it over the long table in front of twenty assorted people. "Thanks. Matt and I decided it was time for the rebellion to take a stand against the Empress and bring her down for good." Gabriel stood next to Matt with his hands planted firmly on the table surveying each one with his ice blue eyes.

In earnest, they began to discuss the role each person seated at the table would need to fill and what materials still needed to be gathered before their plot against the Empress could be carried out. All the plans details took over an hour, with much violent shaking of hands and fists pounding on the table to emphasize points, but – eventually – they clapped each other on the back with excitement while others nervously patted dampened brows or wrung their hands.

He didn't know until the secret passage became filled with palace guards that someone betrayed them. The most prestigious of all Medicée's guards, infiltrated the hidden chamber with uniform precision. With chains, swords, and daggers, the men stomped in throwing cataclysmic noise across the stone walls. Over thirty entered and dragged the rebels, beaten and bruised, into the dungeon; they were locked under high guard and tortured for high treason to the Empress.

***

I'm to be executed tomorrow, Gabriel thought as he put another check mark in the dirt. Thirty in all to mark his thirty days of imprisonment. *At least it will be a good death. Make a stand. But I'm not ready to die. I wanted to see Medicée six feet under before I went out.* Gabriel sighed heavily and watched the figure of a guard shuffle by on his rounds. He curled into the scratchy damp hay and tried to sleep, but it didn't come. Instead, he thought back to Miranda and Thaddeus, his foster parents. He wondered if they would be proud of him or ashamed. They certainly gave him all he ever asked for and even loved him as they did their daughter. Gave him the best school money could afford, taught him religion, and even the defensive arts – not that he was any good, but it helped a little. Until they perished in the fire which began in their neighbors' house, they did everything for him and even got him his first position as the House of Lords private priest.

The fire, they said, started from a candle burning on the table that tipped over and caught the curtains, but every person in town knew this to be a lie. The fire spread too quickly and moved inward from three different sides spreading to the neighbors' houses. Miranda and Thaddeus' neighbors were known to be activists against Medicèe. The entire town mourned their deaths in silence for fear something would happen if they openly remembered their lives.

For Miranda and Thaddeus and the other neighbors, they held an entire day in their honor later on, but Gabriel still missed them. *I will be joining them soon.* Gabriel sighed and prayed some more to Atropos for his death to be quick and easy and for the deaths of his comrades to be the same. He curled his knees up to his chest and tried to sleep again, but once more, sleep wouldn't come. Then something began to bother him.

Something seemed off and suddenly it occurred to Gabriel the guards had stopped their rounds and that never happened – especially before an execution. Light usually shined in at some point, but the torches stayed unlit. It was silent.

Gabriel shifted uncomfortably in his cell and the hay rustled as a soft blue light shined under his door and went out. The priest held his breath, thinking his nearly thirty years were up. He heard a light click and the heavy metal door swung open on silent hinges.

Silent door? Gabriel wondered in confusion. *That door is never silent.* His heart began to race in fear of what he thought was coming, but as he looked out the door, only darkness greeted him. "Who's there?" He questioned with a constricted voice.

"Shhh," someone hushed and a darker shadow entered the cell, making its way to where Gabriel sat on the hay, "Gabriel, follow me."

He gulped in shock, "Follow you? Who are you? How do you know my name?" Gabriel heard a soft chuckle and, finally, could see the outline of a man dressed all in black. He felt almost a nudge in his mind telling him to follow the man, but he hesitated slightly.

"I'm one of the same," the man said in a clear melodic voice tinted with impatience.

Gabriel sighed in pure relief, *'One of the same.' A part of the rebellion* he thought silently to himself, but aloud whispered, "Thank Atropos, my prayers have been answered. Maybe Angels are real after all."

"Wonderful," the man replied, voice dripping with unleashed sarcasm. He put his hand under Gabriel's shoulder and lifted him into a standing position impatiently. "Now hush so I can get you all out of here."

"All of us?"

"Shut it. Just follow, *quietly*," the man hissed under his breath as he led Gabriel out of his dank and damp cell. He bent down in front of the mass cell and shoved something into the key lock and a soft click echoed down the darkened empty corridor. Then pulled a small black cloth out and rubbed it on the hinges before he pushed the door open. Gabriel watched as he entered and came out followed by the members of the rebellion a minute later.

The man in black led them silently down the darkened hallway of the dungeons and past the open door to the guards' chamber. A soft snore echoed out, but otherwise nothing emerged from the room. Quickly, he led them to the end of the passage and made a sharp turn to the left by the staircase and a rank smell issued up to meet them from the sewage entrance by their feet. The young man pulled open the heavy metal disk closing off the entrance and gazed down into what appeared to be a black abyss. He spread his fingers wide and a brilliant blue orb of fire came into existence and floated above his palm. The light sent a dull glow down the shaft and illuminated the ladder for the rebels to climb down. He waved for everyone to continue down the slippery ladder.

The rebels hesitated for only a moment before they heard a loud click from a door being opened and closed above them and they began climbing down as fast as they could. Gabriel still hesitated though, unsure about the young man, although he knew he was on their side. He couldn't help but wonder how he even knew about the passage and who the young man actually was or how he created blue fire. Finally, his fear won out and he questioned the young man, "Who are you? And are you really on our side with all of these tricks you seem to know?"

He turned to face the priest and raised a dark eyebrow, "I'm helping you, aren't I? Sometimes doing the right thing involves a little crime. Weren't you locked up for treason? I can put you back in if you would like."

"No," Gabriel exclaimed louder than he intended, but he was scared to go back. He wasn't ready to die just yet. "No. I realize you are helping us." His eyes followed the spinning and swirling flames of the fire orb, "But who *are* you?"

"Tamynaen Jacob. TJ," he lowered the orb and it softened more as he spoke again in his melodic voice, "we must be quick now. Otherwise the guards will awaken at their posts and we run the risk of someone coming down here and catching us. Come on."

Gabriel looked away from the orb and into the young face of his rescuer and his dark blonde eyebrows disappeared under his bangs. *How can such a young man have rescued fifteen of the most highly guarded prisoners in Medicèe's castle? And how is he able to create blue fire seemingly without thought?*

"When we get out of here, I want a better explanation, but right now I just want out of here," Gabriel admitted.

The younger man flashed a smile, "Then after you." He waved to the hole in the ground wafting up smells of feces and rotten foods. He gave a small chuckle as Gabriel made a face and descended.

TJ quickly swung himself into the hole and closed the hatch before making his way quickly down to the front of the scared group of rebels. He waved for his blue light to bounce up and down in front of him. The group threw dark menacing shadows on the walls and their feet were soon drenched by the stagnant water which covered the ground. They followed him through the twisting passages for a quarter of an hour before he turned off into a darker tunnel and crawled through a smaller hole leading further down. Gabriel felt his hands slide on slime covering the walls and his stomach would have emptied itself, except nothing filled it.

Soon the tunnel grew larger and they could stand once more. It felt like hours passed before they angled upwards and it was even less time before the priest's calf muscles seemed to scream, but the young man dressed all in black didn't slow his pace.

Gabriel licked his dry lips and struggled to keep up. His chest hurt and his broken rib ached, but he didn't complain to the young man. *I don't believe he would care either way. Even though everyone here is beaten and bruised and we haven't seen a decent meal in weeks. He has probably never been on this side of the rebellion though.*

Gabriel swallowed and once again licked his cracked lips and realized they, finally, slowed and the walls of the tunnel widened out into a cave. A light shined at the end and it seemed like forever before the light streamed into the mouth of a cave where a tent stood. He gazed in shock at the multi-colored tent flap and began to wonder where they were as a woman the size of a child came out with a tray filled with covered bowls. She greeted the young man with a broad smile on her sunburnt cheeks.

The little woman smiled in delight at the young man as she placed warm food in the rescued rebels' hands, "So good to have you all here safe and sound. TJ, I can't thank you enough."

The young man shrugged, "No problem. Thanks for the food Reida," he disappeared into the sunshine without another word.

Reida sighed, "Well, glad he's being so talkative. How about you all come this way. We have some logs set up around the fire. Get you all nice and dry." She smiled kindly, "Fed… a bath would be good for you all too. Come on, follow me." She waved them through the mouth of the cave and into the sunshine of afternoon.

They sat on logs surrounding a campfire and Gabriel prayed quickly and began to eat hungrily, "Who is that young man?"

"TJ?" Reida smiled. "Probably one of the best spies or scouts we have."

Gabriel chuckled, "Clearly, since he rescued all of us so easily. I meant where did he come from? He seems so young."

The small woman rubbed her freckled nose, "Couldn't tell you, but he's been around for maybe five years now."

"So, he was very young then?" Gabriel asked as he swallowed his food.

She shook her head, "Looks exactly the same actually. He's a half-elf." She said as a way of explanation.

Gabriel almost asked another question, but the half-elf entered the circle of logs cutting off the conversation. In the sunshine, it was much easier to tell how young TJ looked and as Gabriel watched he began to wonder even more. The young man couldn't be more than twenty and he moved with a grace and dexterity that spoke of martial arts training. He possessed a lean build, but that could just be the clothes which gave him that appearance. He wore a dark red t-shirt and loose black jeans with a silver chain reaching from one pocket to another. It was impossible to tell what it was attached to. Gabriel watched Reida say something to him and he nodded and smiled – a crooked smile that didn't reach his eyes.

TJ finished his food quickly and strode over to Gabriel, "I'm sure you are all tired, so if you would like I can walk you over to your tents where clothes have been put out for you and baths."

"That would be great. Thank you," Gabriel sighed and rubbed his eyes. He followed the half-elf in silence for a time before he decided to question him, "Are you from Layendria or Astèndre?"

"Astèndre, I guess," he muttered quietly.

Gabriel raised a questioning eyebrow, "You guess?"

"It was a long time ago. Haven't been back in a while."

"I see. You can't be that old though. Even elves only live a little longer than humans."

TJ shrugged, "You'd be surprised." He waved a few people into an open tent, "The baths are at the end of this row," then continued on.

"So, how did you create that fireball? I've never seen anyone do that before. Even the Empress' magician."

"Magician?" He snorted, "That's just tricks. What I do is real. And I'm not the only one. I've seen others capable of stuff like it."

"What do you mean, stuff like it?"

"I've seen elves control air and my older sister was the best Seer there ever was," he waved another handful into a colorful tent with a beaded front entrance.

Gabriel sighed, "What about us? How did you know where we were and the secret passage?"

"Looked for it," TJ answered simply.

"You looked for it?" The blonde man questioned, hands on his waist. Gabriel wasn't used to people not fully answering his questions – or giving him complete respect. This young man, however, seemed bent on disregarding him.

TJ shrugged, "In a manner of speaking. This one is yours." Gabriel looked at him in confusion for a moment, but decided he should stop interrogating his rescuer. "Someone will come and get you tomorrow morning."

The next the priest knew, he stood alone in the opening of a canvas tent. He had never camped before. The thought unnerved him, but he refused to let it show. Instead, with grim determination, he smiled at his new neighbor before striding into the darkness. Enough light filtered in that he could see a small table holding a lamp and a bedroll with a pillow in the corner. Someone had already placed a rough wool sweatshirt and drawstring pants for him in the tent. Grimacing, Gabriel pulled his filthy clothes off and wrapped a towel around his waist. He picked up a rough bar of soap and his new clothes and went out on heavy feet to the bathing area with a towel wrapped around him.

***

"I can't believe the Empress has never found out about this place," Gabriel admitted in awe as he looked around at all the tents of different families, couples, and friends which covered the clearing and spread into the beech and maple forest.

One of the members of counsel laughed, "You actually think she would? It's too close to her castle; she feels safe and is arrogant. She wouldn't think people would dare come so close." He laughed and dug in the dirt with his stick and sat on the log in the circle around the fire.

"True, she is very arrogant," Gabriel admitted. "I'm happy to see all of you here. Glad you have all found somewhere safe to hide out. This is the group in charge of the rebellion? Or rather the main front of it?"

Reida shrugged, "Guess so. This is the mastermind, Karter. He is in charge of weapons and our strategies."

"Gabriel," the large bear-like man clasped hands with the priest. "Good to meet you."

Gabriel gazed around for a few moments while everyone sat and, finally, realized who he was looking for, "TJ. That young man isn't here. Shouldn't he be?"

Karter laughed deeply, "You expected him? TJ claims nowhere as home. He comes and goes as he pleases. What we need to do is make a plan of action. And I say it's time to fight."

***

He looked out at all the tents and small children running to and from a fire to the circle of their friends. *Life shouldn't be this hard for them. We are only going to make it worse when we send their older brothers and fathers to war. Can't theses children grow up in peace?* Gabriel sighed as no definite answer came from his plea to Atropos.

A week passed since the meeting and they would have another in a few minutes. Gabriel sat in the circle of logs waiting. The group of ten gazed at one another and chatted, until Karter stood and began speaking, "Let's begin," he paused as TJ slipped into the empty spot on the log next to Gabriel, "Good to see you again. Let's begin our plans. We know Medicée is going to send out another group of her army in a few months. At that time, we should attack since her numbers will be depleted for a few days before she gets her defenses up again."

"A few months?" One of the women questioned. "That's not nearly enough time for us to gain enough to properly fight."

"All we need is to take down Medicée," Karter said with a resonating voice.

Gabriel shook his head and began speaking, "It's not just Medicée, but her advisors as well."

"How many?" Karter questioned.

Gabriel bit his lip in thought, "Probably five of them, but they are rarely in the same room."

An argument of ideas suddenly shot up like a lightning storm. Gabriel tried to quell them, but for once no one heeded him. It went on for a few more minutes before TJ stood. All he did was clear his throat and one by one they all looked up and quieted down. When he began to speak it wasn't loud, but everyone heard him, "Her advisors are strong as well. We need to defeat her fortress. All of them must go down if we are to win. I will travel to the other places hiding the rebels and bring them here. Plan a few weeks, but try and have as much ready as possible for when I get back."

Karter raised an eyebrow, "How will you get to them and have them get here, with enough time to spare?"

"Don't worry about that," TJ sighed. "The best place to gather is on the edge of the forest. Move there."

"I can help plan a strategy for attack," Gabriel added and looked to Karter, "With your help of course."

"You should help with moral of the troops as well. Need to keep everyone positive," Reida threw in with a motherly smile.

Karter chuckled, "You all can figure out the rest, but I need to start weapons training."

As he stood to leave, TJ stood with him, "Before you leave, I think it would be in everyone's interest to train the women as well. I realize this is against what most of you are used to, but the times change. It is time for all of us to change with them." There was rumbled argument, but at a look from TJ everyone quieted down. "I will follow you."

Gabriel looked with confusion to Reida who smiled at him as he stood. She came over and waved him to follow her, "What is it Gabriel?"

"I just don't understand. What is his position here? He can't possibly be just a scout."

She chuckled, "No, he is also a spy."

"Even still, how does a spy have that much authority?"

"Look, you have only been here for a week, but TJ has been here… well, he showed up at the old camp a couple of years back. Karter and I had just gotten in a month before and we were still settling. He just appeared, took a few looks around as if to get his bearings, then strode confidently straight into the tent headquarters," Reida stopped in front of her tent and waved him to follow as she ducked inside. She continued talking as she began to organize her medicines, balms, and pastes. "I remember a shout and then the old leader quickly quieted. A few yells were issued from the commander, but then all was silent. From the shadows, we could see the young man gesturing and the commander wringing his hands. After a few moments, they both began leaning over the table. They were locked in there all night and come morning he was giving orders for us to all pack up and head out. Whatever TJ told him, it made the commander change our entire tactics and living quarters. From then on, every so often, TJ would come back and, always when he did, something would change and sometimes he would even bring us new refugees and supplies. He found out I was a doctor and so began bringing me medical items and, in turn, I taught him a few simple things." She paused and Gabriel sat stunned by this news.

"You mean he just waltzed in one day and is suddenly one of the highest advisors of the rebellion?"

"No, I never said that. What I said is, he brings us news that no one else could ever gain. He brings us the essentials and is always kind to us. Helpful. He has no family and no friends – that we know of. He has nothing, like all of us – except at least we have each other. He does what he can to help though and knowing he has nothing, he risks everything. No one could ask for more. You judge him too harshly," Reida smashed her mortar against a few red berries and they exploded into her bowl and dripped sticky sap down its sides. "And aren't you a priest?"

Gabriel bit his lip feeling guilty, "Yes. I am sorry. I shouldn't be acting this way, but after being in that cell... I don't know."

She smiled kindly at him, "It's alright. We got you out. Well, TJ got you out and we will take care of you now. Do you have much training with weapons?"

"No," he shook his head.

"Why don't you go down to the training yard then. They can help you out and give you some lessons. Should be useful in the weeks to come."

***

Gabriel watched as TJ threw his backpack over his shoulder. He was in all black again, instead of his normal red, blue, or green t-shirts and the chains were attached to his baggy jeans. Gabriel knew at the end of those chains were blades so sharp they could cut through flesh like butter. Yet, as Gabriel watched TJ disappear into the shadow of the trees, he couldn't help but feel like the young half-elf was still just a boy. After all, he appeared to be only seventeen. *He may dress up for war and people may listen to him, but that doesn't mean he should go off to war. He is too young. But he plays the part well. Where I still look like a priest.* He knew he did, even though he traded in his robe for a wool sweatshirt of dark green and brown pants.

The thirty year old man turned around and faced the campsite of the main force of the rebels. TJ would return in three weeks, but until that time he needed to focus on his skills with the staff and sword and the moral of the people. Gabriel had always been able to read the emotions of a crowd. He knew how to lead them to his own purpose, but he always tried to make sure that purpose was Atropos' and not his own. He hoped he did that well, but he would never know.

As TJ left, Gabriel straightened his shoulders and began to do what he did best, he encouraged people and talked to them. He found out about everything and everyone. Gabriel was a sieve of information, not only the everyday lives everyone else saw, but also their hopes, dreams, and their greatest fears. The priest knew about the strategies of war – strengths and weaknesses – about the amount of food, about the best doctors, and even about the Astèndrian's and elves helping them. Nothing escaped his knowledge and his hands reached out everywhere to aid those in need. His mind was his greatest asset and he used this and his knowledge of their hopes and fears to keep the people of the rebellion thinking positively. He knew it could change an entire war.

***

TJ looked around the woods and tried in vain to peer through the underbrush. Shadow upon shadow made seeing difficult, so he waited until his eyes adjusted and everything took on a monochromatic quality from the silver stream of moonlight filtering through the canopy of trees. Slowly the path the half-elf looked for became clear. A thin trail led out of the almost non-existent clearing he landed in.

On silent feet, he began striding down the path to a larger clearing a few miles away. As he walked, the trees gradually became larger and grew closer together until it was almost impossible to see between them. Suddenly, he stood at the clearing and froze, watching, as all around he saw other elves or half-elves standing on other hidden paths.

He smiled, *more than last year. That's great! Maybe that means this war will finally end. It will make the Festival of Lights much better than last year too.* As one, they all looked up to the stars and watched the moon creep out over the edge of the canopy and as it did, its silvery light spilled into the clearing reflecting off the small lake. The flutter of hundreds of tiny wings began to fill the air as the fairies flew out toward the lake and to land on the water lilies and call them to light. Once the lilies began to glow, the elves stepped forward to create a circle by linking hands, in an attempt to complete the circle, they stepped into the water. There ware supposed to be at least fifteen, but only eight made it from Layendria or Astèndre into the sacred forest in Medicée's realm.

Better than last year, there were only three of us to represent the old clans from the beginning, TJ thought. They clasped hands and began to sing as the final lilies were called into light. The fireflies began to twinkle as the fairies started to dance in the air and the elves combined voices lifted into the heavens as they sang thanks to the world for providing them with light. TJ smiled as they finished singing and released hands. The feeling of calm and peace washed over them as they turned to sit on the edge of the lake to watch the moon rise to its zenith. As silently as they could they stripped down to their under cloth's and slipped into the surprisingly warm water and basked in the moonlight until it passed out of sight under the canopy above. Then they disappeared back into the trees, without ever saying a word.

In years past, there would be a full clan waiting for each member of the ceremony, surrounding the center of the forest just for this one night when all the lights came out to dance. Now, they all walked silently back and attempted to hang on to the peace and calm as they snuck back over the border into Astèndre and Layendria. TJ made it back up to the top of the canopy of trees and grew his wings before leaping into the sky glittering with stars.

For a little time, he just enjoyed the feeling of moon and star shine on his face and the cold wind as his wings hummed around him, but he knew it couldn't last. He needed to go back to the rebel camp and he had bad news to impart. His smile slowly transformed into a frown and he sighed, tilting his wings in the direction of the camp twenty leagues away with morning coming up on the horizon.

***

"Atropos is watching over us and has given us strength in numbers as well as in spirit. We may seem small, but we are mighty. Many of you doubted the others would make it here in time, but watch them as they join us out of the forest. Watch as they gather with us to fight and destroy Medicée's hold for good! Atropos is here with us now and he has heard our prayers! He answers us! Let us thank him for all he has done. For the peace he is leading us to," Gabriel bowed his head in silent prayer and the mass of people joined him. When he raised his head, they dispersed in the growing darkness to their campfires.

Gabriel climbed down off the log he balanced on and walked away to his own tent. He bowed his head and prayed with a few of the people, but was quiet, other than that. *I hope I am interpreting Atropos' will correctly. What if I am wrong?* He looked up and jumped in panic at the shape of a dark figure coming out of the woods.

"Just me Gabe," TJ mumbled and Gabriel relaxed at the sound of his melodic voice. "Do you mind if I share your fire for a little while?"

Gabriel chewed his lip in thought, waving at the fire – surprised at the request, "No. No, it's alright. Where have you been? I didn't see you at my sermon tonight."

The half-elf shrugged, "It's the elven Festival of Lights. I went to the sacred forest."

"You went to the forest? That's so far away! Twenty leagues at least. How did you get there and back in a day?"

"I feel no need to pray to Atropos. I've never been particularly religious. He hears and see's all anyway," TJ sighed as he deliberately ignored his question. "I need to talk to you about something else."

"What?" Gabriel asked as he set another log on the fire. The sparks flew up like the fairies unseen in The Empire in almost a century, knowing TJ was avoiding.

TJ bit his lip in worry, "I might sound a little crazy telling you this, because I am pretty sure you haven't been around elves much."

"Okay," Gabriel said hesitantly, "That's true, but I also studied them. How crazy could it really be?"

"I think we shouldn't go to war tomorrow. If we do, almost everyone will die," TJ said in a rush, as if afraid that if he didn't say it quick enough, he wouldn't get it out.

Gabriel froze in the mid-action of setting another log into the growing flames, "After all our work? Why would we postpone it?"

TJ hesitated and in his soft voice responded, "I saw it in a vision. You die alongside two other major advisors and a few of the other advisors die. Not to mention half of the warriors perish and even more are injured."

"You saw it in a vision?" He rubbed his hands together. *Maybe he has lost it. He never did answer how he got to the Forest of Lights – and visions? Only the Old Blood Lines ever had that talent... and he is a half-elf.* The older man shook his head in confusion, *but he had mentioned his sister having been a seer.*

"I told you it would sound insane, but please believe me. I don't want it to be a massacre. Do you?" He nearly pleaded.

Gabriel's mind fought with his own desire not to fight, "No, I don't, but if we postpone we may never get the chance. It's too late to change tactics now. The moral would be lost."

"And that's more important than lives?" TJ questioned bitterly, his eyes black in the shadow cast from the fire.

"I have no reason to believe you."

"I wouldn't lie about something like this," his eyes flashed dangerously in the dark. "She has more troops than normal. This isn't a good idea!"

Gabriel chewed his lip nervously, but he had never trusted TJ. Something was off about him – he knew it, despite what the others seemed to believe. Gabriel shook his head, "You are so young. I don't think you fully understand how the world or men work yet. You will in time."

"I'm not nearly as young as you think I am, but you are right in one thing. I will never understand people – I didn't before and I still don't," TJ sighed and followed it with a deep breath while standing. As he walked into the shadows beyond the fire, he said quietly, "I hope for your sake the future changes. It always is, but hopefully, for once, I will see something other than death."

He watched him leave, but stared after TJ for a long while, deep in thought. *Why would he say something like that on the eve of battle? Doesn't he realize, if we back off now it could possibly ruin everything?* Gabriel chewed the side of his lip in distress, *Why Atropos? Why would you do this to me now? Leave me with this burden to decide the fate of others?*

Gabriel sat in silence for a long while and let his thoughts take him. He tried desperately to think of something other than TJ's haunting words, but couldn't. Eventually, music cropped up in the center of camp and Gabriel decided he needed the company and the festivities called to him.

Following the rhythms, he saw someone playing in the glow of the fire light. They played an ancient sounding instrument and, as he approached, he saw a circle of people surrounding TJ in a halo of light from the campfire. Gabriel watched the young man's fingers fly across the neck of an acoustic guitar which went out of style over a hundred years ago and this style looked about that old. Most people only listened to woodwinds or the forged flutes of delicate metal; they didn't like the sound of stringed instruments, but as TJ played, they couldn't take their eyes off him.

Gabriel saw him close his heavily lashed eyes and take a deep breath. *What could he possibly sing with that guitar?* His thoughts died as TJ began to sing a ballad just as old as the instrument in his calloused hands. His voice was beautiful and strong which was unexpected and lifted the old words he sang into new life. It was ethereal in sight and sound – angelic. As he sang, more and more people were drawn in, but the half-elf didn't seem to notice they hung on his every phrase, word, and note.

He sung of the change which happened in Astyreian over the years like he watched it all happen. Every word came alive and it seemed to Gabriel, and the others, like they saw the images dance across their vision. The entire time, TJ was lit in the background by the firelight, head bent forward, fingers skimming over the strings, and foot tapping out the time to his music seemingly without thought.

He moved from ballad to a folk song where the people gathered to dance then changed easily to a love song. The tunes merged into each other like a brook merges into a stream, into a river, and then on into the ocean. Hours passed before he, finally, gave everyone an easy smile and swung his guitar over his shoulder to disappear into the night.

***

The march began at dawn and by noon they all made it to the edge of the forest where Medicée's fortress lay in wait. They – so far – were undetected. Gabriel sighed in relief. A good sign. He crouched behind a tree on the frontlines ready to attack at a moments' notice.

"He's nowhere. Damn," Karter swore in Gabriel's ear. "Have you seen that cursed half-elf?"

Gabriel looked around in shock and disbelief, "No. I haven't, but…" his voice trailed off as he remembered the warning TJ gave him the previous night. "He may have left. He told me this was suicide."

Karter growled, "Flighty creatures. He just – " a rustle in the leaves above them caught Karter's attention. They looked up and their eyes widened in shock. TJ stood perched on a branch, his chain weapon freshly polished thrown over his bare shoulders, with the forearm length knives held in his long-fingered hands. He looked down at them and they realized how much his demeanor had changed. His emerald eyes pierced them through and his stance was perfectly balanced. He was ready for a fight; he looked annoyed and furious. He tilted his head up in a soft jerk.

"Guess we can start now," Gabriel murmured.

Karter sighed and waved his hand. Within seconds, hoof beats pounded against the leaf covered floor of the forest. Their large bodies leapt gracefully over the fallen trees and onto the open terrain separating the rebellion's forces from Medicée's fortress. Directly behind the riders, came the bowmen. They sprinted, with their hands ready to pull their long bows over their shoulders at any moment.

Bells rang out in a hurried warning from the fortress and a mad scurry could be seen from the towers and balustrades. Gabriel smiled, *excellent. We might be fine after all.* He looked behind him quickly, as the rest of the rebels, a thousand strong, sprinted across the field. Arrows began to fly from the parapets as the horses stopped just close enough to begin firing. The first man fell from The Empress' side over the edge and crumpled upon impact with the ground.

The large wooden doors opened for a mass of guards exited onto the field, in an attempt to disperse the rebels. It was time for Gabriel's forces to begin action. They charged in with zeal as the ladders were secured and other men began their upward climb. Gabriel ducked a sword and thrust upward with his own. The man dropped and the priest felt suddenly sick, but he didn't question it as another guard swung at his chest, he barely dodged the blow and engaged in battle. Everything became a blur as they fought hard against The Empress and it seemed, for a time, they gained the advantage, but it didn't last long as the doors opened once more and a horde of guards entered the field of battle. Gabriel pulled a blood smeared hand over his sweaty brow and glanced quickly around for the other leaders. Karter was easy to find as he swung his axe and cleaved a man's head in two.

Reida could be seen firing arrows onto the fortress wall. Gabriel parried someone's sword and quickly disarmed him, spinning the sword up to slit the man's throat. He looked around for the half-elf, but TJ couldn't be found. *He must have left. I haven't seen him since the battle began.* Gabriel shook his head in anger.

Hours passed and the onslaught of Medicée's guards never stopped. Just as the rebels thought they gained the upper hand against the trained guards, those heavy doors would open and more would come onto the field dressed like death. Every one of the rebels knew they couldn't last much longer. They knew they didn't have any advantage. A dark shadow crossed over the sun as a musical hum drifted on the wind. It swept over the battle field coming closer. It wasn't until the shadow became even with the towers that its presence drew attention. A gasp issued from everyone and both rebels and guards alike paused in shock and wonder at the magnificent sight – never before witnessed in Astyreian. Large pure white wings beat the air in a rhythmic pattern which seemed to be the cause of the music, but these wings didn't support a bird, but a man with black pants, golden skin, and black hair. As he soared closer to the field an angry red scar became visible on his lower abdomen of angel wings that seemed to mimic the pure white feathers sprouting from his shoulder blades.

Gabriel gasped once more as he suddenly realized his constant prayers to Atropos were answered all along with TJ. *How is it that the half-elf never told me he was an angel or even gave me a hint that angels were real?* A grin spread across the angel's face as he whipped his deadly chained daggers out at his first victims. Blood spurted out and they fell, eyes wide in shock at the vicious angel shinning in the afternoon sunlight. This ended the momentary pause in the fighting. Realizing the angel was on their side, the rebels fought even harder. Yet, TJ made the biggest impact. His weapon slicing down from the sky couldn't seem to be defeated and only arrows could reach him, but he was fast, despite the greatness of his wing span and the arrows that appeared to be about to hit him simply burned in the air. He was untouchable.

It's not enough, Gabriel thought as dusk began to encroach on the sky. The large doors opened once more to let over a thousand guards out and only five hundred rebels remained. TJ landed next to Gabriel as the rebel forces backed away to reorganize themselves.

"I warned you. Now, be smart and run," the angel said with venom audible in his voice.

Gabriel licked his dry lips and abandoned the heavenly image in his mind of angels, "I know. I should have listened, but you should have told me."

TJ shook his head, "No. It would have given you false security."

Opening his mouth to respond, Gabriel paused as TJ gasped suddenly and his pale blue eyes fogged over. They cleared quickly and he began sneezing violently, "Call a retreat. We need to run.

Now!" Gabriel stood in confused shock until he felt a small nudge in his mind and heard the other leaders start yelling to retreat as the guards began to charge.

The remaining rebels sprinted toward the forest, but Gabriel knew everyone wouldn't make it to safety. He knew it could have been different, if only he listened before. He felt an arrow pierce his shoulder and he stumbled and gasped in pain.

He caught himself and kept running. *Can't stop now. Got to keep going.* A younger boy fell in front of him and with his uninjured side he pulled him to his feet, "Keep going! The forest is only fifty paces ahead!" Gabriel shouted above the noise and the boy kept running, but adrenaline can only go so far and they had been fighting all day. Heat and a searing pain exploded on Gabriel's back and a shadow fell across his face as he fell. A man stood over him about to give the death blow, but his neck suddenly spewed red and he fell. TJ shook his head and spread his wings as he frowned. He took the boy and left. Gabriel tried to stand, but he couldn't even move or feel the pain anymore. His spine severed, he was unable to move. He watched his fellow rebels run by. Some escaping, while others lives ended in the violence. Black spots began to bubble up in Gabriel's vision.

The world spun and then became eclipsed in the black before a golden light infiltrated his quiet darkness. Gabriel suddenly felt a presence lingering over him. It touched his shoulder, causing him to snap his eyes open. Immediately, Gabriel knew the figure and, with a shaking voice, he murmured his praises.

"Hush, my son," Atropos commanded softly. "I have come with a simple question." Gabriel swallowed and began to cough. "Will you become my second angel and be willing to step in where I cannot?"

"What TJ does?" He choked out between his coughs.

He thought he saw a silver glint out of the corner of his eye, but Atropos began speaking again, "Yes. You would do what Tamynaen does. What is your response?"

"Yes," Gabriel's vision went black almost immediately, but not before he saw a self-satisfied smile on Atropos' face.

7

Chapter 7

"Morning sunshine," TJ slammed a tray of food unceremoniously next to Gabriel's head, causing him to jerk awake. His mind felt foggy and moved sluggishly as he blinked slowly.

"What? ... Where am I?"

TJ laughed in a surprisingly musical way, "Atropos' Sanctuary. His sacred haven. Welcome to your new home." Gabriel still looked confused and TJ remembered feeling like that. He helped Gabriel pull himself up, "Eat and I'll explain what's going on. First, I'm not seventeen, at least not technically. I was born in Astèndre in 1993 and died in 2011. You see to become an angel, first you must die. After that, your body won't age, though sometimes it feels like you have. Second," TJ smiled crookedly as Gabriel swallowed a bite of the egg pie, "I have no idea why we were picked over all the others, but we were and that means we have a lot to do in a short amount of time. Are you going to eat that?" Gabriel looked at the apple and shook his head. TJ picked it up and took a big bite. "See, time moves differently here. Sometimes slowly and other times fast. Your training will start just as soon as you finish and I show you around."

Gabriel bit his lower lip in thought, "Wait. So, you are truly the only angel? And what happened to the rebels?"

TJ took a deep breath and let it out before responding, "Two hundred made it out alive. Karter survived and is now taking charge alongside Rieda. Most of the women and children made it out since the women were able to defend themselves." He gave Gabriel a piercing look with his blue eyes. Gabriel looked away and began munching on a piece of toast. "They are beginning to reassemble themselves now, but hardship is headed everywhere. I saw it in the pools." He paused and Gabriel gave him a confused look. "Sorry, you will see later. Oh, and yes, I am the only, well, until you, I was the only angel."

"So, what kind of training do I need? I can already fight. Maybe not as well as you, but I can," Gabriel wondered aloud before gulping down his orange juice.

TJ gave him another crooked smile, "Flying lessons for starters. And I don't think you have been trained in martial arts. And the elementals you need to be shown. Possibly telepathy – that's what Atropos calls it – speaking in someone else's mind or being able to read their thoughts. Sometimes push their thoughts."

"You can do all of that?" Gabriel asked in awe.

"So can you, I'm sure, but we'll see," TJ stood and clasped Gabriel's hand to pull him up. "Come on and I will show you around your new home."

The half-elf walked to the door with a grace Gabriel wouldn't have thought possible with his large wings. His felt cumbersome and he knew they couldn't possibly be the size of TJ's. His elder smiled at him like an older brother and patiently held open the door. After a few more steps, Gabriel became adjusted to the weight and TJ led him down the white stone hallway with colorful tapestries lining its walls. Gabriel paused at the scene depicted on one of a swirling universe with links forming a border. TJ smiled, "I'm sure if you asked you could move it into your room, but Atropos will probably help you decorate. I am actually quite surprised there wasn't something else in your room besides the bed, nightstand, and chair."

Gabriel shrugged, "As a priest, I am used to not needing much. What was in your room?" He was curious about the half-elf and he got the feeling they would now be spending quite a bit of time together. The more he thought about it, the more he realized he knew nothing about TJ since he always avoided any personal questions besides admitting to having a sister. Gabriel knew he played the guitar and sang, but when TJ opened his black door Gabriel realized he played much more than that.

TJ crossed the dark wooded floor to the black piano and ran his long fingers over the ivory white keys, "This, my guitar, and," he paused for a minute and took a deep breath, "the dark violin."

"Were they all things from your home or did Atropos put them here?" Gabriel asked.

TJ shrugged, "The piano he put here. The other two instruments were from home, I guess. He knew they meant a lot to me. It might be that we came under different circumstances too, so he felt I needed something to – well," he grimaced and his fingers pushed down a few keys creating a sweetly melancholic melody. "Take a look around if you want. You don't have to stand in the doorway."

Gabriel came in and turned his head to gaze in awe at the room covered in different instruments from all over Astyreian's past and present. They were in all colors and shapes. Someone had painted designs on a few of the stringed instruments that Gabriel didn't know the names of. The piano's beautiful black surface was covered in sheet paper and pens with a few notebooks and hardbound books. His nightstand held a glass of water as well as a lamp, while a flute leaned up against a leg. His bed was neatly made with a red and black quilt covering it, unlike Gabriel's white one. He turned and looked at the opposite walls and realized a few bookshelves lined one wall with an odd assortment of history, music, art, and classic books.

It surprised him that TJ would read as much as it appeared. Any wall space not taken up by a book shelf or hanging instrument had paper stuck to it with a picture sketched or painted on it. Underneath all of that, the walls were a dark red with veins of dark blue and green running through it, the complete contradiction of the idea of an angel and it made Gabriel laugh. Gabriel turned toward TJ who sat at the piano and sped through a piece without music. *Must be an original, but how is it possible an angel could be so sad?* He chuckled slightly to himself, *how could an angel also seem so opposed to the color white?*

"I really can do anything to my room then?" Gabriel questioned bringing TJ back to the present.

The half-elf nodded and stood, "Yes you can. I apologize about the next room. It has just been Atropos and I for quite some time so a few of my things ended up in the main room," he snapped his darkened door shut and led Gabriel to what appeared to be a common area with squishy pillows leaned up against the walls and a sofa surrounded by pillowed armchairs. An oak coffee table sat covered in sheets of paper and a notebook with a few pens lying on the open book. "I was just out here working when he told me you had woken up. He would have been there himself, but he had a meeting with his brother. He sends his regards and is glad you are doing well with the transition."

"What is through there?" Gabriel questioned as TJ led him down another hallway covered in tapestries. "And his brother?"

"Yes. His twin brother is Lucvoyeur. You know... the keeper of the hell realm?" TJ paused out front of a pair of dark ominous doors, "That is Atropos' garden. I don't know if you are allowed in just yet.

We can ask him later. Over here though are the three pools. And once you see that, I think we should begin your lessons on flying. Be warned I have never taught anyone but myself. I can't promise I will be good at teaching you how to fly."

Gabriel gulped a little nervously, but he was excited too. He followed TJ into a moss-covered room decorated with hanging vines and plants of all colors, but what drew his attention were the pools and when he looked into the first one he saw the face of his mother holding him tightly in her arms. He quickly looked away to see TJ leaning against a wall completely at ease.

"You aren't crazy. These pools grant everyone the ability to see the past, present, and future in the same time flow as that of Astyreian," he pointed to each pool in turn. "I was always able to see the future, so to me that still comes the clearest. But with these pools I am able to see glimpses of the past and present though I have a lot more difficulty directing them to what I want."

Gabriel looked back into the water and saw the faces of his friends while playing outside of the church yard at thirteen years old. He felt odd seeing all of them from this perspective and yet it made him wish he could go back to that place and time when things seemed so simple and easy. He sighed and stood. He wasn't ready to face the death he knew he would see in the pool that held the present and he was scared of what he would find in the future, "I am ready to learn how to fly… I think."

TJ gave him a crooked smile, "Then follow me."

***

Lucvoyeur glared at his twin with steely blue eyes, "You are walking on dangerous ground! You must stop!"

"I must stop? I mustn't *do* anything. If the Gala hasn't come yet, they clearly do not care what we do. We were exiled anyway," Atropos reminded.

"Exiled for disobeying their rules and creating alternate planets, but this," the silver twin waved his hands at the two angels – one attempting to fly while the other attempted to teach – from the balcony of Atropos' castle, "This is going too far. You can't do this!"

"And what is it that I am doing exactly?" Atropos questioned. Lucvoyeur had always been the more nervous one of the two.

He shifted his weight, "You can't take the genetic code of a creature and manipulate them onto another plane of existence. Extending a life is one thing, but having them die to live again is another. You cannot make them into something they are not. It destroys the natural chain of things. Like taking Hayle away from Tamynaen Jacob, you messed with the Empyrean and you will pay for it… eventually."

"No, I won't. The Gala hasn't stepped in for direct punishment in eons and the Gala won't now," the golden twin snorted. "And who are you to talk anyway?"

"I don't change or alter them. I just let them stay in my own realm that you kindly call Hell… it's Halendonia, by the way. I give everyone the option to move on through the fog, though not everyone wants to. So, I don't make them – and some of them can't without their other half," Lucvoyeur shrugged nonchalantly as he raised an eyebrow accusingly at Atropos before returning to his watch of the two angels. "You won't be able to hold the Infinite. He grows more powerful as we speak. Eventually, he will break free."

"He will not. I will not let him," Atropos growled as he grew tired of his brother.

Gabriel, finally, rose into the air and flew a few yards before he caught the wrong air current and tumbled to the ground. TJ ran after him, trying to hide a laugh. Lucvoyeur kept his face trained on the two angels, "It won't help. The Knowing has seen it. Every thread of the future will eventually lead to it. You can stop many things brother, as can I, but this one you can't."

Atropos licked his suddenly dry lips, "Watch me."

Tamynaen Jacob looked up and tilted his head in confusion and Atropos felt a question enter his mind, "*What's going on? Everything alright?*"

"*Lucvoyeur and I are just speaking, it is alright. We had some things to discuss. Don't worry he would never try anything here,*" Atropos turned to his twin and smirked. "Already he is under my control. We will see if his sister is right, because it certainly doesn't seem that way."

A sigh issued from Lucvoyeur, "Just remember to limit yourself. Especially since this world is dying."

"Speaking of a dying world, we should begin another soon. We will want to be prepared for when this one comes to an end," Atropos added as an afterthought.

***

"I don't understand what you are talking about! Music? What music?" Gabriel sighed in frustration and gripped TJ's hand. His elder pulled him to his feet. Gabriel heard laughter in his voice when he answered, but, looking at his face, he looked like a statue for all the emotion it gave.

"Maybe that isn't the best way for you to learn."

"How did you?" Gabriel questioned. TJ looked over to the rock outcropping spearing into the middle of the silver lake, "I jumped off that."

Gabriel snorted, "Of course you did. Maybe I should try."

He began to walk over, but TJ stopped him, "Possibly not the best idea. I never said it was smart. You almost have the hang of it. Just try a few more times and if you still don't get it, then you can jump off and just hope for the best. Sound good?"

"Fine. I think you are overestimating my flying abilities though."

"I don't think so," TJ watched Gabriel close his eyes and think. He calmed himself down and TJ saw him take on a bronze orange color before he spread his wings and began to run off the hill and take to the air. He smiled broadly as Gabriel began to laugh as, for the first time, he stayed in the air. "TJ! I'm doing it! I'm – ahhh!" He yelled as an air current pushed him.

TJ flew up next to him and began coaching him through the process of flying with air currents and wind. Gabriel coughed and spit out a bug.

***

Dirt was smeared into his face again and he spit out a clod before rolling over to glare at the half-elf who sent him spinning to the ground for possibly the hundredth time that morning. No sympathy showed on his face. "Come on. Get up," he said impatiently.

Gabriel pushed himself up into a sitting position and rubbed his head, "Give me a few seconds to breathe," he knew he wouldn't get it though as TJ's foot began tapping. "How can you be so cruel? You're an angel!"

He laughed, "I wasn't always. And this isn't cruel. I could kick you when you're down. That's what the dragons did when I was being trained, but I'm not. This is me being nice. Now, get up."

Gabriel spit on the ground and pushed himself all the way up, "Okay. So, I need to grip your wrist and-"

"Stop thinking. Just do," TJ interrupted.

Nodding his head, he acted and ended up on his rump, but his face wasn't full of dirt. Good start. TJ drilled Gabriel non-stop for what seemed like ages before his Elder believed his martial arts skills good enough to defend himself and others.

Next, came training his new powers. Unlike TJ, he could not command the elements. Instead, he was a healer and could feel the emotions of others – unless they hid them from him. He couldn't heal himself, but any other living being he could heal broken bones, cuts, and burns – although it took a lot out of him to do so. His other power intrigued TJ, because he never understood how to speak well to others. The first angel was not a great communicator, but Gabriel could speak to the multitude without ever feeling uneasy. With this power, he understood he could sway an entire village into following him by gauging their emotions.

TJ showed him how to store power in his wings and although he couldn't really explain where their power came from and why, he tried anyway. The half-elf gathered his straight from nature and from his stored power.

The second angel, finally, concluded that TJ was an anomaly he would never fully understand. Through living in close quarters with the half-elf, Gabriel began to understand he was also a bit shy. He didn't talk much and kept to himself quite a bit, spending hours playing his instruments, swimming in the Silver Lake, or soaring in the sky. When the older angel went into these bouts of silence, Gabriel would sit and read through the different books TJ collected and learned about the generations that passed in Astyreian before being born and before the two brother's Nor-Ten and Medíc came to despise one another. It fascinated and yet horrified the priest.

These books, also, talked about the old guardians who lived in Astyreian, the dragons. These dragons gave advice and cared for the people who took over the world, but, as time progressed, they became upset with what the men and the elves did to the world and left. However, in the margin was a single name, Herok. Gabriel wondered what the name meant, but by the time TJ returned he forgot to ask.

Sometimes Atropos would take meals with the two angels and other times he would stay locked in his garden for days. He was always kind and questioned Gabriel on his progress. Unlike TJ, Gabriel couldn't enter the garden without being invited, but Gabriel didn't mind. He respected his Elder and knew he needed to work up to it. The second angel followed Atropos his entire life and realized one day, he would be rewarded with his trust – just as he already had been rewarded with wings. Atropos always made certain the two men needed or wanted nothing and, as TJ predicted, the god helped Gabriel decorate and furnish his new room.

Gabriel designed it with a larger bed, a nightstand, lamp, bookshelves lining the walls, a simple light wooded desk, and a squishy sofa in a corner. In contrast to his elder, he liked the color white. Almost everything in his room was made of light colored wood and the bed sheets and sofa were made of lighter fabrics. The two laughed at the difference and TJ smiled, saying it suited him and that Gabriel should have been the first. Gabriel just rolled his eyes.

***

Years passed in what TJ called Haven, but as the two angels peered into the pool showing the present, they realized even more time passed in Astyreian. Soft moss cushioned their knees and hands as they clutched at it in dread.

It's all out war! Gabriel thought in shock. He looked over to see TJ's reaction, but as usual his face was distinctly emotionless. *How can he not seem to care at all? It was his home once too. How could this have happened in such a short amount of time?*

TJ stood gracefully and looked pointedly at Gabriel, "Are you ready?

"For what?" Gabriel asked warily.

TJ smiled his crooked smile, "To attempt to stop the end. It's time for us to return."

Gabriel licked his lips nervously, "I'm ready."

"Good. Go pack your bag. You won't need much."

"Aren't you packing too?" He questioned.

TJ shook his head, "We have to make a stop on the way to Astèndre. I need to visit an old friend and I have things there."

Gabriel nodded and left, but TJ returned his attention to the pools. He stood watching and couldn't help but feel useless. *No mat-*

ter what I do, it is never enough. I pulled Gabriel and his rebels out of prison. I set them up with 1,000 soldiers and yet on the eve of battle I see them die. Before that, I made friends with Medicée only to have her begin a war not only against my kind, but all creatures. He began pacing in frustration and let his guard down. *Nothing is stopping it. I still see death. For everyone.* He bent down to look into the pool holding the future and wished his older sister could be sitting with him. She could have told him every thread and which he should follow.

A knife seemed to wedge itself between his ribs and his throat constricted. Instead of seeing the future reflected in the glassy surface of the pool, his worst memories played across his mind. He crumpled to the ground and hugged his knees tight to his chest. He couldn't tell how long he lay there before he felt someone shaking him and warmth began to spread across his body.

Gabriel knelt by his back with a wide hand on his shoulder and a look of worry and fright on his face. Atropos just looked worried, but TJ knew who the warmth came from.

He knew he shook uncontrollably, but TJ couldn't seem to stop. Taking a few deep breathes he slowly pushed himself up, "I'm fine."

Gabriel raised an eyebrow, but Atropos beat him to a response, "Don't lie to me. What happened?"

"Same as always," his first angel muttered.

Atropos gripped TJ's chin and forced him to meet his eyes, but the angel refused by turning his now yellow green iris' away, "Look at me Tamynaen." TJ obeyed, "Tell me."

He took another deep breath just as Gabriel held his, "I was staring into the future or I was going to, but I thought of my sister. If she were alive, she would be able to tell me which thread to take. Every turn I make still ends in death. I saw their deaths again. First Heather, then Hay – Hayle. Kali and Erinn next. Even Oreal. I still feel tied and their blood. It's on my hands. I'm still marked.

Branded. Why else would all of Gabriel's scars be gone, but mine still be there? It won't go away. I can't get away. The blood won't wash off..." he continued rambling and it no longer made sense as he shook violently.

Gabriel, finally, understood as he watched TJ's eyes turn a brilliant clear blue and a tear snuck out of the corner to slide down a golden cheek. *He watched his sisters die and blames himself. No wonder he is so closed off. It is his way of coping... until it obviously becomes too much.* Gabriel sighed and wished he could say something, but he knew TJ wouldn't want to hear it.

Atropos placed both of his hands, on TJ's shoulders and a golden light glowed around him, filling the air with tranquility. TJ stopped babbling, but still continued to shake as more tears slid down his angular face, "I wish I could bring them back for you. Truly I do, but you are going to have to learn how to move on. Things won't always be so hard. You are cared for here. That is more than you can say about where you came from. Isn't that enough?" Atropos smiled and handed TJ an apple that appeared out of nowhere, "Eat something. It will calm your shaking. Then you may leave. Gabriel come with me," he said as he stood. Gabriel obeyed their maker and followed him out of the large wooden door and stopped. Atropos waited for the door to close and turned his perfect face on the new angel, "TJ will most likely never mention this to you and will pretend this never happened. He suffered severely when his sisters died. He is still trying to cope."

"Did they all die at once?" Gabriel questioned. "What can I do?"

"His four sisters all died at separate times – except for the twins – but he watched all of them perish," Atropos sighed as Gabriel looked at him in confusion. "Yes?"

"But he mentioned five."

Atropos frowned, "He had four sisters. The other girl, Hayle, he watched die as well. Just a friend. What you need to do is watch his emotions. His eyes will let you know," Atropos smiled. "He is a hard person to understand, but still human, well half-elf." Atropos, this time, smiled tenderly and Gabriel knew who Atropos' favorite would always be.

"I will take care of him," Gabriel nodded and returned the smile, "After all he is my brother. My family now. He took care of me and now it is my turn to return the favor."

***

Gabriel and TJ left for the Orcana Islands and Gabriel, finally, discovered what the mysterious name of Herok meant. He was the Golden Dragon and Astèndre's princesses, Ruby and Caladria, lived with him. The two women greeted TJ with easy smiles and waves, but Herok gave a tremendous roar and proceeded to scold him for not returning sooner. The three laughed; the first time Gabriel heard a true laugh from the other angel, a pure and beautiful sound.

"This is Gabriel. He is also an angel. Once a priest and now a warrior," TJ ruffled Ruby's dark red hair. She smiled up at him with a sweet face. Caladria looked Gabriel up and down and gave him a soft smile as she strode over on long legs to properly greet him, "We can't stay long, but I did want news and to share a meal."

"Of course, you are always welcome to them both," Herok grinned from his rocky perch near the cliff edge and swept his golden tail across the vacant ground. Gabriel shifted uncomfortably under Herok's milky blind stare. "I smell your fear Gabriel."

TJ clasped his broad shoulder in a surprisingly brotherly gesture, "Herok has helped me in many a troubled time. There is nothing to fear from him. Unless, of course, you do something to deserve it."

Gabriel nodded his head as TJ helped coach him through making his wings trans-missive, then handed him his shirt. It amazed him the difference TJ's wings made on his age and stature. With the wings he looked so powerful and almost intimidating, but without wings he looked like just another teenage half-elf, until his eyes and serious face shined a warning.

"What?" TJ questioned as he looked away from his pack.

"Just trying to understand how you could look seventeen and yet have the complete respect of a dragon," Gabriel explained. "So where are we supposed to go? And how do you know the princesses?"

TJ waved for Gabriel to follow, "Well, dinner is in the courtyard of their home. So, this way." TJ took him down a small path away from the cliff edge Herok had cleared with his powerful tail. As they crossed a small stream and entered a wooded area, the half-elf began an explanation, "About a year before I came to dedicate my time to the rebels, I spent quite a bit of time trying to help the Regent and King Rupert. Unfortunately, they didn't want to hear a thing I had to say, but I was able to learn enough about their plans from Caladria and Ruby – who happen to be Rupert's younger siblings. They came here to safety many years ago, when I was just starting out. The Orcana don't want to be a part of the war anyway, so it is relatively safe here." He slid open the side paneling of the door, giving Gabriel his first look of an Orcana style home.

"This is beautiful," he said, his blue-grey eyes widening in surprise. The home was decorated in earthy tones, but with silks woven in elegant swirls and shapes. Carved bowls and statues took up the corners or sat on tables and long expensive flowing drapes hung at every window. The home was very open with cushions decorating the floor in a sitting area that could be mistaken as a dining room which Gabriel discovered was, when TJ muttered in his ear that they normally ate by the pond, if weather permitted.

Instead of sitting on cushions and silk pillows inside, they sat on them outside around a shortened table with the background music of water trickling from a small brook into the pond. The princesses joined the men quickly in silk robes tied around their waists with large colorful bows at their backs and loose pants of a darker shade than the robes. Each girl had their deep red hair pulled away from their golden skin, giving Caladria an oddly severe expression while Ruby just looked sweetly innocent. They each placed a tray of food down on the table and everyone – but TJ – blessed the food in Atropos' name.

It didn't take long for the meal to be over, but they lingered, discussing new developments over herbal tea. The war still raged, and Rupert refused to take charge of the country. He still wanted to fight and the Regent – for the time being – agreed to take his place until he felt decided to settle into his role as king.

They decided for a little while Gabriel would travel with TJ and gather his connections. Once TJ felt Gabriel could handle everything on his own, the half-elf would go off in his own direction collecting the histories of Astyreian, and whatever else he felt he should do, while Gabriel did the same.

A little nervous about the coming events, Gabriel went in to the guest bedroom and lay down on the pile of silk cushions. He closed his eyes and heard the sliding door open and close. *TJ must be going somewhere.* The image of the giant golden dragon popped into his mind as he drifted off to sleep.

***

A low growl greeted him in the dark as TJ stepped onto the rock by Herok's head, "I hoped you would come."

TJ slid to the side of the ledge and dangled his legs over, sighing at the perfect clear night. The sky mirrored in the sea was breathtaking, "You always seem to. What did you need to say?"

"It's a warning," Herok said in his vibrating voice, "Atropos and his twin."

"I already know. Atropos told me," TJ said and Herok flicked his tongue out in annoyance.

"Not what I am talking about. They play a game Tamynaen Jacob. A game with the people of the worlds they create. If Lucvoyeur wins he takes charge and Atropos is stuck in his sanctuary. Lucvoyeur is the observer, but if Atropos wins, he stays in charge of the world to control it with his inflexible will. His will becomes law. Lives are mapped out from life until death. That is what he does. He isn't what he has claimed himself to be."

"So, you are telling me that everything I have lived for is a lie?" TJ asked as his anger boiled to the surface like lava.

Herok shook his large head slightly, "No. I am saying he caused what happened in your life to happen. But he tricked you into becoming his first angel. You need to be careful. Especially since we both know this world will not be saved."

TJ set his face in a hard line and glared defiantly at the stars shining so brightly in the black sky. "I know," he growled and swallowed past the lump in his throat before repeating in a whisper, "I know. That still doesn't change the fact that I want to try and stop it."

"You're playing into his hands," Herok grumbled.

TJ sighed, "How do you know this about him? How do I know your version is the true one?"

"You don't, but my answer is that Lucvoyeur visited and told me about a game they play. However, I have also seen what they do in the creation of the next world. It's true Tamynaen Jacob."

"Why? What game?" He questioned as bitterness crept into his voice.

"Do you really want to know?" Herok turned his giant face so an eye the size of TJ's own head stared at him in a blind question.

The half-elf bit a lip, "Just tell me why."

"For fun," came the dragon's short reply.

He stood and paced by the cliff edge wringing his hands and trying to find a center. *Why? Why would that be fun? Isn't there a rule somewhere?* TJ clenched and unclenched his fists. *There should be. That's wrong. It's all wrong. There has to be a mistake. That's what it is.* He thought as he neared hysteria. He felt like he was falling and cold began to spread from the base of his neck. Thinking about all the wrong he endured in his life and putting it into the context that Atropos damned him, was too much. *It's not true. Otherwise Atropos would have lied to me. And gods don't lie. He wouldn't do that.* TJ shook his head as he gripped onto the only thing he could and jumped off the cliff edge before making his wings appear. Herok spread his wings on land and dug his claws into the rock and jumped, the powerful sinews of muscle rippled along his tree sized legs as he soared into the sky. The dragon listened for TJ's wings to appear just before he hit the black ocean water and flex them against the wind until he reached a level with the golden dragon. *"I can't believe you Herok. I'm sorry, but I can't. Maybe someday I will be able to, but I need to see the proof for myself."*

"He is all you have just now," Herok replied in the same manner through the connection TJ made into his mind. *"I understand. But remember my warning. One day, you will wake up and see the power inside you and not fear it, but embrace it. And that will be a great and terrible beauty. Now, may the stars guide us."*

"And the wind lift our wings," TJ added with a brilliant smile as they caught an updraft and sailed higher into the sky.

***

A quake shook Gabriel and the ground split open, as rocks fell, the rumble tore deep into his body. The noise was deafening until a hum infiltrated his mind and started pulling him away. Gabriel's eyes slowly flickered open as he came to from his odd dreams, "What do you want at this accursed hour?"

"Get up. I want to show you something," TJ threw Gabriel his loose fitting knit sweatshirt. "TJ, it is four in the morning," he pulled the sweatshirt on anyway.

TJ grinned, "Which means we have just over an hour to get there. C'mon!" He scampered out of the back of the house and, befuddled, Gabriel followed. He led him out of the back and down a winding path through the forest of the island. About ten minutes passed before they started climbing up into the rockier area and their pace slowed.

Leading Gabriel over the dew-covered field and then under and over gates, TJ hummed to himself seeming to enjoy the early hour. Grumbling slightly, Gabriel didn't say a word as he followed the half-elf over some rusted iron and rotten wood gates – crumbled in from lack of care. The worst were the ancient stone walls that once marked the property lines of the Orcana. Breathing hard, Gabriel pulled himself over another wall and jogged carefully over the uneven ground as he tried to keep up with the younger man.

TJ looked back over his shoulder, "Almost there." He scurried around a few piles of slate and then slowed to let Gabriel catch up with a huge smile on his face. Gabriel looked up at him in annoyance which quickly faded as he saw the reason the Orcana always longed, for home.

Spread out behind the half-elf, a cliff edge sprawled along the coast, unlike anything he had ever seen. It was shaped like a horseshoe with outcroppings every so often to make it possible for the daring to climb down to the ocean, but – more than anything – it was the colors just beginning to appear. The first rays of the sun turned the sky to a deep purple and velvety blue as the clouds and cliffs turned to peaches and pinks. The ocean no longer seemed so deep as near the rocks swirling teals and turquoises mingled with vibrant sapphires and the waves catapulted crystals high into the air when they boomed against the edges. TJ smiled as his plan had the effect he wanted and turned to sit on the edge.

The priest sunk down next to him, unable to find words to express what he felt, but for the first time, Gabriel understood that sometimes words were unnecessary: the feeling of a place and time mattered more.

The sun rose higher in the sky and, finally, TJ broke the silence, "Happy I woke you?"

Gabriel nodded, "Yes. No wonder you always come back here – aside from Ruby, Caladria, and Herok."

TJ nodded in return, "The ocean has always called me home."

"Understandable, it's beautiful," Gabriel paused and became curious. "Even when you were still alive? Did you visit the ocean?"

TJ looked up and raised an eyebrow, "I lived in VeeCee, by the ports. I thought I told you that."

"Oh. Well, maybe," Gabriel fell into a comfortable silence again as he watched the waves rolling in and out in a timeless rhythm. Yet, even with the wonder that surrounded him, it felt like the calm before the storm.

***

The market was packed. Portico never seemed so crowded before, but with so many men off to war, the women sought the safety of the capital to sell their wares. Colors were beginning to become scarce along with the delicately crafted beads and hand carved items. Iron took over everything with dark reds, browns, oranges, and greens dominating the market place.

"TJ, who exactly are we looking for again?" Gabriel questioned as they pushed their way through the press of people – elves and humans alike.

The half-elf looked around, "Short man, hunched slightly. Plain face, long hair tied with leather. Wire glasses. Goes by Matthias.

Historian that works in the palace library, but he isn't here. He is at a small café."

Gabriel dodged around a large woman and her herd of children, "But I don't understand why. What is so important about seeing a historian?"

TJ stopped suddenly and turned quickly to face the man taller and broader than him, but Gabriel felt much smaller under TJ's severe stare, "Take a look around and tell me what you see."

"What does that matter?" Gabriel questioned, but began to look around. "There are people selling and buying things. Children playing and food cooking. That idiot tried to steal something."

"No. Look past that," TJ shook his head as he tried to get Gabriel to look past the immediate things people noticed.

Gabriel sighed impatiently, "Fine." He was quiet for a moment before he realized what TJ meant, "I see kid's using tin cans as toys and scraps of fabric to make dolls. I see stalls holding weapons for protection when it used to be a jewelry stand. I see the food stands with half empty shelves and beggars trying to pick-pocket. The only blues I see are the hint of blue that is the Orcana's natural state."

"Correct. That is why we need to see a historian," TJ turned abruptly again while he continued talking, "Our world is dying, Gabriel. We need to begin to collect its history lest it all disappear."

Gabriel licked his dry lips, "Dying? But we are supposed to stop it!"

"Hush! We can't. No matter what we do, we can't," TJ rounded a corner and the bustle of the market place quieted slightly. "I know it sounds harsh, but we can at least preserve its memory by gathering something that holds memories that are harder to alter.

Mind reeling, Gabriel took in the new information, "How… how do you know?"

TJ tapped his temple, "Sight… visions and Herok saw it too." He walked into a small café and went straight out to the back patio,

"Here is our man." Both men pulled chairs out and sat. The other man nervously picked at a frayed hem of his once nice over coat, "Hello Matthias. I'm TJ and this is Gabriel." He held out his long fingered callused hand. The man nervously shook it.

"So, I understand you wish to take a look in the library?" Matthias shifted and clutched his tea cup. TJ inclined his head slightly, his face set in his normal emotionless manner with his body perfectly aligned under him, "Why?" he stammered.

TJ sighed and, in his quiet way, replied, "We are doing research on the history of Astyreian."

"I've never seen either of you before at conferences or meetings. Where are you from?" Matthias questioned.

TJ sat completely still, body set, "VeeCee. We aren't very well known."

"You look seventeen," Matthias added.

"Half-elf," TJ retorted.

Matthias began picking at his worn sleeve again, "I can't let just anyone into the Palace library. Especially since he clearly looks to be from The Empire."

Gabriel sighed as he saw exactly where things would end up. *How can he have lived so long being so horrible with people?* Gabriel shook his head internally. *His body language says it all – I don't trust you. If he acts like that no one will trust him. Great fighter, horrible people person.* He covered a chuckle. *I guess you can't be good at everything.*

"Look," TJ began, but Gabriel cut him off. "I did come from there, but I worked for the rebels as their map maker. I can prove it too." He gave Matthias a slight smile and the man began to relax a bit. "How about I show you some of my maps – maybe donate a few – if you let us in to the library? Show that we are honest, trustworthy."

Matthias shifted his attention to Gabriel and visibly relaxed this time, "Show me those maps first. Do you have them with you?"

The blonde angel shifted his knee to touch TJ's thigh. He needed the physical contact in order to speak mind to mind – unlike his only elder, *"Can we get them?"*

"Already have them. Do you think I go around completely by memory all the time?" Came his reply along with the accompanied pain.

Gabriel shifted as TJ handed him his beaten and faded backpack, "Of course. We have some right here." He reached inside and pulled out a roll of ten small maps. "Take a look."

Matthias looked around hesitantly, "Not here. I trust you, but let's… I'll take you to the library." He laid five coppers on the table to pay for his mug of tea and stood with his brief case in hand.

Replacing the maps, Gabriel returned the backpack and stood, "Thank you. We appreciate it."

"How did you do that?" TJ questioned silently.

Gabriel smiled at the man he considered family, *"I was a reverend. People just seem to trust a man of Atropos. I know how to make people believe anything I want and make them feel at ease."*

"I've never been good at talking to adults," TJ shook his head.

"You are an adult," Gabriel said with concealed amusement as they followed Matthias up to the palace library.

The half-elf shrugged, *"Some days."*

Dusty shelves lined every space in the vast expanse of Matthias' domain. Tables crammed in-between bookshelves with chairs cramped about them – wooden and straight backed – held even more books. Unlike the library in Medicée's palace, this library didn't have tapestries lining the walls for extra color and warmth, but it didn't need it either. The space was so jammed the three men felt the warmth immediately after entering. The books were the color, the color that drew the eye from across the room. The purple dyes unseen in years combined with the blue's which had disappeared decades ago attracted the vision of many. The angel's fingers twitched wanting to pick up each one.

"This way," Matthias waved and scuttled along to the back section while keeping his eyes peeled for one of his underlings. "The histories aren't read very much anymore. Quite a shame really. Many of them are filled with such beautiful writings and – " he paused and the hidden angels saw his cheeks flush, "Wonderful drawings."

TJ smiled, "I happen to love pictures in my writings. They get the point across better sometimes."

"You, boy, go gather a few lanterns and set them about. These two have clearance to the library and anything else they need," Matthias looked to Gabriel.

"A few scribes might be nice," Gabriel smiled. "If you can spare them."

***

We have been here in the library for a few weeks now and even though it seems we spend every waking moment together there isn't much talking. I was hoping the time we spend together would help me better understand TJ, but I don't. I am getting glimpses of his personality and the things he likes, but nothing else. Nothing about his past, where he came from, or who the people were he grew up with. If I didn't know any better, I would say he didn't even have a past, but I do know better.

I found out on the third night while staying in the palace that TJ knows King Rupert and the Regent. It amazed me he knew him well enough to reach out and shake hands with him and give them both his crooked smile. It is hard for me to understand how he can know so many people and have their trust when he seems to have none himself. It bothered me that he had mentioned before when on the Orcana Islands that he knew them. I took it to mean they wouldn't trust him. Apparently, they just didn't want to give up on their war.

With the well wishes of the King, we have been given full clearance to go anywhere we want in the Palace. We can have whatever we need and come and go as pleased. When I questioned King Rupert why he gave us this freedom, he just looked at me and questioned back, "Would you not trust TJ with your own life?" I couldn't exactly respond to that. The king just smiled and replied further that TJ had protected his sisters and had helped him numerous times in the past. He knew TJ wasn't simply a historian and that he was much older than what he appeared, but nothing else seemed to matter to him. TJ had his full trust.

I wish I could be satisfied with just that knowledge, but I'm not. I want to be a part of his life. After all we will live forever with each other and if I know nothing about him, how can we truly become family?

~ Gabriel

2233 Day Right

10 years passed working in the library. Every few months TJ would take Gabriel out into the world introducing the priest to various people the first angel knew. Finally, Gabriel was beginning to get a handle on the way things worked. His sheltered life before had made it seem as if everything were possible – just by being a reverend. He had begun to realize this was not the case. In The Empire, people trusted religious leaders irrevocably. Anything they said was taken at face value, but Astèndre was completely different, along with Layendria. These two countries had religious affiliations, but it was run more by those who had power and wealth – which was

spread out in a more equal level than that of the country he had grown up in.

As Gabriel's mind worked around this change, TJ began to open up. He taught him the mechanics of horseback riding while laughingly telling stories about his twin sister, Oreal, and the riding trips they used to take. When he taught him about the Fairy folk, TJ began to introduce his little twin sisters and when Gabriel first met the elven people of Layendria and TJ painstakingly taught him the musical language, Gabriel learned more about TJ's incredibly smart and talented elder sister.

It was almost like being constantly with a mute at other times. Gabriel, in turn, traded TJ's silence with stories of his own. He explained that growing up in his adopted family had shown him the power of what love and treating others with constant kindness could do. At a very early age, Gabriel made the decision to live his life in a devoted manner. He never let his personal ambitions get the better of him – or he tried very hard to not let that happen. Once the fire had devastated his hometown, Gabriel realized he couldn't stand by and let the injustice of what the Empress was doing continue.

TJ nodded along to this admission with an impassive face.

"Was it similar with you?" Gabriel questioned intently. "I just knew I could do something. I have always seemed to have an affinity for working with people and getting people to talk to me and believe what I say. I knew I could infiltrate her castle. I knew what that could do for the rebellion."

Shrugging, the half-elf continued cleaning the hooves of his stallion, "I couldn't care less at the time and the war with Medic was just beginning. It didn't really matter who was in charge. Here or the Empire. I don't know if being in Layendria would have made much difference either. Poor is poor. And my family spent their entire existence on the bottom of that long list. I worked three jobs at seventeen just to scrap together rent and barely enough food to keep my sisters from being malnourished. That was what occupied my time and thoughts… not fighting a war that would make no difference to me or mine when it was won."

Gabriel froze with the comb partly through the mane, "Then why fight now?"

"Because now it matters. I don't have two little ones to care for and money isn't an issue. However, this world will end if something isn't done. I am not convinced we can stop the end, but at least I can try and that affects everyone," his eyes stayed down as he wiggled the dirt out.

That seemed to be how their conversations would go when Gabriel tried to force them. Eventually, he learned to either stay silent or just tell his own stories. TJ seemed more than happy to just listen. The more that time went on like that, the more Gabriel realized he was learning about TJ anyway.

One morning on the way to the Palace Library, Gabriel and TJ were speaking philosophy about history and its relation to the present. How past mistakes always seemed to duplicate over time of their own accord. TJ believed it could be side-stepped or even passed up completely with the correct learning and application of knowledge. Gabriel, however, believed it had to do with Atropos and the destiny he had in mind for everyone. He believed through trials of loss and complication everyone became stronger and it would lead toward a better future. It was an ongoing debate between the two.

Their debate continued as normal for a few more minutes, until they passed by a small shop and a bushy brown-haired girl around their age came flying out, tripping and falling into TJ – who caught her without thought as she neared the ground. Gabriel paused in mid step and watched their eyes meet. The girl began hyperventilating. TJ almost threw her away from him as he stumbled backwards.

Gabriel stepped in and placed a hand on her shoulder – imbuing her with calm.

"Keep him away from me! He is a murderer!" She screamed while shaking.

TJ shook his head and moved no closer to her. His eyes wide in horror as if he watched a different scene winding its way past his eyes.

"He isn't going to hurt you. I promise," Gabriel looked over his shoulder at his elder, completely confused. "TJ – what?"

TJ had begun shaking his head without stopping. His eyes still wide, had taken on a clear blue color with a hint of golden yellow in them. "I need to go." With that he turned down an alley and disappeared.

Turning back to the girl, Gabriel blinked heavily while chewing his lip nervously. "See? He's gone. Okay? Are you okay?"

Her breathing slowed and she looked around cautiously, "Yes. Yes. I'm alright. I should – I should be going. Thank you. I- I'm not sure... Thank you." She ran off leaving a very confused Gabriel in her wake.

A few days later, Gabriel was beginning to become worried. TJ still hadn't returned after their brief, but strange encounter with the brunette. Gabriel kept trying to read the book in front of him debating if he wanted to transfer a passage into his records, but he had read it five times without retaining a bit of it.

That's when TJ stumbled in, throwing his bag down on the ground, and dropping into the seat across from Gabriel. His eyes looked slightly bloodshot and bruised as if he hadn't slept since the abrupt parting. The worst was his ashen complexion – so opposite from the normal golden tan. Before he could even ask TJ if he was alright, one of the kitchen workers came in with a large plate filled with cheese, fruit, bread, and oat cakes. Behind him was another worker holding a tray with a tea pot and a steaming mug of herbal smelling tea.

"Thanks," TJ took the mug with a brief smile and nod of thanks. Once the workers left, TJ glanced at Gabriel, pushing his sleeves up before reaching for an oat cake. "I asked them to bring enough for you too."

Gabriel looked at the food and his stomached growled. He snatched up a clump of grapes and some creamy brie cheese, then his eyes froze on a deep bruise visible in the crook of TJ's arm, "TJ, what is that?"

TJ balked, snatching his arm back quickly, almost knocking over his mug of tea, "I-I – do-do-don't know…" he bit his lip and closed his eyes breathing deeply. "Don't worry about it. I'm fine. Just tired and hungry."

Letting the moment pass, Gabriel popped a grape into his mouth. *Great. My elder brother is a heroin addict.* He thought naming the newest drug created in Astèndre. *And I know nothing I say or do will make him stop. There is no way to help him and it all goes back to that girl.* Gabriel bit into the cheese as TJ pulled out a notebook and began scribbling in his elegant handwriting. Gabriel pulled the book back over to him, but the words on the page meant nothing to him. He wanted it to tell him how to fix his family member, but nothing in these books could cure the past – only help in the future and only if there was enough time.

8

Chapter 8

"Who is that man?" A husky voiced elven woman asked as she elegantly strode over on long legs to the practice field.

The officer followed the general's inquisitive gaze, "Half-elf, ma'am. Name is TJ. Not sure how old he is. In fact, other than that and his great skills, I know nothing about him. He just turned up one day."

She turned abruptly and walked into the arena, "You. Over here. Blade boy! Come on!"

The young man spun the chains slower and caught the handle of the shining daggers as he walked over. He stopped in front of the tall deadly elf and inclined his head in respect, "General Lysandría."

"You have impressive skills. Who trained you?" Lysandría questioned as she watched his face closely.

"The dragons," he responded with a completely impassive face.

The officer snorted, but was silenced almost immediately by a look from General Lysandría, "Go and train our troops." She returned her gaze immediately to the half-elf, "They tell me your name is TJ and that you haven't been here for very long. How old are you?"

"Older than I look," he answered vaguely.

"Walk with me," she commanded and turned on her heel, head held high. TJ followed with his face emotionless. "You may have talent and ability, but that won't get you far in my army if you have arrogance and lie. So, tell me, TJ, who you are."

The young man frowned, "My name is Tamynaen Jacob. I was born in VeeCee. I don't quite know how old I am; I could figure it out if you really wanted me to, but, it doesn't really matter."

"Go on," Lysandría said as he stopped speaking, "Tell me more."

"Like what?" He questioned.

Lysandría stopped at the edge of the lake and turned to face him. Wind blew her hair into a tangled mess as she gazed into his face again, "Why did you leave home, what happened to your family, who trained you, why are you here, and will you be of help or hindrance to me?"

A crooked smile twitched at the corner of his mouth – his first show of humanity – just as his eyes changed from a blue-green to a brilliant clear blue, "I left because I didn't have a choice. My family is all dead." He paused for a moment and took a deep breath, "That was a long time ago," he pulled his long fingers through his dark hair, "I already told you who trained me, the dragons."

The general cut him off, "This is what I mean. Don't lie. You have no place here if you lie." She expected the tell-tale signs of lying or being caught in one, but the only change in his face was his eyes melting from that brilliant blue to an amused lime green.

"I'm not lying, but I don't care if you believe me or not on that point. However, I am here to help you."

As he spoke, Lysandría's mind began to whirl. His mood showed in the iris' of his eyes. *Those eyes... I've seen those eyes before.* She delved into her memory and, finally, it hit her. Keldar, the King of Layendria, had eyes just like TJ's. *The shape, the full dark eye lashes, the ever-changing colors. This young man has royal elven blood. It is how we determine our ruler. The Old Bloods. How can he be one of them?* She reigned in her thoughts, "I believe you, but first you said you are older than you seem. How old?"

"I'm not sure..." he bit his lip in quiet contemplation. *How much do I tell her? I don't think she is the type of person I can just not answer. I need her trust.* TJ pushed her minds boundaries to catch her thoughts and felt reassured in what he already came to believe about the long-legged elf, "I was born in 1993 Day Right."

The shock on her face was visible for only a split second. *It fits. Rumor was – according to mother – that Keldar fathered children when he ran away for a time. Maybe he is one of them and just doesn't know it, but he is royalty. With his eyes like that he is direct in line for the throne – he should be our crown prince.* "You said your family is all dead... how did they die? How did you survive?"

Lysandría immediately realized it as a question she shouldn't have asked, but he responded in a monotone voice, "I had four sisters. One was my twin. It was violent. I couldn't stop it. My mother committed suicide a few years later. I don't know about my father, but I don't know why I lived."

She looked out over the water and shifted her weight from one foot to the next as she contemplated her next question, "How..."

"Am I still alive?" He laughed suddenly and the sound struck a chord in the general. It was a beautiful sound and unexpected. She nodded. "Atropos needed me alive. I am his man. Ironic since I'm in no way religious."

She pulled her curling red hair around the side of her head and attempted to braid it in the wind, "Run that by me again."

"I should have died with my sisters, but Atropos needed my help. He let me live and made me well again. In return, if he asks me to do something, I do it."

"But you aren't religious?" She questioned.

He shook his head, "Wasn't before and am not now. It's just politics. But don't take my views on it. Make up your own mind."

"Why are you telling me all of this?" She asked suddenly.

TJ flashed a crooked smile, "You would have known if I was lying. I need your trust if I am going to help you."

I know he is telling the truth, but how can that be possible? Lysandría wondered as she thanked Atropos for her being able to recognize the similarity between TJ and King Keldar. The young man turned from her and bent his wiry body toward the stones at their feet and picked up a smooth one. He rubbed his thumb over the water polished surface and threw it horizontally across the lake. It skipped across the surface and disappeared, leaving ripples against the windswept water. *Atropos must have really needed him. I know I could use his help.*

"What's it going to be?" He questioned in his emotionless voice as he skipped another stone out into the rippling water seeming completely at ease.

General Lysandría shuffled her feet a bit before answering, "I believe you, but I feel you are a wanderer." He didn't answer and she knew it would be like that with him a lot. "I won't tolerate your wandering. If I am going to use your help, then I need to be able to rely on you."

"Understandable. Sometimes I may need to leave. I don't always get a choice," he admitted.

She smiled at his back, "And I can understand that," she paused for a moment, hesitating at what she wanted to ask him. "Will you help train me and my army?"

He threw one more stone before turning, "Of course, but you may come to hate me."

***

In an empty field, two men who looked completely opposite from one another smiled. The one was clearly not meant to be in The Empire. He was tall and wiry with a skin tone that said he spent a lot of time outside since it was tanned golden from the sun. His hair was dark – which spoke of the enemy countries people, but the other man greeted him like family. This other man was tall, but broad and paler in his coloring. Blonde with icy blue eyes and a tendency to smile, his gestures were wider and freer. He laughed without thought while the other had complete control of his body and he smiled only once when they first saw each other. The little girl watched from the window of her parent's farm house in confusion.

She knew Gabriel. He was a priest and worked for the Rebellion, a group against the Empress, but she had never seen anyone from Astèndre before. Her father came up behind her, "Isabel what are you doing?"

Isabel looked around, "I saw Gabriel walk across the field and wanted to know why he was leaving, but then that other man came out."

Her father chuckled and patted the girl's hair, "It isn't polite to spy on people, but I understand you were just curious. Make sure that curiosity doesn't get you into trouble someday."

"I will Papa, but..." she glanced back and saw the two men coming back this way. "Is he staying here with us?"

"Yes. He is a part of the Rebellion as well," her father smiled. "Reverend Gabriel wouldn't ask unless it was important and safe."

The door opened and the two slipped inside. Gabriel touched the other's shoulder carefully, "Jonathan this is TJ. I've told you a bit about him. He is like a brother to me and works for the Rebellion. Currently, he is in the Elven Army under General Lysandría."

"Nice to have you here," Jonathan smiled kindly at TJ, his leathery skin creasing, but TJ didn't smile back. Jonathan watched Gabriel squeeze his shoulder slightly, "You seem young to be in the Army and working for the Rebellion."

Another tighter squeeze and TJ turned to raise an eyebrow at Gabriel. He looked back at Jonathan, his face a mask, TJ explained, "I am older than I look. I appreciate your generosity in opening up your home to me. I know how dangerous it is in times like these to house someone like myself."

"Everything is dangerous. At least you aren't elven."

This time TJ glared at Gabriel, before turning back to Jonathan, "I am a half-elf."

"Oh," he looked shocked as TJ took the bandana, previously concealing his pointed ears, from his dark head. "I-wow. That's alright. No – really. It's alright." Bewildered, he took a moment before speaking again. "I apologize. It's just, I've never seen an elf before."

TJ smiled crookedly, "I'm half-elf, but that's alright. Don't worry about it."

"Wait! There's an elf here? I want to see!" Isabel ran around the corner from where she eavesdropped. She froze as she looked up at TJ, whose eyes changed as she watched from a blue green to lime green as the girl's mouth fell open. Her father reached out a hand to stop her. Frightened about what the half-elf would do.

"Hello little one," he slowly bent down to her level and held out a long-fingered hand, "My name is TJ and if it's alright with you I will be staying here for a while. Is that okay?"

"I'm Isabel. You can stay here," she cautiously raised her hand to place it on his, but looked up again. Even though she knew from her family that elves were not terrible creatures, her school always taught the opposite. His eyes changed again to a deeper green with a hint of lime in the ring around his iris. They were peaceful and honest. Isabel smiled and knew, despite his carefully monitored actions and his oddly even speech, TJ was a good person. She put her hand in his and smiled, "Why do your eyes do that?"

Laughing for the first time, his entire face changed, "Because I am partly elven."

"I like you. I'm glad you are staying," she squeezed his hand, "Maybe we can make you happier."

He blinked in surprise and smiled, "Maybe you can Isabel. Thank you."

Gabriel swallowed hard. Children always saw more of people than adults, but they also didn't filter things – they were honest to a fault. The old priest always believed that was why TJ liked kids so much. Somehow, they saw past the carefully constructed mask he created for the world. Sighing Gabriel looked down at TJ, "Come on Tam, we need to get moving to the base camp. It's a few miles from here."

Standing with an easy grace, TJ nodded, "Thanks again."

The two angels left through the back door and began to stride through the field to the woods. They walked in silence for a time until they made it to the darkness and became hidden from view, "Tam, how are things with Lysandría?"

Normal in his ways, TJ was silent before he spoke, considering, "I would say good. We have Medicée's troops stopped at the line, but it is only a matter of time before they break through if we don't get more troops soon. Medicée knows this as well as any of us."

"Does she know anything about you? Why did she just let you leave?" Gabriel questioned.

"Yes," TJ said simply before explaining further. "She figured it out right away. Lysandría is something special. She just knows. Not sure how, but she just does. I knew she would know if I lied and so I told her the truth when she asked. She lets me go when I need to and doesn't ask questions."

"Interesting arrangement you have there," Gabriel smiled at him, "She must be something special."

Laughing, TJ shook his head, "Not special in that way. To someone she might be someday, but not to me. She is just a friend. Nothing more."

"Why not?" The Priest questioned.

"I can't Gabe," he frowned.

"Why not?" The older looking man asked again.

Shaking his head, TJ sighed, "I can't love her. I never could. There is – There was… I just can't. She deserves someone who can always be there for her. I'm not that person." TJ frowned and looked about at the thick forest of silvery beech and the young maple trees trying to spring into the light shed between the leaves of taller trees. "Who is in charge of the rebels now?"

"Samuel and Jayden. Samuel is in charge of all the battle plans and Jayden all the medical and transport things," chewing his lip, Gabriel shrugged. "They are good at what they do, but no Reida or Karter. However, in some ways that is a good thing too. Not as daring or risky."

"Definitely a good thing," TJ nodded as they strode into the base camp. His experience with Reida and Karter had been different than Gabriel's. While Gabriel remembered them as being great tacticians, dedicated, and wonderful trainers of men and women, TJ knew them as risk takers, dangerous strategists, and dedicated to the point of idiocy to a cause.

Gabriel led him to the main tents where everyone sat around a table loaded with maps. "Samuel, this is TJ the second in command of the Elven Army. He is here to help out with the plans and a bit of training."

"Gabriel, I already told you we don't need help with the training. TJ, I apologize, but you look incredibly young and inexperienced," Samuel grunted naming TJ's one main fault.

Rolling his eyes toward Gabriel, TJ let out a rare burst of emotion, *"If only I could have waited a few more years to be killed – perhaps people would take me more seriously. Does it really make that much difference a few years? Please tell me, because it has almost consistently been my experience that children are not only more honest and trustworthy, but they also learn so much quicker. It is adults who have gotten us into this mess to start with and I hear a young man around my age – or death age – is moving rapidly up in the Astëndre Armies."* He let out a huff of air, *"Seriously. People piss me off."*

Using the link TJ had built into his mind, Gabriel bit back the pain rolling into him from TJ. It always happened that way, but it had been awhile since he had spoken to TJ in this manner. *"I don't know TJ. For some reason people think maturity can only come with age. Stupid, but that's how most people seem to think."* Sighing in annoyance, Gabriel shook his head and spoke aloud to Samuel, "He always has that problem. Fine. TJ since you are so very young, then clearly you need more training. Why don't you go to the practice ring and have someone teach you something." A smile tugged at his lips.

TJ smiled back crookedly, "Of course. I can use all the training I can get." Rolling his eyes at Gabriel, he spoke back into his mind, *"And of course that means I will just have to be extra tough in order to properly gage how much I still don't know right? Can't hold back or they won't know what I need to work on."*

Gabriel brushed his wrist against TJ's, *"True. Just don't injure anyone. We need everyone healthy and in one piece."*

"Sure thing Gabe. See you in a little bit," TJ whistled merrily as he strode off to the practice ring untangling his chains as he went.

"You have no idea what you just unleashed, Samuel. TJ was trained by the Dragons and not even a Dragon can defeat him. I guess you will witness that for yourself though since Verit is the

Red Dragon and Terrance is the Silver Dragon," Gabriel laughed. "If you want a show, I suggest you go and watch." He strode even closer to the table though as everyone hesitated before running off after TJ. Metal already sounded from the arena as Gabriel began talking with Jayden.

***

The tent was dark, but cozy. The light filtering from the single lamp lit up the meal of bread, cheese, and apples. It wasn't much, but TJ didn't mind and neither did Gabriel. The boys lounged on the blankets packed in to make the confined area warmer and talked. Gabriel's face took on a reddish tinge as they talked that impressed TJ.

"You are so pessimistic!" Gabriel growled, but TJ shrugged in response biting into his apple instead of replying. "That's all you have to say?"

"If you don't lower your voice someone might hear you and, if they do, we both are going to have a lot of explaining to do," TJ chewed and swallowed before raising his eyes to meet Gabriel's.

"You are the most insensitive being I have ever met," he retorted, but lowered his voice.

"Then you clearly haven't talked much to Atropos. Get into an argument with him about the path this world is taking and all he says is, 'Well, that's a bummer. Guess I'll have to make another. Maybe the morons won't mess up this time.' Does that guy have attachment issues or what - and not the kind where he *hangs on* to people. If you think I am bad, just go back to Haven and have a chat with him. Fuck, it makes me look like the most caring and loving person in the world."

Gabriel laughed despite himself before becoming serious again, "You really think this world is ending?"

"You know I see visions. Gabe, since I was a teenager all I have seen of the future is death and decay. Nothing has ever changed that. No action has ever been made that changes it. I am not saying we should stop trying, what I am saying is we need to prepare ourselves. That is why I had us copy those books down and write the histories," TJ sighed and tossed the apple in the air. "I have had my whole life to come to terms with it and I will always miss it when it is gone, but well, maybe the next world we will be able to stop things from getting this far."

"I understand. I just feel like we are useless," Gabriel bit into the bread and chewed quietly for a moment. "So, how long are you staying to help train?"

"Till the end of next month and then I need to head back. Lysandría needs help still," TJ muttered. "I wish I could stay longer. It's nice getting to see you."

Speechless for a moment, Gabriel swallowed his bite. TJ had never said anything like that to him and it shocked him that the older angel actually said something amounting to caring. He smiled, "It's nice getting to see you too Tam. I'm glad you came."

"You know if you ever need anything," TJ blushed and looked at the ground, "All you have to do is let me know," Gabriel smiled, nodding.

✳✳✳

Disaster sprawled out in front of a handsome young man whose face was masked in dirt and grime. He stood trying to catch his breath from the chaos consuming his past two days. They saved the town, but at a devastating cost. Buildings burned and crumbled as he stood staring and all around him troops dragged bodies into rows which circled around the town, but some went into a mass grave about one hundred meters from the town. Slowly from hidden doors and rooms came the survivors – mostly women, children, and the old – to claim their relatives or friends. At that point the young soldier looked away.

He strode quickly over to a large tree between two houses and emptied his stomach before wiping his sweating forehead and smearing the dirt on his face. He leaned against the tree as he slowed his breathing and tried to remember the reasons he fought. The reasons he killed. Murdered.

"Mister?" A small voice broke into his morbid thoughts, "Are you okay?"

The soldier turned around and saw a young girl of about eight. He frowned, he was a mere ten years older than her, "I'm alright. Are you?"

She shivered and held out a bowl, "Yes. Water?"

"You brought me water?" The young man asked in surprise, his warm brown eyes wide.

The small girl nodded shyly, her tangled mop of hair bouncing with the motion, "Yes. My mother always told me to treat the soldiers as if they were my brother or father. When they used to come back, they were always tired and thirsty. Would you like a drink? It's cold."

He frowned, but he held out his hand and knelt down in front of the small girl, "Thank you." He sipped at the cold water and sighed, "But what do you mean *used* to come back?"

Tears filled her eyes, "My father died when I was six and my brother a year ago. He did it to protect me. But now he is gone."

A lump formed in the young soldier's throat as he remembered telling his sister those exact words, "I'm sorry. I know what that is like. I have a sister back home as well." He handed her the bowl back and smiled, "Thank you, kiddo."

She smiled back at him, "You're welcome. Be safe," she scampered off to find another soldier as he pushed himself back to his feet, remembering people like her were the reasons he fought in this war. *People like my mother and Ella. But I won't die. I won't leave them unprotected. My sister needs me.*

The young soldier jogged quickly to his commander to find out what was needed of him, but, as he went, he made a promise to himself; he would take his fathers' place in the Kings Own. He would end this war and protect the people, just as he protected Ella.

Ella... he shook his head as he jogged around a corner. His father had been a general in the King's Own. The soldier wanted only to be like him, but stronger. Better. It was the only way to protect the ones he loved. His mother and beautiful little sister, Ella. No one else understood his determination for becoming the best. In school, the other kids thought, at first, it was because of how he had received news of his father's death and how his mother had promptly fallen ill. As time passed and he began to meet girls and make friends they thought his over confidence came from his strength and quick mind. They didn't realize it was his shield. His way of dealing with the loss and the focal point of his life – Ella had taken ill and they couldn't find a cure.

The commander came into sight and, frowning, the soldier snapped his mind back into action of the battle, instead of slipping back into memories.

***

A tall man strode quickly through the halls of Astĕndre's palace as a younerg man struggled to keep pace. Listening intently to the young man, he didn't notice the awe in the younger one's voice as he gazed up admiringly at the handsome general who walked as if he owned the world.

"General, Lysandría and her troops are the best trained warriors I have ever seen. Not only is Lysandría an incredible warrior, but her commander-at-arms is heavy handed with the troops. Very good at training and possibly even more dangerous in battle than Lysandría," the messenger said in excitement at being able to give his message directly to the General of the Kings Own.

The General smiled down at him, "I am certain this can't be a bad thing. We need all the help we can get. That's why we sent for the elves in the first place. We will have time to decide just how strong they are, but either way we can learn a lot from them." He flashed the younger man another smile, proud that this soldier had such grand aspirations. No one ever got anywhere in life by believing things like status could stop you. "Just as they can learn from us. Now, why don't you go and wash up. Then get something warm to eat in the kitchen. My orders." The squire looked at the near legendary general in surprise that he had noticed or cared how dirty and hungry he was. "Go on. Get." The boy scrambled.

The General pushed open the door leading down a long hallway to the outside. *I've heard many good things about this elven army, but there is no possible way Lysandría and her commander can be better than I. This should be interesting.* The tall man stood up a little straighter and organized his face into an emotionless mask. The double doors loomed in front of him, heavy and oak. He paused and swallowed in a slightly nervous way, before putting his weight against it and stepping out into the gloomy afternoon. The elven army was already setting up their canvas tents and fires already burned bright, but off the edge of the stone walkway, his own commander talked to who could only be General Lysandría and her commander, but a young man – possibly a half-elf – stood at her right. He frowned slightly. The squire hadn't mentioned a third and as he walked closer, he realized the young man was probably at least five or six years younger than himself. He came to a stop in front of them and inclined his head at the three, taking in their appearance.

Lysandría, a tall elven woman with pale features, stood in a warrior's stance with her feet spread slightly apart and arms clasped behind her back to give her a more solid appearance. Her red hair was tied in a thick braid hanging over her shoulder and at her side an elven made sword hung next to a brown leather handled dagger, matching the one poking out of her calf high boots. The General held out his hand and Lysandría clasped it and turned to the man at her left with a smile playing in her cinnamon brown eyes, "General Micheal, this is Colby. He helps with the training and some of the more technical details." Micheal covered his confusion by extending his hand to the man dressed all in brown with a stocky build. He stood only a few inches taller than Lysandría who already moved on to the question at the front of his mind. She waved toward the young man, "This is Tamynaen Jacob, my commander and trainer."

Micheal held out his hand in shock and raised an eyebrow. *He looks like a teenager; this must be some kind of joke.*

Gripping his hand tighter than politeness allowed, Micheal was surprised to have him step into the handshake, "I go by TJ." He lowered his voice for only Micheal to hear as he looked straight into his dark brown eyes with his own teal-blue one's, "That won't work on me. I may be young, but I am no one to mess with."

Micheal wrinkled his brow and knew immediately, TJ was much stronger than he thought and nodded. Lysandría frowned, "Do you two realize how similar you look?"

The younger man tilted his head and they eyed each other warily. As their eyes met again the sides of their mouths twitched, TJ turned to step back to Lysandría's side as both said, "There is no way." They looked back at each other and raised a questioning eyebrow.

Micheal ran a hand through his dark hair, "Shall we discuss what is going to happen? After all, we only have a few months of training before we are to begin moving out."

"Of course. Where do you wish to go?" Lysandría questioned.

"Let's take a walk around," the young general said, before realizing they might be tired, "Unless of course you have walked enough."

TJ laughed and Micheal looked at him in surprise, it was light and musical, not what he expected from his emotionless face. Even his body was perfectly controlled. He gave off the aura of a warrior and it shocked Micheal he would laugh so easily. Lysandría turned to face him and gave him a silencing look and muttered for him to be polite. "Let us walk," Lysandría said in a louder voice.

"Right," Micheal ran his fingers through his hair again, his mind reeling, "The training field has already been extended for all of our men and women to get to know one another."

Lysandría made a comment in the elven language of Layendrian and TJ inclined his head responding in the same manner. She smiled and said in Astèndrian, "I was commenting on our similar styles of training," her smile turned into a grin, "It's no wonder we are the best."

"Well, thank you," he grinned in response, "Of course, I agree. I was thinking we could start with your troops training mine in the morning, followed by strategy and self-practice, then my troops training yours in the evening or late afternoon."

"I am assuming you just happened to forget about meal breaks?" Lysandría added as the small group made their way through the city of tents being erected around them. Micheal's men interspersed the elves and helped by holding tent poles or hammering in stakes according to his commands. The generals smiled with relief that their troops were getting along.

"Right. Of course, we will have meal breaks. I thought that was obvious," Micheal admitted. "What is your area of expertise?" He questioned the young half-elf as he noticed more about him. *Must be hand to hand since he isn't carrying a bow or a sword. That's great to have an expert in hand to hand, but not very useful when the enemy has swords and bows.*

Lysandría smiled wickedly as TJ answered, "I have martial arts training, but I enjoy playing with swords and bows."

"You enjoy *playing* with swords and bows?" Micheal repeated in a questioning voice, completely at a loss on how to read his new co-worker.

"Yes, isn't that a good thing? Liking what I do for a living?" TJ questioned in a serious tone.

The Astèndrian's General turned to look at him, thinking he might be a little crazy. At first, he only saw TJ's serious look, but then he noticed a playful glint in his eyes and the twitch of a smile, just as Lysandría once more seemed to scold him in Layendrian. "Not quite sure how to respond to that, but may I request to see your specialty. No offense, I just have trouble seeing how martial arts can keep you alive when up against swords."

"Oh, I have daggers too," TJ smiled maniacally.

Micheal raised an eyebrow, "Again, no offense, but I don't see how that keeps you alive."

"Not many do," Lysandría laughed, "Just wait and see."

"I'm not amazing or anything. I'm not the best and I know that," TJ sighed as he looked around at all the troops.

Micheal pointed to the left and their group turned to face a large fenced in arena that was the practice field. A few people dueled in a corner while a handful of others practiced archery. A couple of elves cared for the horses after the long trip to the palace.

"After you," Micheal waved them in. "Jeremy is my second in command and in charge of our training so are you both okay fighting?" They nodded. Michael hoped Jeremy didn't underestimate the half-elf like he had at first sight. "Pick your weapons of choice," Micheal waved at the rack of swords and rapiers as the troops began to realize the two trainers were about to fight, they called friends over and stood in a circle around the practice arena. "Step into the circle," Micheal said.

Looking at the circle of rocks lying in the dirt, TJ stepped in and waited for Jeremy to collect a broadsword from the rack and enter. They both bowed – acknowledging the other fighter – and stepped back, each falling easily into a warrior's stance, taking stock of one another.

TJ stood gracefully, his feet shoulder width apart, arms crossed behind his back. Jeremy held his sword out to the right with one foot behind the other, his left arm tucked against the small of his back. They stood frozen, sizing up each other's body size and possible capabilities. Both men bent their knees slightly, before Jeremy began circling his opponent. TJ never moved. Instead, he closed his eyes and let his delicately pointed ears track the other warrior.

His clothes rustled and the wind whistled off the steel blade, giving TJ just enough time to dodge out of the way. He dropped to the ground and rolled out of the way with Jeremy quickly following him with a downward swipe of the sword. Again, TJ rolled, up onto his feet this time. He followed, by ducking into Jeremy's guard and kneeing him in the chest. The other man coughed, but hit out, causing TJ to step away quickly and duck to avoid the slashing blade.

Jeremy charged, forcing TJ back to the edge of the circle. He pushed the advantage and swept the sword in, but didn't notice that once again the half-elf dropped down to the ground and swept his foot in a circle causing Jeremy to drop. Before he could get his sword up, the half-elf kneeled over him with a shining dagger to his throat. Jeremy knew the fight was over.

"I have no idea how you managed that," Jeremy said taking the hand TJ offered to him. "I couldn't even see you."

"You underestimated your opponent," TJ smiled crookedly as he pulled the larger man to his feet.

Micheal sighed and stepped into the circle, "Do you need a rest or are you alright for another round?"

TJ bit his lip, realizing it was a habit he picked up from Gabriel, "No, I am fine."

The two bowed to one another and stepped back. This time, TJ looked like a true warrior. His stance was farther apart and his knees bent with his arms loose at his side. His eyes watched every movement of Micheal closely. Micheal nearly mirrored the half-elf, except in his left hand he held a long, well-crafted sword.

Unlike with Jeremy, the two didn't play with one another. At least, it didn't seem that way. The two moved and twisted around each other like a practiced dance. TJ, again, got the first hit in by ramming his shoulder into Micheal's rib cage, but he countered by smashing the handle of his sword into TJ's collarbone. TJ danced away and Micheal followed.

By this time, the General came to the realization the half-elf was, in fact, playing with him. Annoyed, he switched his sword to his other hand and attacked with fervor. TJ twirled around him and Micheal heard a whirling and turned to see two daggers connected by a chain being spun in the half-elf's long fingered hands. Micheal swore under his breath and both men began circling each other slowly. They caught their breath after a few seconds and grew more serious about their stalking.

TJ caught the twitch of Micheal's sword and they charged one another. TJ smiled wickedly and jumped into the air flipping over Micheal with seeming ease, his daggers twirling dangerously close to Micheal's face. The young general pivoted and executed a perfect crescent – if TJ didn't jump out of the way.

He's playing with me. Micheal thought and began to try harder.

The fight suddenly became more interesting as the deadly weapons flashed in the late afternoon sun shining through the overcast sky. Dirt began billowing out from beneath their feet as TJ dodged and ducked under Micheal and Micheal did the same. TJ, finally, decided to end it by flinging out his chained daggers at Micheal's sword and capturing it, before flipping over him to rip the sword out of his hands.

Next Micheal knew, he was face down in the dirt, his own sword to his throat and both of TJ's daggers pressing into his back. *I lost,* Micheal thought in wonder, *but I never lose. He is amazing. Wonder where he is from and who trained him.*

"Mercy," Micheal said and the half-elf let him up returning the sword. "It had been a long time since I've been beaten. You truly are an incredible fighter."

A wicked grin crossed TJ's face, "I told you, I am not one to mess with. Now you mostly know why."

"*Mostly* know why?" Micheal laughed and turned to where Lysandría and the others stood watching with a crowd from both sides of the troops. "I've had enough for one day and I can imagine you are all tired."

"Agreed, but if I know TJ at all," she smiled at her second in command, "He will want food."

"Good thing I was just going to take you there. Please, follow me," Micheal led the way out of the training field and onto a path taking them back to the palace.

✳✳✳

Micheal sighed as he entered his home just outside of the palace gates. Immediately, he went to the fridge and took out a dark beer. He stepped through the white trimmed doorway as he twisted off the cap and into the living room where his petite little sister sat reading a book in the faded brown armchair.

She turned her moon shaped, porcelain face on her brother and set the book down, "Mom was already put to sleep. She wasn't feeling well."

Micheal nodded and strode to the armchair. He wrapped his arm around her thin shoulders in a hug and pulled her long raven hair away from her face. She smiled at him and he kissed her forehead in the gesture of kinship, "How are you feeling, Ella?"

She sucked in her lower lip, "I've had my better days. Just dizzy. I don't know why."

"No one knows why dear," he gazed at his sister with a kind and loving look he reserved only for her, as he sat heavily on the sofa next to her chair.

Without much thought, she picked up her book and joined him, leaning against his side as he wrapped an arm around her, "You met the Elven Army today, didn't you?" She watched his dark head nod as he took a swig of the beer, "How did that go?"

His handsome face frowned, "They are very well trained. The general, Lysandría, I didn't get to see fight, but she is very quick witted. Her mind always seems to be calculating. The second in command, TJ, is the most talented fighter I have ever seen."

"Even better than you?" She questioned, her innocent brown eyes turned on him in disbelief.

"Yeah. Even better than me," he said with a sullen voice. "He was playing with me Ella."

"Playing with you?" The frail eighteen-year-old questioned.

Micheal nodded, "Yes. We dueled, but it took me awhile to realize that he was. I would like to think he had to try a little, but I am uncertain if he actually did."

"He is elven though," Ella added knowing her brother's pride stung. *His pride carry's him too much anyway. I wish he would realize being the best at everything isn't why his troops love him, but it's because he cares about them.* She shook her head.

"I have fought elves before though and never have I seen one this adept and he is only a half-elf! They are basically human except for their added senses and a little faster. You know that," he paused for a moment and took a drink. "I swear he was trained by the dragons or something."

Ella snorted, knowing how unrealistic that was. She tied her hair back with a fraying red ribbon Micheal gave her for her birthday, "Sure Micheal. They all went to the Orcana Islands almost fifteen years ago and didn't pick any one to follow them. If they are still alive, they are very old." He tapped his beer bottle, "Although, I did hear a rumor that a few of them were back in the country not too long ago... don't know how he would have managed to find them though – or be trained by them so well in such a short amount of time."

"I don't know Ella. He is nimble like one and graceful. Humble too. He doesn't act like he is as good as he is. I ate with them tonight and Lysandría made a comment about his talents and he blushed like he had never been complimented before," he ran a hand through his hair and watched the butler turn off the electricity and light a lamp in its place. "He just seems like a completely genuine person. Although he is very quiet."

"Maybe you should get to know him better," Ella suggested as she covered a yawn.

"Maybe I should," he admitted.

Ella sucked in her lower lip again as she contemplated her next question, "Micheal, I want to go back to school. Can I?"

Micheal sighed and closed his eyes. It was his sister's only request. She didn't care about the pretty things he bought her and, although she loved books, she really wanted to go to university and he always denied her that. For the past four years, he had denied her request and it killed him inside, because they both knew she was brilliant. "You know I can't let you Ella. Not until the doctors can figure out why you keep fainting or your dizzy spells stop."

"But what if they never do?" Ella questioned in frustration – tears pricking the backs of her eyes. "Am I just to be kept locked up?"

"Don't do this to me. You know I would do anything for you and if I could figure out a way to make you better, I would. For now, I need to keep you safe. I promised that to our father," Micheal gazed down at the person he cared about more than anyone else. She was the reason he fought for Astèndre. "How about I find you a tutor?"

She covered another yawn as she looked up, a smile brightening her face, "Really?"

"Yes. Would that be alright?"

"More than alright!" She yawned again. "You are the best."

"Good, but now you should get off to bed," he advised, smiling warmly at her and putting his cheek on her silky hair.

Ella turned and gave him a hug before pushing herself up. He smiled at her as he propped his feet up on the coffee table, chipped and fading from age and use. She walked off down the hall to her room and he heard the door snap shut and sighed. He loved his sister dearly, but he knew the tutor wouldn't stick around. They tried it before, but Ella always scared them off with her constant questions and with how quickly her mind worked. *Maybe I could talk to the palace librarian... what's his name again?* He thought about it and, finally, remembered, before drawing on the bottle of beer again, *Jack. That's right. I will talk to him tomorrow.*

The butler returned an hour later and smiled warmly at the young master of the house who had fallen asleep with his feet on the coffee table and an arm hanging off the side of the couch. The butler leaned down and picked up the empty beer bottle and quietly woke him up to send him off to bed. He couldn't help but chuckle slightly as he remembered doing the same, when Micheal was a young boy.

Micheal grumbled as he stood and thanked the man who had served his family for almost twenty years as he stumbled off to bed.

9

Chapter 9

Atropos stood in his beautiful garden watching his world fall. He felt his brother enter and frowned, but Lucvoyeur said nothing, just walked gracefully to his side. Silence reigned for a long time, until Atropos finally broke it, "What are you doing here?"

"Why did you break our contract?" Lucvoyeur retorted.

"I didn't break our contract," Atropos turned to glare at his brother. "Why do you believe I did?"

Lucvoyeur's perfect face looked astounded for a moment before becoming statuesque once more, "You destroyed the reincarnates. If the Gala demands one to be created you know you must leave it alive. If the Empyrean demands it, you know the Gala will come."

"Prove that I killed a reincarnate," Atropos sneered at his silvery twin.

He sighed in annoyance, "Why do you always have to do this? You are being defensive. That always means you know you did something wrong."

"Except *you* are wrong. I have not killed a reincarnate."

"Oh really? You didn't kill Hayle's reincarnation?"

Atropos smirked, "No. I did not. She died of natural causes."

Sighing heavily to show his annoyance, Lucvoyeur rephrased his question, "Although you know what I meant, I will spell it out for you. You entered Hayle's reincarnate through her mind and shattered it. No, she did not know who she truly was, but that is beside the point. Atropos, you broke the girl's sanity."

"I fractured her reality for a mere few minutes. You make it sound like I destroyed her entire life. She is one in many," he waved a hand at his brother and stepped away a few paces squishing his toes into a moss garden.

Striding over to the fountain, Lucvoyeur reached in with cupped hands before bringing the silvery pool to his lips and drank, "You know you did wrong and she does matter. She will be the one to destroy you. You cannot break the chain without severe consequences."

"And how do you know I broke the chain. You are not able to see that?" Atropos raised a pale eyebrow in question.

"Cabala told me," Lucvoyeur met his gaze steadily.

Atropos looked over his shoulder as if expecting her to enter his garden without warning, but his older sister did not appear. He brushed a speck of dirt off his golden shirt sleeve, "And she can read that now? Why do you believe her?"

"Because she can. As can The Knowing. Why do you have to question everything?" Lucvoyeur sighed. "All I really need to know is that The Gala would find nothing if they looked? Remember, if you draw their attention we are both lost."

"They would never come here," Atropos said suddenly angry. If there was anything he hated, it was being caught and he feared what The Gala would do to him. He didn't believe his brother could actually prove it though, which meant the council of the gods wouldn't be able to either. "We have already discussed this."

"Either way. You have broken the rules of our game. We both know this."

The golden twin spun to face him, "Prove it." He sneered, acting like a small child.

Lucvoyeur smiled broadly at his brother. It was what he had been goading Atropos into saying this entire time. If Lucvoyeur couldn't push his twin into behaving, only one other person might be able to, "Gladly. I will call upon my witness: Cabala."

Atropos shivered as a cold like death entered the room with a sheet of white fog which quickly dissipated. He licked his lips in fear and anger as a young woman appeared in the middle of the pond, normally showing him images of Astyreian. She wore a shimmering dress glowing in the color of mother of pearl. Placing small feet on the surface, she strode with precision across the water, leaving not a single ripple in her wake. What looked like dew drop shaped seed pearls clung around her thin neck and collarbone. The same dew drop jewelry shined at her earlobes and around her dark hair loosely twisted at the back of her head and cascading down in ringlets. The woman was small in comparison to the two men, but she held herself with an authority making her seem much larger.

"This had better be a good answer coming from your mouth Atropos," Cabala said through her misty sheen in a voice resonating power.

Atropos gulped, "Answer for what?"

Cabala turned her large green eyes on him, he backed up a pace, "Don't fool with me little brother. You know how I hate to get involved in your feuds."

"Then don't get involved," Atropos said boldly and quickly realized it was a mistake.

Her eyes flashed dangerously and tendrils of mist reached out to attach to his wrists, pulling him into the air like a marionette, "Did you forget why I was given the name Puppet Master, dear little brother? Do not test me, because I could be *your* master. However, I prefer the dead now. They are quieter. More at peace," she smiled sweetly and her serene beauty returned. "Lucvoyeur, I don't know how you can stand being with all those waiting to cross over to my realm."

"Some of them are quite a handful, I will admit, but most aren't bad," he glanced at Atropos still hanging in the air. "Especially Tamynaen Jacob's siblings. They are wonderful. Kind and loving, although they miss him terribly."

Cabala smiled, scaring Atropos even more, "I can imagine. The Knowing, I wager, keeps an eye on him and the Elementalist can probably see glimpses every now and then."

"Yes, to both," he watched his brother being flipped around effortlessly in the air by his elder sister, as Cabala watched in seeming serenity. "Hayle won't move on without him. In fact, I'm not sure if she even could, but his sisters all took her in. They love her and she loves them."

Turning to Lucvoyeur, Cabala twirled a ringlet and stated, "Of course she can't move on. The Empyrean ordered her with the Infinite. She cannot move on until they are reunited, but some idiot," she dropped Atropos to the ground, "Messed with that. Until that is rectified, nothing will change. She won't be able to find peace."

"Will the Gala come to fix it or punish us for breaking the chain?" Lucvoyeur asked in worry, ignoring his twin.

"Not just yet. They have larger things to worry about," Cabala thought for a moment and began to fade into the growing mist, "Maybe if they knew you held the Infinite and his match separate, they would care more. In truth, if they knew you messed with the order of the sixes lives, they would come, but they don't...yet."

"Are you going to tell them?" Atropos questioned in fear from the ground.

Cabala raised a delicate dark eyebrow on her younger brother, "Have I any reason to?"

"How would I know?"

"Well, I don't. So, no. I won't tell them, but I warn you Atropos, they will find out eventually and when they do – you will pay for it. You have been warned," Cabala evaporated into her mist.

The twins watched the mist disappear, leaving glistening water droplets in its place. Lucvoyeur smiled, "Told you so, but you just couldn't listen to me."

Atropos threw sparks of electricity at him in anger and Lucvoyeur laughed as they bounced off a shield he erected from his own power.

"We need to end this world and quickly," Atropos finally admitted.

Lucvoyeur nodded, "First, shouldn't we begin the creation of another?"

"Yes," his golden twin frowned in thought. "Let us start that process now."

***

The ground was incredibly muddy and slick, but the half-elf didn't let up on anyone. He continued drilling Micheal's troops at a relentless pace just as the sky opened once more. The rain had poured down on them all day. It would stop for a brief moment, sometimes as long as a half hour, but then would start up again in a torrential down pour.

It didn't take long for his reputation as being hard and un-sympathetic to spread to Micheal's troops and it was days like this which made them realize the honesty of the elven troops. It also made them appreciate Micheal much more. He wasn't an easy general, but he also would have relented slightly in this weather, but not TJ. The half-elf still expected their best performance, where Micheal and Jeremy would possibly have even let them leave early.

Finally, completely drenched and looking like mud creatures, the combined troops left, exhausted, just before dinner time. TJ sent them off to the baths as he waited for Micheal to finish talking to one of his commanders before walking over.

"Are you trying to kill our troops?" Micheal questioned with exaggerated heat in his voice.

TJ shook his head like a dog and his nearly shoulder length, sopping hair clung to his mud streaked face, "Course not. They haven't died yet, have they?"

"No, not yet, but we have only been through a few skirmishes," Micheal admonished.

"True," TJ looked thoughtful. "We should actually be getting sent out to battle soon."

"Looks like it. Things are beginning to get hot at the border, more than usual."

TJ nodded, looking like he couldn't care less, but Micheal knew it was an act. Through the months they trained together, he came to this conclusion about his new friend: he cared a lot – too much sometimes. It was an odd thought for Micheal since he never had a real friend before. Most people from his school years always associated with him to either get his rebound girlfriends or some slight popularity. The general had always been at the center of every spotlight and, to be honest, he liked it that way, but what he always craved was someone to just be his friend and TJ became that. The half-elf didn't care that Micheal got the girls when they went to the bar and didn't care that he always told the stories or relayed the strategies to the troops. None of that mattered to him. Micheal smiled at the thought that Ella was right.

TJ glared at him as he realized Micheal had drifted off into his own world. He bent down and scooped up a handful of mud and splattered it into his face. Micheal spit and wiped it out of his face –

a vengeful look came into his eyes, "You have got to be kidding me. You will pay for that."

"Then make me pay," TJ grinned as Micheal drew his sword. TJ whipped out his chained daggers and spun them in the air, cutting through the water droplets.

The two dueled until the rain came crashing down in sheets and they could barely see. Not wanting to injure each other, they called truce and laughing put their weapons away. They clapped hands breathing hard.

"Well, Mitchie we should be able to cool things down in a bit. Don't you think?" The half-elf said using his nickname for the 23-year-old general as he returned to their previous conversation.

They began walking back toward the palace and nodded at a few of their troops as they passed, "Of course. I mean, we are the best." He grinned in a self-impressed manner, "Let's go grab some food from town. I would love to eat well before we head out in a few days."

"Agreed," TJ looked around. "Should we ask Lysandría to come along?"

"Good plan. I still don't see how you and you alone can get her to act like a real person," Micheal admitted.

"What do you mean?"

"She is terrifying and had no humor around everyone but you," Micheal explained. "You can get her to laugh, smile, and even joke. Me, on the other hand, just gets dirty looks from her. This is a first for me. I don't know what to do with myself."

"I can imagine," TJ laughed – a rare full laugh, "I've seen all of the women you attract and of every kind. You normally can get the shyest ones to talk. I couldn't tell you why Lysandría relaxes around me, but she did mention to me once that I remind her of a family friend back in Layendria."

"Well, I guess we should wash up if we are to be let in any-where," Micheal sighed and the two boys headed off to the baths.

Once clean and in dry clothing, the boys wrapped oil skins around their bodies before running for the carriage waiting for them. Lysandría sat in the dark inside waiting impatiently. "Took you forever. And they say girls take long." She raised an eyebrow at Micheal, "They never met you apparently."

Micheal tried to give her his winning smile, "I just wanted you to see how handsome I can be."

The elven woman looked him up and down, "You should have taken longer."

Micheal blushed and looked down at his feet. He was at a loss for what to say to her. It wasn't that he wanted her to fall in love with him, but he wanted her to like him. Everyone liked him. The troops he was in charge of, the medics, his commanders, the kitchen staff, even the king. Micheal had never met a soul who didn't like him – until Lysandría.

TJ touched his shoulder, "You are just trying too hard."

She pulled her long red hair over her shoulder and ran her fingers through it, completely unabashed, "So, I chose The Red Wagon. Is that alright?"

Micheal nodded not meeting her eyes. TJ looked up at her as she lit the candle and put the top back on. It was a fairly quick ride, but riding in the dark didn't appeal to her. *You could be nicer to him,* TJ said into her mind. *He is trying to understand you. He wants to be your friend. Why is that such a bad thing?*

She looked away from his strange eyes and she hesitated – as she always did when they changed colors about telling him what that meant. After having known King Keldar for over thirty years now, Lysandría had seen the similarities between Keldar and TJ. Their appearance was drastically different. Keldar had blonde hair and long features. He was prone to smiling and laughter, but their long fingers were both quick to pick up instruments. Their expressive voices equally entrancing. Their eyes – identical. She had never said anything to the King, but as no heir appeared, Lysandría worried that she may have to someday soon. If the King died, they would be lost, but would her people accept a half-elf to rule them and one who was technically dead? The elven general shook her head and raised her eyes to see TJ studying her.

"You were miles away," he gave her a rare smile that she couldn't help but compare to her King's. Again, they were the same – smiles that warmed everyone around them.

Giving TJ a smile in return, she glanced over to Micheal who sat in the corner with a frown on his handsome face, "Micheal, I am sorry. I just – I'm not used to people speaking so, well, freely with me."

Micheal raised an eyebrow, "I guess you wouldn't be. You've been a general for nearly 30 years now."

Laughing, TJ shook his head, "That's not why she isn't used to it. She is the cousin of the King. A princess, distantly. They do their royalty a bit different, but still." He laughed again at the look on Micheal's face, "People just don't speak that way with her. It offends her sensibilities."

Lysandría slapped his leg, "I am not that kind of royal. I wouldn't have joined the army if I were. Just talk to my sister if you want a 'sensible' royal."

"Then don't get all in a huff when Mitchie talks to you like a normal person. Sheesh. I mean some of the things I have said and done in front of you are ten times worse than things he has said and you never tell me off."

She blushed slightly, "You-you're different though."

"How so? How am I any different?" TJ questioned.

"You remind me of someone," she looked out the window refusing to meet his steady gaze.

"Who do I remind you of?" TJ asked curiously.

"I, I can't say. If I could tell you, I would, but the repercussions if I did would be great," she shook her head and suddenly remembered the story of his family's deaths. She had met the other angel – Gabriel – very briefly, but the memory of the things he told her about TJ had stuck. She knew never to mention who she thought King Keldar was. It very well may destroy TJ.

"Just tell me. How could there be repercussions? What would the problem be?" TJ rolled his eyes at her concern, completely baffled.

She shook her head, tossing her long curls into shadow. As TJ opened his mouth again, Micheal gripped his arm and gave a squeeze, "Don't. Whatever it is, whoever it is, I think she has a good reason for not telling you. Just let this one go."

Their carriage stopped and Micheal opened the door. Thankful for the rain, as it stopped their conversation. They sprinted into the building and were greeted by a warm crackling fire and bright lanterns. After a few drinks, Lysandría began to warm up to Micheal. TJ smiled at Micheal and leaned over to whisper into his ear, "I told you she would warm up eventually. It just takes some time."

"You could have told me she was a royal. That may have helped," he laughed.

The tall general crossed her long legs and reached over to grip Mitchie's hand, "Thank you for inviting me. I needed this."

The conversation drifted into easier matters of childhood memories and war stories. TJ didn't really know what to add, but he was happy just listening. Micheal glanced over at him, "What about you? Who was your first girlfriend?"

Lysandría froze with her glass to her pink lips. TJ smiled distantly, the alcohol keeping him in a warm protective haze, "Hayle."

"Tell us about her," Micheal downed his whiskey and waved to the bartender who brought another round. TJ slammed his back and set the glass on the rough counter. "Come on, you haven't said much since we got here."

TJ looked down at the beads of sweat drifting down the sides of the glass making patterns like cracked ice. He liked Mitchie a lot. He was the first real friend he had since Lysandría – and before that not since Gabriel, but his relationship with Gabriel was different. It was more like that family member who you liked, but could never truly relate to. Mitchie always seemed to understand TJ without trying. He didn't usually press him on topics and they could fight and get mad at each other, but, the next day, were laughing together about some new trainee or swimming down at the lake. TJ wanted to tell him everything, but he couldn't. He decided on a half-truth, "I just come from a very different world than yours. My stories aren't about peace and comfort. I didn't live a life of luxury. Have you ever been to VeeCee?" Micheal shook his head. "I didn't think so. I was born there. I don't think I ever told you that, but up until sort of recently, they were sticklers about the class system. They didn't like them mixing. Hayle was from the Mercante Guild. I was from the Dead Lands."

Micheal watched him and saw the minute lines of stress that pulled at the tiny muscles around TJ's eyes and saw his fingers begin to tap. He hesitated at changing the topic even though he did want to hear more, but TJ went on. Lysandría watched him carefully – as if afraid of something.

"It wasn't all bad though. I had friends from all the different districts. Hayle and I were happy, but then – I don't know. I pressed her to make a choice and she ended it. Said she couldn't pick me over her family. Her decision lasted about a day and then she wanted to talk again. She was coming to tell me something when she was murdered in a back alley near the Shop District. I saw it happen in a vision… it – it wasn't an easy death." TJ frowned and looked at Micheal. A tear slipped out of his eye, "You see? My stories are a bit different. I would rather hear yours." A light entered his eyes which hadn't been there before and they changed from clear blue to a deep blue the color of the ocean. "Thanks."

Micheal tilted his head to the side, "For what?"

"Listening. I've never told anyone that before."

Lysandría leaned over and kissed him on the forehead, "Aida, that is what we are here for. We will be here for you, just as you are here for us."

Micheal nodded and ruffled TJ's hair, "I would say you are more like the brother I always wanted."

TJ and Lysandría met each other's glance and burst out laughing, ruining the moment.

"What did I say?" He looked around as if someone else could help him, but the only one who looked over was the bartender. TJ waved at him and he poured them another round.

"Aida means family. Well, not literally," TJ answered and attempted to control his laughter. "It literally means 'precious one' but it has come to mean love for a family member."

Lysandría giggled into her drink before leaning over to kiss Micheal on the forehead, "You are a dear one. I wish I had seen it before."

"You are such a royal. I can hear it now in the way you talk. I wish I had known that," Micheal laughed and sipped at his beverage. "We should do this more often. Once a week."

The other two nodded in agreement, feeling at ease despite all the reminders of war surrounding them.

***

Three weeks later the two armies marched west to the border between Astèndre and The Empire. Micheal wove his chestnut stallion through the mass of his army, checking up on them and making sure everyone stayed well. They would give him smiles or stiff nods and usually not much more. What Micheal liked most about his experienced troops was they knew what could happen. They knew what battle and war held for them and, yet, they still continued to keep their heads held high. The air stayed slightly light with bursts of songs and laughter. It shattered now and again with the dread of battle and images from each man's past, but it wasn't hesitant like it would be with green troops.

As camp was set the two generals began discussing strategies in the war tent. They knew the strengths and weaknesses of their troops very well and it didn't take long for them to figure out a plan of action. This was a place where battle had gone on since the very beginning and they needed reinforcements. Ditches and dugouts interspersed the grounds and dead trees lined one side of the field while a river lined the other. Micheal knew the area well. To him this would be an easy and a perfect battle to test their training.

TJ began playing his wooden flute by the fire outside as Lysandría and Micheal left the tent, pleased with the decisions they made. Both sides of the troops gathered around the campfire to listen to TJ's soft playing and tell old war stories, reminiscing about the almost myth like tales of when there was peace in the world.

Tomorrow, they all knew, would be hard. They would set up around the border patrols campsite and the following morning set off for battle.

***

An arrow went wide and missed Micheal's left side by a few feet the following morning. He gazed angrily over the crowd of people fighting in a bloody mess for the shooter. It wasn't that the arrow would kill him, since he wore a protective leather jerkin with metal disks sewn into it, but it would hurt. With little thought, he swung his sword about in a great arc and caught a man at his neck and stabbed another in the chest while looking for the man as the other two fell to the ground. Micheal saw Lysandría roll around a man who appeared to be the size of a bear and thrust upward with her short sword. He gurgled and slumped to the ground as she darted off to her next victim. He turned his head slightly and arced his sword in a crescent, catching a man across his back. Nerves cut, the man twitched violently and fell. TJ's shinning daggers caught Micheal's eye and he watched the half-elf spin his deadly dagger over his head and lash out in a half circle stilling the onslaught of The Empires troops coming at him. He grinned viciously at the ones lined up to get at him and they hesitated to come closer.

Micheal sighed in wonder at the young man and, finally, caught sight of the archer. He charged forward on his horse and leapt off, catching the woman in mid swing with his long sword. The other warrior barely raised an arm in protection before Micheal caught her in the throat and decapitated her.

Astèndre came out victorious over The Empire two days later. The Empire retreated in a hurry, leaving their dead in order to preserve the living. Micheal and Lysandría pulled their troops back and looked them over for wounds. Those appearing in good health, they sent back out to collect their dead for proper burial and to mass bury the enemy's corpses.

"We could have lost more," Lysandría commented, as the generals and their second in commands watched their troops being dragged in. "You were right. It was a basic and easy fight."

Micheal nodded, his jaw clenched, "I still don't like watching my troops not walking themselves out."

"This is war. It happens," Lysandría admitted harshly. She had been at it for much longer.

"True," Micheal turned his face away, "But it doesn't stop me from knowing that a message will be brought back to some little boy that his father is dead and he is now in charge of the family. It's unfair they will have to go through that."

"Yet, life goes on," TJ said bitterly. "Even if it is unfair, that, also, is life. Get over it and get used to it."

Micheal and Colby looked at TJ in shock at the bitter words spoken in his melodic voice. Lysandría simply frowned. She knew enough about him to at least understand he had good reason to believe his words true, "I tend to have more hope for the populations even though I have morbid thoughts toward our generation."

TJ shook his head and walked away toward his tent. A few moments later, his flute could be heard playing a ballad filled with mourning.

Lysandría met Micheal's eyes, "Ignore him. We should go check on the wounded."

Micheal nodded, but couldn't help but wonder what caused TJ to be even more morbid toward life than he was. He followed her into the medical tent with Colby just behind.

***

A few months later, Micheal looked about at the people in the training area and saw Colby put the troops through their paces. He turned to see Lysandría nod to TJ before he sprinted off. The tall elven woman approached him on her long legs, "How goes it for you this morning?"

He looked out to the practice arena and remembered his sister. She fainted at breakfast that morning and he worried about her, "Could be going better. Is TJ alright? He seemed in a hurry."

"Had to leave this morning. Received an urgent message," Lysandría said easily, as she watched all of the troops moving with definitive movements.

"You just let him go?" He questioned.

Lysandría eyed him with a raised eyebrow, "You think I could stop him?'

Micheal shrugged, "He is your second in command."

"Yes and no," Lysandría admitted. "He isn't paid. He helps me because he is good at it. No one owns TJ's allegiance. He is completely his own. On paper, Colby is my second in command. I thought you knew that." She watched him closely and saw stress lines on his forehead, "Ella okay?"

Micheal ran a hand through his hair, "No. They still can't figure out what is wrong and I worry about her."

"I know," Lysandría muttered in a husky voice. This rare show of sympathy and emotion almost scared Micheal. Despite their friendship, she only showed that when it was just Micheal and TJ around.

"Yes, well, not much can be done about it. Some of the best doctors have tried to figure it out." Micheal frowned and changed the topic, "I know you all have to head out in a few days," he looked sadly at his new friend.

She nodded in his shared sadness and realized their troops mirrored their downtrodden feelings.

The general hoped TJ would return before the elven army had to leave. He was shocked that TJ didn't come and say farewell to him, but Lysandría assured him it was a very pressing matter. "His brother sent him word that his help was needed immediately by the rebel army deep in Medicée's Empire. Only TJ could get to them and help. He only had a few days to get there."

"How could anyone get there in three days – without being stopped?" Micheal asked her.

She just shrugged, "I have no idea, but if anyone could, it would be TJ."

The elves dispersed three days later back to Layendria to defend their own land being invaded. It was a sad departure and the head of the column was missing a very important half-elf. The troops shook hands and there was some slight hugging from the women as they left through the gates. Lysandría rode up on her chestnut mare to where Micheal stood vigil at the gate and jumped down.

"Wanted to give you a proper farewell," she held out her hand and he took it. On impulse she raised her free hand and set it on his shoulder, "You're a good man Micheal. No matter what happens, remember you can't always control everything. I wish you all the best in the future."

Micheal smiled slightly at the tall elven general, confused by what she said, "Thank you, Lysandría. You have taught me so much. I wish you the best as well." He looked around, but knew TJ wasn't there, "Give TJ my thanks when you see him again."

Lysandría nodded and they let go. They knew they would never see each other again and yet, the two generals held their heads high for their troops. She gracefully swung herself back into the saddle and kicked her mare into a gallop to lead her elves out of the capital of Astèndre.

***

Hooves pounded against the dirt road as the messenger ran his sweating horse through the palace gates trying desperately to outrace time. He slid quickly to the ground and sprinted through the doors being held open for him. Micheal met the exhausted young man in the main entrance. The general pulled the envelope from his fingers and sent the messenger off to sleep as he ripped it open and quickly read the letter addressed to him by the general of the Princes Guard. He began swearing.

"What is it?" Jeremy – his commander – questioned.

Micheal pulled paper out of his back pocket along with a pen, "They are going to be overrun with Medicèe's finest. They need our help."

"That's a two days hard ride away!" He exclaimed.

"Then we had better get moving," Micheal sighed heavily as his mind changed to war strategies. "Give this to my sister. Tell her I love her and not to wait up for me." He said to the messenger hovering nearby.

Micheal turned and sprinted off to the war room where he knew King Rupert waited. *We have only been back for a month.* The guards opened the door as they saw him coming and he gave a quick bow and handed the letter to King Rupert.

The king read through it and told his servants to go collect the gases for Micheal's troops, then turned to his general, "I expect you want to leave tonight?" Micheal nodded, "I wish you luck. Send me word when you get the chance. This won't be an easy battle Micheal. Be careful and keep the troops safe."

"Yes, my King," he ran his hand through his dark hair.

The king knew it as a sign of stress and nervousness in his general, "What is it?"

"Nothing, my King," Micheal let his hair fall in front of his face.

"Look up at me when speaking," King Rupert ordered kindly, "And don't lie to me. I know you too well. What is on your mind?"

Micheal looked up and sighed, "My younger sister, Ella, she is really ill. I'm worried she might die while I am gone."

The king thought for a quick moment before responding, "I will send for your family and have them come live here. They will be treated as a part of my own. Atropos knows you have done so much for myself and our country… as your father did before you."

The young general visibly relaxed and flushed slightly in gratitude, "Thank you, your majesty. I cannot express how grateful I am."

He nodded, "For all you have done for me, I wish I could do more. Now, you should be on your way. The troops will want to see their beloved general moving about them."

Dismissed, Micheal stood and bowed again before turning and walking quickly out the door of the war room.

When he reached the fields, the city of tents was already packed away. His troops rushed about collecting gear and packing the horses and the few carriages with supplies. He smiled bitterly with pride, but it quickly fell as Jeremy came running over.

"The Plains of Gean are too far away for us to get there on time and actually be able to fight," he said in a rush.

Micheal nodded, wishing Lysandría and TJ could be there with him, "We will make it. We have to and we will be ready to fight when we get there."

"But sir, you will condemn us all," Jeremy tightened up in an uncomfortable gesture.

"No. Our troops will be ready. We will double time it and just shorten sleep a little bit," Micheal began walking quickly in his normal cocky way, "Don't worry. Everything will turn out alright. We are all way to pretty to die. Didn't you know that?"

Jeremy laughed nervously as they entered the torn down campsite of their troops, not quite certain if what his general said should make him feel better or if it was meant to be a joke.

***

Blood ran in lines toward the water, dying it a deep red in the growing darkness. Fire lit up the sky in brilliant oranges, yellows, and reds. It almost looked like a firework show, except instead of cheering, shrieks sounded out; instead of clapping, yells and death groans battered the ears. The smell of soot, chemicals, blood, and decay penetrated the air, but as Micheal and his troops gazed at the battle covering the plain – their eyes wide in shock at the ferocity – they couldn't smell anything. Their masks already covered their faces, protecting them from the two chemicals created by the palaces alchemists in defense against The Empire.

Bravely, Micheal took off his gas mask, but left his goggles on and called the attention of his troops. The fighting began to die down as he yelled, "I know we are all tired and I know we are all sore and hungry, but as we stand here The Empire is already shaking and scared. Look at them running back to their tents across the plains! They know we have come! They know we are here and that we hold the power to defeat them! Now let us go and help our kinsman reclaim what is rightfully ours!"

Micheal charged up to the general in charge of the Prince's Guard on his chestnut mare and promptly saluted. The other general's eyes widened, as without being told Micheal's troops began to intersperse his own, helping drag the wounded off to the medical tents and restock ammunitions. It hit him suddenly that this was the famous general of the King's Own striding toward him like he owned the world and leading the mare he jumped off. From all he heard of Micheal, even though he appeared outwardly cocky and self-important, he truly cared about his troops and deeply loved his younger sister. He became a general five years back at the age of nineteen and a quick mind caused him to rise in the Army faster than any before him, but it ran in the family since for the past three years he held his fathers' old position in the King's Own.

The older general snapped to attention, but Micheal just held out his hand, "General, how may my troops assist you and your own?"

"You came, I couldn't ask for more. In fact, I didn't think you would even make it here before we were all slaughtered," the older man took his hand.

Micheal gave a sideways smile, and knew he picked it up from TJ, "Of course we came. We brought more of the gases. I can have my troops launch them. I'm having them set up now and my medics are going to help the wounded and restock your supplies." He paused as a strain of silence suddenly went over the armies. Micheal looked out across the Plains of Gean. He couldn't stop himself from running a hand through his dark hair. "Shit. They just got reinforcements too."

In the light shed from the moon, shadows of Medicèe's troops could be seen marching into position directly across from them while the cannons were being loaded. There were at least a thousand more of them than of Micheal's troops.

"Ready the troops. Load the gases. Prepare to fight. Come on men!" Micheal smiled as one of his commanders arched a delicate eyebrow at him, "Come on women!"

He nodded at the older general and pushed his horse to the front lines and, gracefully, pulled his sword from its sheath climbing up. He swept it in an arc above his head. It caught the light from the moon and glinted silver, giving the silent signal down the line for his troops to fire the deadly gases only supposed to cause the unmasked enemy to perish.

This gas, however, was not one of the other two. This one lay tucked away on a shelf and forgotten for years. This gas penetrated their masks and crept in under their goggles. Their eyes began to bleed as their noses and ears dripped red fluid. Then the cannons hit mixing in a deadly combination with the gases. An explosion of sound and fire echoed out in a mushroom cloud and the thousands who entered the plains died, leaving Astyreian to Halendonia, the place in-between.

10

Chapter 10

Except Micheal.

He felt as if he floated in darkness with a ringing in his ears that wouldn't stop. A bright light pressed on his eyes and, with a slight pain, he forced them open and gasped. A man shining golden in the night knelt by his side, "Micheal. Do you know who I am?"

The young general coughed slightly before responding, "I – I think so. You must be a god. So, I would suppose that makes you Lucvoyeur. Come to collect me from the living." At the mention of Lucvoyeur a silver light began to grow just behind him.

"No. I am Atropos. Lucvoyeur is my twin brother," Atropos smiled kindly, but to Micheal's trained eye, he could tell it was slightly forced. "I am here to offer you the chance to be one of my Angels."

"What?" Micheal asked stunned as he tried to figure out what the silver light was and listen to Atropos at the same time, "Why?"

"I have always admired your strength and your quick mind. I would love if you used that to help people in the future. What do you say?' He smiled at him again.

"How could I say no to an offer like that? Anything and anyway I can help others, I will take it," Micheal coughed. "Yes."

Atropos turned his head to look over his shoulder at a glowing silver duplicate of himself just as Micheal's vision went dark.

*

Atropos has finally called me home. TJ is – of course – already on his way back. We have another angel. A general of the army. I am happy to be going back to Haven. I miss the peace of Atropos' Sanctuary and I feel that I can do no more here. Unfortunately, I am losing my hope that something can be done to stop the end. Atropos will be displeased. I hope I haven't incited his anger. I will admit, that is my greatest fear.

I had previously been with the Rebel's deep in The Empire. We had become so desperate that I needed to call TJ for help. I flew to the Astëndrian border and sent word to *TJ from there. It was a few days before I saw him flying desperately over-head and I launched into the sky to meet up with him. On the way back, we talked over what had happened and I felt that the rebel forces were at an end. Medicée was determined to wipe us all out this time. When we returned, disaster lay before us.*

After leaving, The Empire's forces must have come upon them and decimated all who had stayed behind. The tents were burned, the medical supplies stolen, the food crushed under their heavily booted feet. Corpses lay in the paths and they were not just the corpses of warriors, but also of the simple folk who could not escape to the Orcana Islands or even to King Rupert's realm. Layendria would have even taken them in if they sought sanctuary upon entering their forests. I cried out for those I had known, but they were no longer with us. The Rebel Army was done. There were none left in The Empire with the courage or spirit to fight. It was time for me to seek elsewhere for work.

With TJ, I flew to Layendria where he introduced me to a number of other doctors and healers who would let me help create supplies in mass quantity for the armies. These people were nice and kind and it was a new experience for me to be among the elves. Even when travelling with TJ, we had not gone into Layendria very often. It was more peaceful and it rejuvenated my spirit being with the elves, but my heart still cried for the Rebel Army and I couldn't help but feel the hope of winning dwindling away.

~ Gabriel

2328 Day Right

***

A loud rustling and thunk woke Micheal from deep sleep. Before that everything had seemed so quiet. He listened intently and heard a familiar laugh that sounded incredibly musical, but a hush quickly covered it up. Micheal opened his eyes and found he lay on a soft bed face down in a room filled with white.

His door snapped shut and he pushed himself up on the bed to see Atropos walking over, a smile on his perfect face, "Everything will be set up to how you like it soon enough. How are you feeling?"

Micheal shrugged, "Sore, but that's all."

"No headache?" Questioned the god.

Micheal shook his head as Atropos looked at the door behind him that had just shook, "Where are we?" He asked.

"My sanctuary. It is a place away from everything," Atropos smiled, waved his hand, and the door opened. A tall broad-shouldered blonde fell through the door, his wings in slight disarray and snickering sounded behind him. "Gabriel, please pick yourself up. Must you two always act so childish?" Atropos said to the blonde, as the shadow disappeared from the doorway. Gabriel did so and smiled sheepishly at Micheal. "This is my second angel, Gabriel. This is Micheal. Will you help train him?" Gabriel looked a little worried, but nodded as without being asked a black-haired half-elf with a wiry frame entered with a tray of food and giant wings tucked neatly behind his back. Atropos smiled like a father would at his pride and joy, "And this is Tamynaen. I believe you have already met?"

Micheal's jaw dropped as he recognized the young man. Suddenly, it all fell into place. He stuttered in disbelief and TJ laughed, "It's okay Mitchie. You're in Haven now. And now, I really am your elder. We will get you trained and back on your feet in no time."

"Alright nurse maid Tammy," Gabriel said ruffling the younger looking man's hair.

TJ turned and rolled his eyes, "At least I am kind enough to realize he might be hungry."

Atropos sighed, "They bicker like actual brothers, but you are one of them now. You all should take care of each other like family."

Micheal watched the two angels with confusion. He had never seen TJ act so comfortable with anyone before. They let him eat and answered a few questions, but the moment he finished, they pulled him to his feet to show him around his new home and train him.

***

The first training session didn't go as Mitchie hoped, since flying came so easily to TJ. When he flew it looked so natural. He could be walking one moment and in the next he was in the air. It was nearly the same with Gabriel, but Mitchie – as TJ called him – couldn't get the hang of it.

Finally, as the first day ended, Mitchie understood. The wind parting around his wings made air pockets to cushion them. He flapped against them and rose skyward. He pushed down with his right and tilted the left higher and spiraled down to the ground.

Gabriel congratulated him and TJ nodded with a smile on his face. The rest of his training wasn't as peaceful as flying. Through his martial training, he began to realize just how much he changed. His body became harder and more flexible and even though he always possessed a sharp analytical mind, it began to move quicker. Gabriel too, helped train him. He taught healing and culture. TJ taught him history, tactics, weaponry, and martial arts.

Mitchie witnessed, with his own troops, losing your temper with TJ wasn't smart, but never experienced it himself, because when they trained before it had always been in front of their troops. TJ and Mitchie had been guarded. He couldn't help it though, since TJ wouldn't always explain things. He just expected Mitchie to understand what came so easily to him. Mitchie exploded only once – a mistake he never wanted to make again.

Gabriel bit his lip in the background and held his breath as TJ's face – already emotionless – smiled crookedly. His eyes flashed dangerously as the wind picked up and he strode over to Mitchie and gracefully bent down. He didn't say a word just reached out and gripped the front of Mitchie's shirt with a burning blue hand. The flames didn't hurt Mitchie, but it did terrify him, since this was nothing he ever saw before. He understood now why TJ was the first and knew he would forever be the strongest. For once, Mitchie felt okay with not being the leader. TJ was good at what he did.

"Okay. Okay. My mistake," Mitchie gulped and TJ released him as he climbed to his feet. "Will I learn to do that too?"

TJ shrugged, "Perhaps. Gabriel can't control fire, but has healing powers and can bend emotions."

"What about you?" Mitchie questioned.

TJ shrugged, "I do fire, earth, a little air, and I can dapple with water. I'm not the greatest healer though."

"He forgot to mention he can read peoples thoughts, speak into their minds, and push ideas on them," Gabriel chuckled.

"So can you," TJ rolled his eyes and looked at Mitchie whose eyes went wide. "You probably can too, but you may need physical contact to do it, unless it's with me. That's the way it is with Gabriel at least."

"You can read people's thoughts?" Mitchie asked in shock.

"Yes," TJ answered simply, then realized he should elaborate, "I don't do it unless I feel that it is necessary and I never flat out make people do anything. I just give them a slight nudge and only if it is for their safety."

Mitchie ran a hand through his hair, "Bet that comes in handy. You could probably save a lot of people that way. Could you do any of this before you became an angel?"

TJ's voice became vacant, "A bit, but nothing useful." He took a deep breath, "Maybe we should stop and take a break." He turned and quickly walked away back into Atropos' castle.

Mitchie looked over to Gabriel and met his icy eyes, "What did I do?"

"I can't say, because he never really told me," Gabriel paused and waited until the heavy oaken doors closed behind TJ. "I know that you worked with TJ before, but I don't quite know how close you were to him. Did he ever mention his sisters?" The old general raised an eyebrow and didn't answer, "I will take that as a no. He watched his sisters die. He blames himself for it. I don't know how it happened, but even now he has trouble dealing with it."

An odd note coated his voice that Mitchie caught immediately, "What do you mean he has trouble dealing with it?"

"Track marks. I've never caught him shooting the heroine, but I have seen him drugged up. I hope you never have to witness him like that. Just a forewarning. He may seem completely calm and tranquil – like he is emotionless, but that is far from the truth."

Mitchie digested what Gabriel told him and the fog that hid TJ's past began to fade away, "I am assuming I am to never mention this to him? Pretend like I have no idea?" Gabriel nodded in confirmation as they began walking back toward the castle. "When are we going to be allowed to go back to Astyreian?"

"I am staying here. There is no reason to go back. That world is dying and no one can save it except Atropos, but he won't. It isn't his way. TJ will bring you there though. There are a few… beings he will want you to meet."

***

TJ's fingers flew across the neck of his maple bodied acoustic guitar with a rosewood neck as Mitchie and Gabriel played a game of chess. Atropos slid in and appraised his angels with his sculptured face, "You all seem to be doing well."

His long fingers slowed, "How are you doing? How much time is left?"

"Not much longer. Most of the populations have left for the islands of the Orcana. The world is falling apart. Tamynaen you asked me to let you go down one more time. If you are still wanting to, go now, but don't stay long."

Mitchie looked up in hope and TJ nodded, "Come along. It's time to go."

The clouds were thick and heavy, blocking the entrance into Astyreian as TJ and Mitchie stood on the cliffs. Mitchie looked a little wary as he gazed down, "So, we just fall?"

"That's the basic idea. Is there a problem with that?" He questioned with a twinkle in his eyes.

"No, just making sure," Mitchie gulped as TJ spread his magnificent wings wide.

"Ready?" TJ questioned. The third angel nodded, spread his own wings, and watched as TJ took a nose dive off the rocks and into the cloud cover. He mimicked his elder and watched as, within minutes, he soared by his side in Astyreian.

The young men frowned as they looked down at the barren landscape. They watched the pools before they left to prepare for what awaited them, but it was nothing like seeing the real thing. Everything lay dead or dying and looked red and brown. Animals decayed where grass used to be and the water was stagnant or so horribly polluted it ran in a red brown toward the ocean. Even the ocean became dirty from where the rivers and streams ran into it. Mitchie shivered, "It looks like the rivers are running with blood."

"Even the ocean is turning red," TJ muttered.

Mitchie agreed with his silence and followed the half-elf blindly until they began crossing the ocean, "Are we going to the islands?"

"Yes. There is someone I would like you to meet," TJ said and continued to fly steadily, appearing to float on the air currents.

Mitchie gave him a curious look and sped up to keep pace with him. As they reached clearer water and eventually the booming metropolis, once home only to the Orcana, TJ led them to the northwestern part of the smallest island. TJ circled just below the cloud line, before descending. Following, Mitchie saw a glint on the barren cliff edge. He tilted his head and stared at what appeared to be a sparkling boulder. TJ glanced back and began to laugh as they came close enough for Mitchie to realize the glint were the golden scales of a large dragon. TJ landed by the dragon's head and smiled, "Herok. I am glad to be able to see you one last time."

"Tamynaen Jacob, I wish I could say the same, but I am glad to hear you once more," Herok growled in response and tilted his head. "Who have you brought with you this time?" He sniffed the air, "Ahhh. It has begun. The Three Brothers will reign supreme till the end of the beginning."

"What?" TJ questioned, but knew better than to wait for a response. "This is Mitchie or Micheal."

Mitchie stepped, hesitantly, toward the giant creature and caught a glimpse of one of its giant milky eyes not knowing what to say.

"Why are you afraid, Fearless General?" Herok questioned and Mitchie was taken aback by the dragon's forwardness.

He shifted uncomfortably, "How do you know that about me?"

Herok boomed, "Tamynaen Jacob did you forget to mention that I am a Seer... again?"

"Maybe," TJ smiled maniacally.

"Why must you always do that? The poor people you bring here will think they have been watched their whole lives. Must you always frighten them?"

TJ laughed, "Of course. Think how I must have felt when I first met you. It's only fair."

"No, it's not. You had the help of knowing your older sister who was the greatest seer who ever lived – save maybe one," Herok seemed to whisper.

TJ sobered at that and scratched at the tender scales around Herok's blind eye, "Sorry Mitchie." TJ tilted his head as if listening intently to something the dragon said and nodded, "I need to go visit the girls anyway. I will catch up with you later." TJ turned to Mitchie, "Come and have a seat here. Herok wants to talk with you."

Mitchie watched as TJ left and, tentatively, sat on the boulder by Herok's large head. *What could this ancient dragon want to say to me? I didn't even know there were any dragons left... especially one so powerful. Of course, TJ would know him though.* Mitchie laughed inside and began to calm down from the initial shock. Neither broke the silence which followed TJ's absence. Instead, they let the sound of the crashing waves encompass them.

It had grown dark when Herok, finally, swept his tail back and forth across the ground causing a wave of dust to lift into the air, "This is what your world will become. Are you prepared for it?"

"Yes," Mitchie said immediately.

Herok moved his head back and forth, "No, you are not. Don't let that pride carry you. There are many other qualities you should embrace first. You have always been in balance Micheal. Don't fall the other way because of your pride."

"What does my pride have to do with anything? I thought you were going to give me some insight as to what is happening to our world and maybe how to stop it. I thought that was why I became an angel!" Mitchie released the confusion and anger that had been building for what seemed like years.

Sighing, the dragon collected his thoughts, "That is what I am talking about. First, I am going to answer a few of those questions, but then you are going to listen to some things which need to be explained. Can you handle that?" Mitchie sobered. "Good. Now, there is no insight I can give you for this world, but Atropos and his brother are creating a new world. A world filled with green and life. Take care of that world. I have already told TJ what will save it or at least protect it for a time. But everything – apart from one – has its season. It's time to grow and die. When TJ is ready, he will share that with all of you, because there will be more of you when the new world is created. There is no stopping the path of destruction Astyreian has gone down. Understand?"

"I understand," Mitchie ran a hand through his dark hair. "I just don't like it."

"That is what is horrible – and I know TJ would agree – you don't have to like what you need to understand."

"Gabriel would too, but he would at least hang on to some hope," Mitchie added in a melancholy tone.

Herok grumbled, "Yes, Gabriel would hang on to some hope. That is just how Gabriel is. He evens the two of you out. Now for a little understanding. Have you ever encountered someone you thought you might know before? They reminded you of someone who had died before?" Mitchie nodded. "That is because they were a reincarnation. They were that person, but reborn in a sense. These people may not always look the same or act the same and it can only happen to people who don't cross over from Halendonia to the final death. These are the people you will recognize and I give you this as a warning so you can prepare yourself."

"Prepare myself?" Mitchie interrupted. "Prepare myself for what?"

"That I cannot tell you. I can only give you a warning. Am I making sense?" Mitchie nodded although he was only barely keeping up. "Good. Next that pride of yours. It makes the rest of your character hang in the balance. No one is just good or evil. Not even Medicée. She was an adorable child. I watched her grow up, but her father fed her ego and never once told her no. You know how the story goes. She eventually wanted the one thing Medíc could not give her, his empire. Medicée poisoned her father and took it for herself and yet still wanted more to feed her insatiable appetite for power."

"I know the story. Why are you telling it to me?" He asked in slight annoyance.

"Because, you ignorant creature. Open your mind. You were a loved child just like her once. You had everything handed to you until your father died and you were left to care for your young sister and then mother. Yet, you still progressed with your talents and took your fathers old position at a very young age. You know what it is like to have power and pride. Don't let that go to your head. Don't become worse than Medicée. It is a careful balance that you stand on."

Mitchie ran his hand through his hair again in deep thought as he watched the waves crash ceaselessly against the rock cliffs far below, "What about the others?"

"Gabriel is different. His family was killed in the rebellion, but he was raised with love by an adopted family and has always been religious. He worked for everything he gained in life and worked hard for it. He is not prideful, because that is against his faith and tries hard to stay humble and do good for everyone before himself. His fear of disappointing is the only thing that may sway him."

"And TJ?"

"He is a special case," Herok paused as if unsure of what to say for the first time. There was a silence then and Mitchie was uncertain if he would continue his explanation. After a while, Herok nodded his head as if in an intense conversation with someone Mitchie couldn't see.

"Heather? How are you doing this?" Herok questioned across the vast space and time that separated them.

Heather laughed – a golden sound, "Don't question our combined powers, but I needed you to know something."

"About your brother I am guessing?"

"Of course," Heather's smile entered her minds voice, "When isn't it about him? You need to tell Mitchie about his past – at least a little. Mitchie needs to know why his character isn't in the balance and about who our parents are."

"The Old Blood lines were never to cross though. They made you all demi-gods."

"Yes. They did, but Mitchie needs to know. He will be the one to plant the seed TJ needs to come into recognizing who he is. One day, he will challenge Atropos, but not until he recognizes his full potential. He must recognize it Herok."

The dragon growled in understanding, "I will do as you say Heather. Please send the others my greetings and let them know that TJ... misses them."

"I will. And I know. I see his pain every day. As does Hayle and Oreal... she feels it. As for the twins, they see what we show them, but one day they will see it too. Thank you Herok for all you have done for my family. A greeting awaits your arrival." The connection severed.

"I apologize for that. Must have dozed off for a moment," Herok tilted his head as if looking up at the stars, "What I am going to tell you must never be revealed to anyone. Not even TJ can know that you know this about him, because some of it even he has never even guessed at."

"I understand. I won't disobey you," Mitchie swore in relief, he finally would get some insight.

"TJ's life was a tragedy. His mother, Annah, never loved him. She wanted a daughter, not a son and his father, Keldar, never once made her stop her abuse. Heather, his older sister, did everything she could to make them understand and the most Kel did was send TJ's twin sister away to live with an old family friend. Leaving TJ alone, was one of their worst mistakes and it wasn't until he met a little girl, Hayle, when he was four that he spoke again."

Mitchie perked up at the name of Hayle and he remembered the conversation Lysandría, Mitchie, and TJ had about the girl. That was the night the three of them had decided they were as close as family.

"Well," Herok continued, "They moved later to VeeCee. His father left them when he discovered Annah was pregnant again. A few years later, Heather was about to leave to find him, but she was hit by a cart with TJ watching. Then he met Hayle again.

"Do you see a pattern? There is one. There always is... Anyway, they truly loved each other and if *He* hadn't messed with it, everything would have ended as it was supposed to, but instead, Hayle left him. She couldn't give up being from the Mercante Guild for some kid from the slums. However, somehow, Hayle fought back against it and changed her mind. She went after TJ and got lost. TJ saw it in a vision and went after her. He didn't make it in time and Hayle died in his arms. Her killers were never found. After that, he let the drugs take him and became numb. He lived only for his little sisters and his music. When he finally died it was more of a reprieve than anything. His life was more of a tragedy than I could express and it isn't my place."

Mitchie remembered all the little things TJ said about life and how it never turned out how you wanted it to. That life was a bitch and, if lucky, you died in the end. Mitchie never quite understood his morbid friend, but now he did. *TJ hadn't been lucky enough to die, but hadn't he chosen to live? Why?*

"His life was tragic. It is true, but not all of it was horrible. He had friends and family that cared, just not your typical family. His friends cared deeply for him and would do anything for him. If only he would have asked and his sisters loved him too. He was talented and would have gone far, but he never got the chance. And Hayle… she loved him. She truly loved him, more than anything. She showed him what love meant without the label. That is something to keep in mind. You can only feel, as an angel, the emotions you felt when alive."

"I can't believe it. How – why… why did he choose to become an angel?" Mitchie asked in shock and confusion.

"For the same reason you did. To make a difference, but with TJ he also didn't want anyone else to have to go through what he did."

Mitchie nodded in understanding and once again they fell silent. The ocean reflected the stars and crashed the white dots against the rock wall they sat on. The pounding echoed around in Mitchie's head as he tried to digest everything, but two names continued rising to the surface. Annah and Keldar. *Why do those names seem so important?* He thought about it for a long while and then, even though his idea seemed farfetched, he asked the dragon, "Did Princess Annahbelle ever have children? A son, perhaps?"

"The psychotic Princess? Mayhaps," Herok's blind eye twinkled as he added, "And perhaps so did the elven King Keldar or King Kel. Has a sort of ring to it, King Kel… but he would have been a prince then – and during those years they both disappeared from the royal records."

Mitchie froze, "You mean, they had children together?

Herok smiled as he knew the angels head whorled, "Isn't that what you were already thinking?"

"Yes, but," Mitchie paused for a second, "Having thoughts confirmed is different than just having them."

"True," Herok snorted.

"But… but that would mean the two Old Blood lines mixed. So, if one of their children took the throne the kingdoms would be united."

"Not if all their children died," Herok added.

"TJ isn't dead. He was their child…"

"TJ wouldn't want the power anyway. He never liked being the leader. He was happy to sit on the sidelines and watch. But do you recall that *all* their children died – violently. The Old Bloodlines should never have mixed. Do you understand what happened when that occurred?" Mitchie shook his head listening intently. "A demigod was created who doesn't understand just how much power he possesses. Tamynaen Jacob is almost as powerful as Lucvoyeur and Atropos – or one day he will be that powerful and perhaps more. And before you say it, that is not a good thing – or a bad thing necessarily, but that means this world must end. A demi-god with that much power off set the balance and *He* grows bored. Atropos kept TJ alive because he was the most powerful of his five siblings, Heather knew too much, and the twins he never would have been able to control. But if Atropos didn't claim him, Lucvoyeur certainly would have the second he was allowed."

That flew over Mitchie's head, but he logged the information away in the back of his mind, hoping he wouldn't forget it. He didn't know what to say, but he knew TJ was incredibly strong – even for being the first it didn't make sense.

"Never tell TJ this. He must come to the conclusion himself. Unfortunately, he still believes he is only as strong as he is because of being the first. It is just unfortunate he never reached his eighteenth birthday. That would have been a great and terrible thing to see. His coming of age would have been grand indeed…" Herok trailed off thinking, as Mitchie sat and pondered the ways of the world.

As Mitchie lay down to sleep in Caladria and Ruby's Orcana style home, he knew that Herok and TJ were taking a final farewell flight. He, finally, understood why TJ acted the way he did and realized Herok told him more than he ever told Gabriel. TJ would never tell him all of this or at least not for a long while. The worst of it all was he would watch his world end and knew TJ could step up and, with Gabriel and Mitchie's help, they might be able to stop it. But TJ couldn't know he was a demi-god and that was something Mitchie would take to his final death, but he probably wouldn't believe him if he told him either.

***

They tried to stop it, the end of their world regardless of what Atropos said. Nothing they did could forestall the end. The Three Brothers went to war. TJ took out his chained daggers and seemingly lost all humanity. He killed ruthlessly. No thought went into what he did. The first angel whipped his daggers into Medicèe's

army and ignored how young they all were. They fell at his blade –
throats slashed and chest's impaled. As night fell, TJ stood on a hill
and bodies lay at his feet covering the hill like trampled blades of
grass.

Mitchie stepped in after that. His brother was covered in blood
and looking for more. Even though Mitchie was the one who made
all the battle plans and carefully staked out every detail to killing the
enemy troops – he knew when to stop. The General froze before
decapitating a young boy of perhaps fifteen. Stomach jumping to his
throat, Mitchie began only injuring and never anything that would
last. He didn't know what to do, but he fought his way to TJ anyway. All he could think of was getting to him and getting him out of
there. Finally, he made it and found one of the daggers at his throat.
TJ froze just in time.

"We need to get you out of here. TJ this is the third time. Can't
you control yourself? What has gotten into you?" Mitchie frowned
in an unbelieving manner. "Let's leave. Now."

TJ glared, "I don't know what you're talking about. Get out of my
way."

"Gabriel!" Mitchie yelled above the din of clashing metal.

Turning to see his two brothers, Gabriel sprinted to their side,
ducking the blow of another enemy, "What... TJ what happened?"
A young girl of thirteen lay by his feet, eyes wide flat discs.

"We need to get him out of here. This isn't good for him any
longer," Mitchie gripped his arm. "TJ, if you don't get your wings
out, I will drag you out of here." Continuing to glare and look for
blood at the same time, TJ didn't respond. Mitchie pulled his arm
back before slamming his fist into the center of his face, "That is it!
Grow them, now!"

Seeing stars, TJ grimaced as his own blood spattered his face and
he suddenly seemed to realize where he was, "You're right. Let's go.
There is nothing more we can do here."

Standing as one, they let their wings shift back into the space they should always occupy and ruffled them before leaping into the air. They no longer knew what could be done to stop the end.

****

The Three Brothers – as Herok named them – could do nothing more for their world and it nearly destroyed them, as they watched their people murder each other until there were none left standing. The earth had been poisoned with the amount of blood and decay soaking into its soil and water. Those unwilling to fight migrated to the Orcana Islands and overpopulated them. The natural resources could not replenish fast enough and then they too died.

The brothers could only stand by over the middle pool in Haven, the pool of the present, with eyes clouded. Only hours passed since their return, but years had come and gone in Astyreian. Their world had ended, but it was just the beginning of a new one. A new world called Islandrial.

11

Glossary

- Aida: Layendrian for precious ones or a term of love for family.
- Atropos: Literally means 'inflexible will.' The ruling god of Astyreian and twin

  of Lucvoyeur.

- Cabala: The older sister of Atropos and Lucvoyeur. There is no similarity
  between her and the religion Kabala. She was once called 'The Puppet Master' for the works she did in her own worlds and was charged by The Gala for the atrocious crimes she committed.
- Day Right: The second half of the world of Astyreian. The Old Blood lines are
  cemented and the caste system becomes ultimate. This is the time when TJ, Gabriel, and Micheal live.

- Empyrean: The force that determines the balance in the universe. It truly is 'the
Universe,' but has a will of its own which it passes to The Gala.
- The Gala: The council of the gods that hears and sees what the Empyrean wishes
to be carried out. They are the punishers when the laws of the Empyrean are broken and their power is great.
- Lucvoyeur: Caretaker of Halendonia and twin of Atropos. Voyeur literally means
'observer.'
- Moon Right: The first half of the world of Astyreian. When the dragons still ruled
and the world grows and learns.
- Old Blood lines: There are two of them. They are the lines the dragons picked to
rule the different races of Human and Elven because they are the two races that needed the most help. The humans were to be governed by primogeniture (not dependent on sexuality, but on first born). The elves were to be governed by an eye color trait (the eyes of the next ruler would change depending on their mood to keep them honest to their country). The trait did not stay within the specific family of the ruler, but could skip a generation or siblings – sometimes even cropping up in cousins to the ruling family.
- Tamynaen: With a little twist taken from the Latin it means 'Star Lilies.'

12

Astyreian Months

January – Nightmoon
February – Shademoon
March – Shadowmoon
April – Dawnmoon
May – Greenmoon
June – Risingmoon
July – Midmoon
August – Redmoon
September – Fellmoon
October – Bloodmoon
November – Duskmoon
December – Darkmoon

13

Astyreian Days of the Week

Mierten – Monday
Tebuleten – Tuesday
Wisterten – Wednesday
Throwten – Thursday
Frayten – Friday
Sateriten – Saturday
Sunnerten – Sunday

14

About the Author

I grew up in Rochester Hills, Michigan with my mother, father, and older brother. My family enjoyed travelling when I was growing up and my parents always made a point to take my brother and I (and sometimes our dog) everywhere they possibly could in the United States and beyond.

Currently, I live in the Metro-Detroit area with my husband and our pack of animals, adventuring and loving life!